MW01595645

The Treasures of the Promise

To my good friends
Mike + Rebecca

CAROL LEE ANDERSON

Carol L. Anderson

ISBN – 13: 978-1979049542
ISBN – 10: 1979049548

DEDICATED TO

my grandchildren
Grant, Brian, Cambria, and Bronwyn
Manuel and David
Alina and Acacia
Leif and Thane

OTHER BOOKS BY CAROL L ANDERSON

DO YOU KNOW WHAT YOU ARE DOING, LORD?

THE TREASURES OF DARKNESS

CONTENTS

CHAPTER 1

BETWIXT

Tofar gripped the rope handrail as he stepped onto the gangway. After enduring weeks on the open sea, he wanted to rush like a wild animal set free down to the firm ground below, and away from the ship that had held him captive. Instead, he measured each step carefully, alternating terror with joyous excitement.

Standing at last on the worn planks of the pier, his body still swayed with the rhythm of endless undulating waves. A tightly-packed, woven bag hung in the firm grip of one hand. With his spare hand, he drew over one shoulder the outer cape he had worn throughout the journey. It had proven its worth against cool, northeasterly winds and cold, suspicious glares. On land at last, it became a shroud to be shed at the dawn of a new day. He hoped he could shed his fears as easily as the familiar garment.

Warnings there had been in abundance, pleading with him to desist from his quest. However, somewhere beyond his island home was the reason no one would speak the forbidden word—father.

1

Was the world really such a dangerous place? Was the fact that he had no name and no history of importance to anyone besides himself? What harm could come from a knowledge of his family?

Standing tall and brave on the deck, he had dutifully waved as the ship glided out to sea. The sight of his mother weeping tore at his resolution not to give in to the fear he felt. Tofar was all she had left. At twenty years of age, should not a mother expect her son to venture out into the world? Surely she would understand that he had to leave.

*

On land, damp, early-morning fog began to rise in the wake of a languorous breeze. Ahead of him, beyond the town of Betwixt, he could just make out trees rising high into the hills, and he was sure the fragrance of flowers would soon begin to overpower the briny smells of the sea.

Tofar pushed aside the image of his fearful mother and her attendants that begged for attention. The extreme unpleasantness of the journey added to the sum of memories needing to be banished by the promise of a new day. To his left, small fishing boats floated close to the rocky water's edge, waiting for the fishermen to haul the night's catch ashore. To his right, burly sailors caught heavy bags of grain tossed from the ship. Surveying the wharf, with its stacks of wooden crates and assortment of gear—the use of which remained a mystery even after weeks at sea—he spied the way forward and started toward the town.

"Master! Master! Wait," shouted a young voice. Tofar turned his gaze into the white glare of sun penetrating the thinning fog. The familiar maze of masts and ropes, like a tether that would not let him go, was a sight he was anxious to leave behind. The silhouette of a young boy bobbed up and down, one hand held high waving a small, wrapped packet.

"Master, Captain says to give this to you." Breathless, the captain's cabin boy scurried down the gangway and thrust the parcel into Tofar's hand. "Sorry, we did not expect you leave so quickly."

A subtle smirk crossed Tofar's face as he recounted to himself

2

the many reasons he left quickly, hoping that such a trip would never be repeated in his lifetime. Day after day of looking out to a steel-gray sea and sky with nothing much of interest to see, queasy stomach, horrible food, and mocking stares of the crew they did not attempt to hide, had been insufferable.

"Ho, looks interesting. Did the captain say where this came from?" Tofar inspected its exterior.

"He doesn't know, Master. Someone gave it to him to give to you when we reached Betwixt. That is all I know."

"Off with you, then. And good bye." Tofar stooped down and poked the item into his bag as the boy retreated and disappeared into the bowels of the ship.

As he passed the men stacking the unloaded cargo, they sneered and muttered what were now familiar jests about his appearance. Would the indignities never end? He stopped after several paces to fold the heavy cape over his arm. There was little he could do about his other attire. The bright, intricately-patterned shirt and *malab,* or narrow wrap-around skirt that men of his island home traditionally wore, could not be missed among men who dressed in drab, loose-fitting trousers, shabby tunics and leather boots. Then there was the color of his skin and the length of his hair. Since setting out from his home, he had seen no one whose skin color matched his own shade of brown, or seen men with long, black hair braided in his customary style. Tofar bowed his head and stroked his face self-consciously.

The young newcomer continued forward as the sun bore down with greater energy, away from the sea, away from the memory of an unsteady rising and falling of the ship beneath his sandaled feet—feet which much preferred the uneven cobblestone street. With the first leg of his journey behind him, he now preferred a comfortable bed upon which to lay his feet.

Tofar passed buildings of stone and wood huddled together like soldiers in close rank standing against an enemy. The weathered exteriors seemed to hover overhead either protecting or threatening— he could not decide which is was. Betwixt stood in stark contrast to his home where life was lived in open, spacious quarters. Servants in constant motion had made sure every crumb and scrap was swept away and all surfaces scrubbed. Betwixt did not receive such care.

"Sir!" yelled a young lad who looked to be about ten years-old. "Sir! You've arrived on the Lone Wolf, eh?"

Tofar was startled to be addressed by a child in the street. "What is it? Why yes, I did. How did you know?" The boy laughed, then stopped himself and said, "Sir, you're lookin' quite lost, and your clothes—you look like someone from..." he paused trying not to sound disrespectful. "From somewhere else." Tofar felt his face flush with self-consciousness. "I saw the ship come in this morning," the lad confessed.

"By any chance do you know where I may find a meal and a bed?" stammered Tofar.

"Sir! This is your lucky day. Just around this corner my uncle awaits to welcome you to his inn. Follow me."

Tofar smiled and wearily dodged stray dogs, sweepers' crude brooms, and vendors setting up temporary shops in the street. His pace quickened as the smells of fresh bread overpowered the stench of days-old fish.

"Here. Right in here," said the boy as he bowed and backed away.

The innkeeper's short stature resembled the round sign swinging above the doorway that read, The Owl's Nest. A painted, round-bodied owl peered down with wide eyes upon those who passed below. Inside, Tofar struggled to adjust his eyes to the dark. After several minutes, the low ceiling and heavy, wooden beams forming the structure emerged from the murk, and he began to take note of his surroundings. Compared to the dank atmosphere below the ship's deck, the inn appeared as an oasis of comfort.

"Welcome, welcome!" said the innkeeper and waved his arm with a flourish. He looked up and down at the young man before him with what Tofar thought exhibited more exuberance than was warranted. "I see you are..." the innkeeper wore a look of skeptical

4

amusement and paused to find the right word. "...a gentleman of means? You will be in want of a room and a meal. Is that correct?"

Tofar didn't know if he should be embarrassed by the remark. "Why yes, in my country I am a gentleman. And I will be wanting a room and meal," he said, attempting an air of superiority. Interchange with common service people was unfamiliar. What was the right thing to say? If someone were to ask, how would he explain his presence so far from home? Who would he say he was, what name would he give?

Be careful! said the voice in his head.

"That will be two milos. Pay me now, and then it is right this way. A room is waiting for you at the top of the stairs. I will bring you a tasty soup shortly." Tofar found his money belt underneath his shirt and brought out a gold coin. The innkeeper's eyes widened. He rubbed his hands together, his eyes fixed on the shiny object, and asked, "Will you be staying several nights, then?"

"I believe I will," Tofar said after a pause in which he tried to remember if he had a plan or not.

"Is there a name to go with your room?" he asked, "In case someone comes looking for you."

"No one will be looking for me; I am certain of that." replied Tofar. He tried to shrug off the temptation to distrust everyone he met.

The innkeeper led the way to the stairs, passing the entrance to a dimly-lit dining room. Three roguish-looking men sat at a table and turned away as Tofar walked by. Fighting off an apprehensive chill, he started up the creaking, wooden stairs that led to a broad hall and balcony. Narrow doors of hand-planed oak lined the upper floor.

"Where have you come from?" asked the innkeeper trying to appear only slightly interested.

"Far from here," he offered suppressing a yawn. "You would not know my home. It is quite a distance."

Sleeping on board the ship had been a near impossibility. Tofar could barely keep his eyes open by the time he was shown a bed. He entered the small room noting the low, wooden beams that made it difficult to stand upright.

"Watch your head," warned the stocky man. "You are taller than most of our guests, and unusually dressed. Forgive my curiosity, but we have not seen such dress as yours before this." Tofar again felt the heat of embarrassment come over his cheeks.

A young servant appeared carrying a platter of hot soup and warm bread smothered with a sweet fruit preserve. Tofar's eyes glistened with anticipation and joy at the thought of eating real food. Once he was alone, he ate like a greedy animal, his mind in a luxurious fog. Thoughts of his island superiors burst and disappeared like annoying bubbles, as he enjoyed the moment.

Be careful! It is a dangerous world beyond.

Not again. Not now. He savored every slurp of soup and bite of bread, then collapsed into peaceful sleep.

*

Bright sunlight filtered through the narrow, paned window when Tofar woke. He was lost to time. Judging by the position of the sun, he reckoned the day was little more than half gone. A squeak brought him fully awake. He turned to see a large mouse casually finishing the last crumbs of bread. Tofar's sudden jolt of surprise did not startle the brazen creature. Tofar brushed it away with a swish of his hand and watched as it scurried away and hid behind the bulging bag beside the bed.

Ah, yes, my bag and the package. What have we here? His fingers rummaged through the overstuffed bag, then extracted the mysterious gift that had been tightly bound with string. A small knife Tofar carried soon remedied the problem, the heavy wrapping folded back to reveal the contents.

The first to catch his attention was a small, drawstring pouch containing several gold coins. He had brought money for the journey, but perhaps someone knew he would need just a bit more. The second item was an amulet on a leather thong. He ran his fingers over the surface observing the small flowers that surrounded a central stone. It was a beautiful piece that must have been made by an expert jeweler. He smiled at the memory of his boyhood attempts to duplicate in

6

wood the intricate crest of his family. This was no amateur's copy but the valuable relic of some bygone era. *Does he think I need this with me for protection, or to remember the last remaining member of my family? Yes, I will not forget you.*

Tofar opened the letter and surveyed what he expected to be the familiar warnings from his mother. *Why must I be treated like this? I am of age! I do not need your help.*

He folded the letter and thrust it, the coins and the amulet into a small woven bag he wore around his waist. *I will read this later,* he thought, dreading the confrontation once again with his mother's overpowering fear.

Rubbing the dusty window pane with his shirt sleeve revealed a clearer view of the street. With its sunlit beauty and freshness, nature beckoned him. The day was too glorious to waste sitting inside and brooding about all the possible things that could happen to him as he ventured out on his own for the first time in his life. For one afternoon, his quest for a plan could be put aside.

*

"You there, Sir. Can you tell me a way to find a walking path in the forest beyond the village?" asked Tofar of the innkeeper who stood near the front door.

"Indeed! You are going out then? Splendid day for a walk. Wonderful idea!" returned the stout host in a loud voice. "Just go out this door and walk about one hundred paces. You will see a road on your left. Take that road until it branches out left again and up into the hills. Make sure you don't get lost." He turned to stare at the men sitting at the gnarled oak table in the back of the saloon.

"Thank you. I will return soon," said Tofar confidently.

*

Following the innkeeper's directions proved to be simple, and soon he found his way to a well-traveled pathway into the woods. Broad branches of leafy trees reached out over the road providing a cooling shade from the intense sunlight. Rich, earthy smells enhanced

7

by recent rain lured him onward. Like his island home, the forest was alive with buzzing of insects and conversations of lively birds. Tofar closed his eyes and reflected on the joy of being free from the confines of the creaking ship and the loathsome sailors; free from the duties and cares of being the only son of a mother who never stopped worrying about his safety.

The narrow path into the forest wound around and twisted right and left. Tofar climbed over gnarled roots and jumped over muddy puddles, sometimes losing focus on the sights before him. Trying to take in the beauty of the setting, as well as the details of the trail, almost distracted him from the need to remember the way back to the village.

Stopping to memorize the sight of a large, twisted tree as a landmark, he heard a rustling sound in the bushes. An ominous feeling overtook him, despite his determination to resist the fearsome voices that always haunted his mind. Tofar turned to face the tangle of shrubs.

"Is there someone there?" he yelled.

Hearing nothing, he continued, lost in the sights and smells of lush vegetation. The rustling sounds seemed to parallel his path.

"Hello?" he called out. There was no response. He picked up a section of fallen branch from the ground, pondering the possibility of a wild animal stalking him.

Without warning, a large, bearded man stepped into view and advanced steadily in Tofar's direction. His disheveled clothes and haughty expression stirred instant alarm.

"Didn't I see you at the inn?" The bearded man laughed and raised his hand to signal someone to join him. Panic struck, but it was too late for Tofar to run. Before he could respond, the two men rushed at him, one leading with a fist that found its mark on Tofar's jaw. Flashes of starlight filled his senses and he crumpled to the ground. Wincing in pain, he curled up in a ball as the punches and kicks landed on his defenseless body.

Muffled voices in the distance, jostling, pain, followed by quiet stillness. Starlight faded into a brilliant, blinding light. Rearing up before him, an enormous white horse appeared, with hooves striking the air threatening to descend and crush his chest. He tried to turn, but was frozen to the ground. Above the horse, the face of the rider appeared. The light all but eclipsed him, as his bright clothing shone like the sun at noon on a cloudless day. He looked momentarily at Tofar with a bold, compassionate smile, then turned to beckon someone in the distance with a wave of his arm.

The vision evaporated into darkness.

CHAPTER 2

AMETH

Sounds of crackling fire reached Tofar's ears before he opened his eyes to find himself in a small, dimly-lit room.

"Who have we here?" A wizened, prune of a face peered down at the hapless figure Tofar imagined himself to be. "Looks like someone has put you in a sorry state, young man."

The creaking voice continued speaking, but it was not to Tofar this time that he addressed his comments. "He is waking, Barth."

Tofar tried to speak. The old man placed his hand under the wounded youth's head, raised it, and poured a pleasant-tasting liquid into his mouth. The movement of his head caused pain to shoot from his neck down through the muscles of his abdomen. Tofar yelped. He turned his head away bringing even more discomfort.

"Where am I? Who are you?" Tofar wheezed and shut his eyes again in fear of the answers. He began to shiver, then moaned in misery at the realization of his predicament. "What happened?"

"You are safe, my son. Do not fear. We are here to help. You were beaten up badly, but you will survive. Lie still." The old man took blankets handed to him by his servant, Barth, and laid them carefully on the patient.

The flickering fire offered light, its warmth melting away the quaking of Tofar's body. Feeling around the edges of the mat where he had been laid, he detected what felt like straw beneath the rough bedding. This was a new experience as, save for the uncomfortable hammock on board the Lone Wolf, he had never laid upon so primitive a surface.

A round, blackened pot boiled over the fire. The smell of broth reached his nostrils and the sound of his rumbling stomach broke the silence. The old man's merry eyes, dancing with the reflective glint of firelight, turned to stare into his patient's face.

"The name is Ameth. What shall we call you?"

An automatic fear rose once again as Tofar thought about how to respond to the question. Ameth observed a wince and a narrowing of his patient's eyes in the dim light. "You have nothing to fear from me, my son. Others would harm you, but I have no such plans for you. You are safe here." Detecting warmth and genuine sincerity, the fear retreated.

"My name is Tofar," he whispered trying to find his voice.

"Aahh," replied Ameth in a long drawn out manner, as if searching for some significance.

Tofar looked into the wrinkled face that radiated kindness and dignity, the likes of which he had never experienced. His body was bent and thin. Though it was obvious he was no longer physically strong, his senses did not seem at all diminished. Simply garbed in a long brown robe tied at the waist with a sash, he was unimpressive in the way Tofar would expect a dignified, older man to be impressive. In his island country, such a man would be dressed in robes of the finest cloth.

"This is good. This is very good. Just Tofar, then."

"How did I get here? I was in the woods. Those men, they attacked me, I think." A muddled mix of memories jumped in and out of Tofar's mind; the men, the light. What did it mean?

"Barth did not see the men you speak of. He was directed....well, he found you lying in the road," replied Ameth. "He brought you here to my home."

Tofar turned his eyes to the young man who stirred the broth and noted his craggy face and obvious strength. "Thank you. I am grateful. I.....I don't know how to thank you." Tofar fell silent exhausted by his efforts to speak. After sipping as much broth as he could manage from Ameth's oversized spoon, he closed his eyes and relaxed.

"You need to rest now. It is late. Tomorrow we will talk. Sleep in peace."

"But I must get back to the inn. The innkeeper warned me not to get lost. They will be worried."

"You are in no condition to find your way back tonight. It is late. We will talk tomorrow." There was a reflective pause before Ameth continued with a hint of glee, "This might be the first night of a great adventure."

*

Tofar did not sleep well. He could not move without great pain. The faint trill of crickets outside masked his own labored breathing, punctuated by flashes of light when he closed his eyes. He tried to make sense of all his jumbled thoughts, lining them up in as much order as he could remember. He must have been hit on the head with a club, or perhaps punched in the face. The blow had brought the flash of light. But what of the white horse and the radiant rider who smiled at him? Nothing made sense no matter how many times he revisited the scene. Somewhere in the night, he fell asleep at last, not waking until it was fully light.

*

Stiffness and aching greeted Tofar as he woke to bright sun beaming into the room through arched windows. Tofar looked himself over to find that his cuts had been bandaged, dirt had been washed away and his clothes were somewhat straightened. Relief flooded his mind to find that his impressions of safety remained in the light of day.

12

Looking about him to observe the manner in which Ameth lived, a strange security comforted him. The sparsely furnished room was small and peaceful. On a low table, a careless stack of books rested next to several stubs of candle. Close to the straw mat, a washbowl and pitcher had been placed to refresh the unexpected guest.

The clunk of split firewood being placed on the stone hearth roused Tofar from his repose. Barth was busy with his morning duties, and it wasn't long before delicious smells filled the air.

Down a narrow stairway from his upper chamber, Ameth arrived in the room. Despite his age, he looked cheerful and energetic.

"What a wonderful day, Barth, Tofar! What adventure will we find ourselves in today?"

Hearing the word adventure reminded Tofar of his host's final words the night before. Adventure, he concluded, must be the fuel that kept Ameth young and filled with life.

"I hope you are feeling somewhat revived today, my son. You look better than you did last night. Come, drink this hot tea. Bread? Cheese? Ah, fresh fruit from my garden!" Ameth had thought of everything.

Tofar's head ached. The rest of his body was bruised and battered. "I hurt everywhere; other than that, I am sure I will live." Tofar tried to sound positive and adventurous.

"Now tell me, where have you come from?" Ameth asked with such concern and compassion that Tofar found himself wanting his host to know more.

"I arrived in Betwixt on the Lone Wolf, which is now docked at the seaside." Tofar flinched at the pain in his head and reached to steady himself. "Frightful journey." Ameth waited for him to continue.

"Before that, I traveled for three weeks from an island to the southwest. You wouldn't know the place; it is such a long way away."

"Hmm. You would be surprised at what I know. And your family? asked Ameth. "Do you have a family name?"

"I do not have much in the way of family. There is my mother; that is all." Tofar's face hardened and he wondered why the concern about his family name. How did this old man decide to pick on the most sensitive issue in his young life?

"Have you no father, sister, or brother?" Ameth's questioning annoyed him, and after a shake of the head, wished to say no more on the subject.

"You must forgive my questioning you about your family. I seek only to reveal some chance connection. You are much like, " Ameth hesitated, "an old acquaintance. What would be the chance that you and he are related?" he said with a brief laugh.

"It would be a comfort to know I look like somebody, as so far, I seem to be very strange to everyone I've met."

"In this part of the kingdom, that would be true. But there are other places where you would be quite at home," said Ameth, before changing his tone. "Tell me, do you know who attacked you in the woods?"

"I'm not sure, but one of them looked like a fellow I saw at the inn. I have a bag there and have already paid for several night's stay."

"Hmmm. At the inn, you say. I think we can assume your belongings might be difficult to recover. Was there anything of great value?"

"Just clothing, and my cape. It was valuable to me, but not to anyone else," Tofar answered in a weak voice. "This is outrageous. The scoundrels cannot simply walk away with my possessions."

"Perhaps it is for the best. These are clothes which will only bring attention to your foreign origins. We must find something for you that is more in keeping with local custom."

"But the innkeeper," Tofar stammered. "Why would he...?

"Don't concern yourself with that now. It may be best for your location to be kept from the innkeeper and his ilk. Is anything missing from your person?"

Tofar's stiff arm reached for his waist and the small bag of coins and other items from his recent gift. "Is this what you are looking for?" asked Ameth holding up the small pouch. "Barth found it lying beside you in the woods."

"Yes, that is where I kept my money. They took everything I had then," he said through clenched teeth and tightened jaw.

"I guess the robbers did not want this." Ameth held up the letter. "Barth found this at your side." Ameth ran his fingers over the letter, sensing the fibrous texture of island parchment. He squinted to look closer at the seal. "Is this something important to you?" he asked.

"It's just the family seal. It was with my amulet and the gold coins I received yesterday morning. I have not read it fully, as it is probably more of my mother's fearful ramblings. She was, and remains, obsessed with my safety."

"For good reason, don't you think?" asked Ameth. "You received an amulet with the letter? What did it look like?"

Tofar tried to raise his hands to show the size and shape as he described the decoration. "It has small flower patterns carved around a central stone. I suppose it looks like something valuable, so it is no surprise that it was taken."

Again, Ameth looked to be deep in thought, as he heard the details of Tofar's former possession.

"Do you want to read the letter now? It may shed light on your mishap."

"Common thieves. How dare they? They wanted money and it is money they took, though I am not sure why they had to kick the stuffing out of me while they were at it."

"Calm yourself, young man. Anger will not undo the damage. What is done, is done. Now, the letter?"

"I do not think I am able to read it. Will you? Then you will understand what I mean."

"Let me get my spectacles.....ah yes. And I begin.....

To my dear Tofar,

You have been like a son to me all these years. I knew your father well, and we all grieved his loss all those years ago. I have looked out for you and your mother as you grew up. She may have told you fascinating tales of old, I am sure. You must not

15

tell anyone about your past or family. Be very careful as your family has, to this day, enemies who would send you to the same fate as that of your father. I can no longer help you. You made the decision to leave us and now you must find your way by yourself. I know you seek answers about the past, but be warned. Despite what your mother longs to know about the disappearance of your father, you must take great care if you search for answers to the past.

I give you this amulet that belonged to him. May it bring you good fortune. Some say it has magical powers, but it is more meaningful as a symbol of your family. Guard it carefully and keep it hidden.

The ship's captain has been good enough to look out for you and give you this letter. I fear there are always spies about who would bring you great misfortune. You have had enough misfortune to last a lifetime already.

May the gods be with you.
Jopha.

Ameth was silent and held the letter before him for a long while before putting it down. "What do you think it means?" he asked Tofar.

"I know Jopha. He is advisor to my mother. He sounds just as fearful as she, if not more."

"Is this your mission—to find your father?" Ameth asked.

"I shouldn't be talking about this. You read the letter. You see? Everyone is afraid I will find out something terrible, something that will endanger my life as well. But I have to know. Until that time, I do not know who I really am! You can see why I cannot tell you a family name. I do not even know it myself. I have to invent a name, but I can't even think of a good name to invent!"

Tofar's anger brought constricted muscles and increased pain. He had not meant to reveal this dark secret about himself, but it was out. He was no one, of no importance. All the pride that should prop

16

up his sense of family and belonging had been shattered; his family destroyed through some evil scheme that made his name a forbidden word.

"I may be able to help you," said Ameth, again in low voice. "I will send Barth to find out more about your belongings. You must stay here with me until your head and body heal from your injuries. Together we will make a plan."

"But, sir, I cannot repay you," replied Tofar.

"The name is Ameth," he insisted. "And you needn't pay me anything, since now you have no money."

Tofar's anger burned at his helpless state. "But I must. It is only right. I cannot accept all this help from you and not repay you."

"I may have some work for you to do to repay your debt." The young man looked into Ameth's eyes and noted a change from kindly smile to serious concern. "Now you must eat something and then rest. We must get you healed and healthy before we talk of such things."

"You are very kind, and why? I do not know. I am no one here. I have nothing. I do not know where I am going or what I am doing." Tofar hung his head in utter disbelief and regret. "In my island home, I was at least the son of a wealthy Mistress. That meant nothing to me at the time."

"My son, there are several reasons why I want to help you. For one, I have lived a long time. I have been in your place many times and longed for such help. I did receive it, most undeservedly, and now I help others. Someday, you will do the same. You are someone, and perhaps more important than you are capable of imagining." Tofar sighed, unable to conceive of such a circumstance.

"The second reason is, you need some practical help. From the way you are dressed, you appear to be from another age. No one has seen such hair, such clothes, for many years. People are afraid of strangers these days." They both laughed. Ameth turned to stare into the firelight. "And besides that, I do believe you were sent here for a reason. In time, all will become clear."

Tofar did not understand what reason there could be for his

being attacked and almost killed. Through his distress and anger, he heard Ameth continue to address him as "my son." In his heart was an ache and desire to be connected to something, someone larger and nobler than himself. Ameth's face was wrinkled and sunbaked, but humble and sincere. Perhaps it was *his* face that had appeared in the bright light. Perhaps Tofar's own mind had translated the aged countenance into the strong, compassionate face he had seen.

"Barth will help you learn what you need know to help me." Ameth gestured toward the quiet man who smiled as he tended the fire. "You shall know him better soon. He is my right hand, and some days my left one as well."

Tofar turned his head to acknowledge Barth. A sudden sharp pinching sensation stabbed his neck. A bright light flashed in his head once again. Horse's hooves high overhead, noise, pain. He grabbed his neck and fell back onto the mat. Barth and Ameth rushed to his side.

"Are you alright?"

"Who was that?"

"Who are you referring to?" asked Ameth.

"The rider. The white horse. The light," moaned Tofar as he squeezed his eyes together trying to shut out the pain. Ameth and Barth looked at one another and smiled.

"What did he look like?"

"Strong, brave. His face, he looked at me as if he knew me."

"My son, I believe you have seen The Prince."

CHAPTER 3

THE SIGN

The memory of the previous day and night blurred and was all but forgotten the following morning. Tofar rose carefully, hobbled to the fireplace, soaking in the heat for his injured body.

Barth crept into the room, carrying a bundle of vegetables in one arm and wood for the fire in the other. Tofar could see how his own lanky frame could have been lifted from the ground and carried to Ameth's home. Barth was not tall, but he was heavily muscled, no doubt a result of the physical work he performed. His bushy hair was short, with wisps of garden cuttings caught up in unkempt locks. Tofar estimated his age to be several years beyond his own, though he was still youthful. The most intriguing feature appeared to be deep lines etched in his face. It was easy to see that Barth had experienced either an accident or some violent episode that resulted in jagged scars. Tofar's mind went to work immediately concocting one imaginary scenario after another to explain the marks.

The servant stepped forward holding a round object in front of his patient's face. He had fashioned a neck brace from heavy canvas like cloth. After motioning his intent to put it on Tofar, he then gently wrapped the brace and fastened it in place.

"Thank you. I am sure it will help the pain." Tofar paused before asking, "Barth. May I be so bold as to ask how you got those scars?"

"You may, my friend. The answer will not please you. As you have probably imagined, I have been a fighting man most of my life. Were it not for my Lord, the Prince, I may have been one of the men who roughed you up and stole your money. He rescues the villain as well as the victim."

Stunned, Tofar did not know what to say next.

"I have something else for you." Barth reached behind a small wooden chair and brought out a wrapped bundle of cloth. Tofar immediately recognized the lining of the cape he had worn on his sea voyage.

"What is this? How did you find this?" he asked as he hastily untied a loose knot in the ends of the garment. "My clothes! Where were they?"

"I found them behind the inn. It looked as if they had been thrown out after being inspected and found not to be worth much in the street market. Can you tell me what else is missing?" asked Barth in his quiet manner.

"Did you go back there in the middle of the night? Weren't you afraid they would hear you?"

"Did you forget so soon that I am a former thief? That part was easy for me. Now tell me what is missing? Perhaps I can retrieve any valuables you had."

"It looks like most of it is here. Wait, there were gold coins; but I doubt those can be found; they are likely already spent."

"Is that all?" asked Barth again.

"My amulet that was in my small pouch. That can't be very important. I wouldn't want you to risk your life for that."

"I will see what I can find. Do you remember any more about the attack?" asked Barth.

"I can hardly remember anything at all."

"Do you remember yesterday you said that you had seen a light and a person on a horse?"

"I said that? Yes. I can still see his face in my mind. Do you know who it was? Ameth said something about a prince. Is that the one you speak of?"

"Not just a prince; it was THE Prince," replied Barth.

"Prince? Prince of what?"

"He is the son of the High King; the one who reigns above all."

"I have never heard of a high king, but then I have only just arrived in this part of the world. Why would his son suddenly appear just when I've been beaten up and left to die? Why didn't he arrive sooner and save me from this predicament? And why did he leave again?" asked Tofar with a scowl.

"You were not aware of the circumstances of your rescue, Tofar. I did not just find you in the forest by accident. I was headed in a different directions when I saw a bright light. The Prince was there. It was he who stopped the robbers from making sure you did not live to tell of your attack. It was he who directed me to you lying on the path. I think the reason he allowed this attack was so that I would find you and bring you here."

Tofar was astounded by this revelation and was about to reply when Ameth entered the room, unaware of the ongoing conversation. He stared intently at a small scroll.

"Barth, I must speak with you outside for a moment."

Curious as to what the two discussed, Tofar rose from his bed, stepped closer to the door, and tried to listen to the conversation. Ameth spoke very softly, but some of his words were discernable nonetheless.

"...change of plans...the young man must go...this could be the very sign we have waited for." Only a few words made any sense after that. "Ask the Captain...find out...send this message."

As Tofar moved away from the door and back to his place, he wondered, *Is he talking about me? What plans? How is my coming here a sign? Sign of what?* The voices of fear nagged again, warning of danger and

21

threat, even in this serene place. He held his hands to his ears and said, "No!"

"No?" asked Ameth returning to the room.

"Oh, no. I don't mean 'no'. I, well, I have so many addled thoughts. I don't know where I am or why. Maybe I should go."

"To that *I* will say 'no'! You are in no danger here, Tofar. But you may be in danger traveling about in the kingdom. I will explain all to you in time. You are afraid, are you not?" asked Ameth.

"I have lived my life with fear. I want to be free of the voices that shout in my mind that everything is to be feared. I have tried to brush them away only to find that real danger does exist. I cannot ignore that."

"In time, my son. Rest and be patient."

*

Darkness cloaked the land to all who did not know its every tree and knoll. For one accustomed to making the journey at night, the forest did not hide its roots and stones that, to the ordinary day traveler, could trip and confuse. Barth easily slipped behind the inn at Betwixt, once again seeking an unsecured window or unlocked door. He waited and listened.

From inside, he heard someone laughing, a low, evil laugh of contempt.

"Sweet little bauble. Humble, innocent-looking decoration. I know what you are and who you belong to." He laughed again through the slurred speech of one who has been sampling his own strong drink.

Barth peeked around the corner of a small window and saw the rotund innkeeper sprawled upon his chair. The table before him held empty mugs and overturned bottles. A closer look at the man revealed an intricately patterned amulet on a leather string in his hand.

"You can't fool me. I know who you are. I'll find you, and when I do, you will be sorry you ever left that sweet mama of yours. And I will be richer. I will get such a reward for this. Oh, yes I will. Wait and see."

Barth wondered what he meant by these words. The innkeeper's

22

head dropped and then jerked upright again.

"Where are you? Mouse! Butch! Go find him. Where are you? Don't tell me you are sleeping. It's only, it's only. What is it? Oh, its late. Tomorrow! Tomorrow you go find that boy and you bring him to me."

*

Tofar longed to be able once again to go outside and enjoy the sun on his face. After several days of practice, he walked slowly to the nearest window to view the gardens surrounding the house. He held his side firmly to reduce the pain of what he suspected was a broken rib. The throbbing of his head and the dizziness continued, but the joy of being nearer to nature and sunlight cheered him immensely. The anger and sense of violation had faded to a manageable state, in light of the peace and comfort experienced in the care of the wise, old man and his mysterious servant.

The windows afforded a splendid view of the forest beyond Ameth's humble estate. Several paths led away from the building and Tofar wondered where each would take him, should the temptation to wander or explore come upon him.

"Come," said Ameth. "I see you staring out the window. Now you must walk with me and see my garden."

Tofar's unsteady gait and pain made the prospect risky, but the offer was too good to turn down, even if it caused discomfort. He was amazed to see the mystical beauty of the landscape. A gardener with a tasteful eye had planted flowering shrubs of every color and shape. Moss hung from a variety of ancient trees. Everything was neatly trimmed and meticulously cared for.

With the inviting pathways he had seen from the windows at last under his feet, Tofar tread gingerly beside Ameth upon pavement of orange and yellow-hued stones. The care taken in creating such works of artistry fascinated him and absorbed his attention. He turned to look back at the house and was shocked by its animated appearance. The unusual windows he had gazed through only from the inside—arched at the top and flat on the bottom, with one on each side of the oak entrance—seemed to form eyes and a mouth. A narrow stand with a lamp was centered in each window.

"Oh" cried Tofar. "Your house! It looks like an all-seeing watchmen guarding your garden. Did you design it this way?"

"You noticed. Yes, I did. I built this house many years ago, back when I was much younger."

"You have lived here a long time then. What has been your occupation for all these years?"

"I have done many things. In time I will explain in more detail. Right now you must be at peace. Conflict and troubles will come, but today we enjoy the beauty of our surroundings."

Tofar wondered of what conflict and troubles Ameth spoke.

"Can you tell me more about The Prince that you and Barth have spoken about to me?"

"Ah, I have so much to tell you. It is true we must begin, and the sooner the better."

"Why is that?"

"You could be more important than you know. Here. I have something for you." Ameth reached into his pocket and pulled out a small item. He handed Tofar's amulet to him, closing his own hands around the young man's as he received it.

"How did you find it?"

"Barth did the deed. It was in the possession of the innkeeper as we suspected."

"I am amazed. He is a talented fellow," Tofar exclaimed.

"This amulet is a valuable piece, more valuable than you may realize," Ameth said with a far-away look in his eyes. "I believe it holds the meaning of your journey."

Tofar looked closely, as if for the first time, and wondered what Ameth meant. "The stone is unusual. None like it could be found in the land of my sojourn."

"The markings on the back, do you think they mean anything?" asked Ameth. They both peered at the intersecting, engraved lines.

"Let me see. They appear to be very random and devoid of

design. I had never noticed before."

"Curious. Someday perhaps we will know the meaning."

"As a young boy, I attempted to carve a copy of the flowers. I could not duplicate its detail, though I tried with all my skill."

Ameth seemed deep in thought. "You are a carver of wood, then? I will test your skill and put you to work."

"Describe something that would be useful to you and I will make it. That is the least I can do." said Tofar.

Ameth became more serious, "You must be very careful. It appears that the symbol on the amulet has been recognized. We must keep your presence here a guarded secret. The men who beat you may come looking for you again."

"But why? I don't have any more gold to steal."

"What I am about to tell you will sound very strange, since you have heard nothing of the kingdom to which you belong. I think that those around you as a child must have known the story. For some reason, they have kept this from you; I am about to tell you. Let us begin at the beginning."

CHAPTER 4

THE KINGDOM

"Long ago, before anyone can remember, the Kingdom of Illumah enjoyed the rule of Zenith, the High King. He was—and still is—wise and benevolent, merciful and just." said Ameth.

"Can he still live after so long?" asked Tofar.

"Indeed he lives. He is not called the High King for no reason, for he lives on in the great City of Light, far to the north. King Zenith, it is said—for no one I know has seen him in person—is more than just a king. He knows all. Many years ago, he powerfully ruled over the entire kingdom. Peace and contentment reigned in his vast domain. There was no need for King Zenith to have an army to defend the kingdom as there were no enemies.

So that each and every subject of the kingdom could declare their allegiance to the one king, he placed a pome—a glowing, golden ball in the shape of an apple—on a crystal pedestal in front of the throne room. Everyone who claimed him as king journeyed to the City of Light and touched the pome. In return, they received illumination, purpose and hope. The people of the kingdom drew life and health from the strength and goodness of the King. All could take comfort in knowing the High King was on his throne, and their lives and welfare were safe in his care. They belonged to the High King as part of his family. In the days of old, the sacred pome was named "The Promise" because it stood for all that the King had promised his people.

"That sounds wonderful," said Tofar. "Did something change?"

"Ah yes. The King's most trusted and gifted servant—Alpha by name—became jealous of the love and loyalty that all the people had for their king. His loyalty was not to the king, but to his own evil designs. Slowly, his jealousy turned to hatred. He began to plan how he could steal the Promise and destroy it.

Quite accidentally, he discovered that while holding it in his hands, as he formed his scheme, instead of life and hope, he was filled with anger. The longer he held it, the more the anger manifested itself, until his whole body changed into the form of a ferocious dragon. Once the supernatural knowledge of his ability to change temporarily into this beast took root in his heart, he knew he could not destroy the golden fruit. He knew he would use it for his own ends, to gain power over the people of the kingdom.

He began to circulate a rumor that life and goodness came from the Promise itself, and not from the king. Whoever possessed it gained the authority and power to rule the kingdom. When at last he convinced a large number of the king's subjects that it was the Promise they should revere, he then stole it and spirited it, and himself, away in the night."

"Did the servant then claim to be king?" asked Tofar.

"He did not call himself king. Instead, he changed his name, taking the title Ultimate Ruler Malpha, and claimed that he alone had the right to rule because he owned the golden pome, the Promise. In order to prove his greatness, he held it in his hands and let his anger flow until he again turned into the terrible green creature. People were terrified and quickly submitted to his demands. Those who refused were imprisoned, or worse. Word spread that the creature had bested the High King in battle and, as a result, he claimed all authority.

Gradually over time, every small or great village and town recognized the symbol and authority of the dragon."

"What did the High King do?" asked Tofar.

"King Zenith declared that Malpha had committed high treason. Condemnation and death awaited him in the future. Anyone who believed his lies was likewise condemned and separated from the true life that the king alone offered."

"Does King Zenith propose to reclaim the people who have turned away from him?"

"He does, indeed. Instead of an army to win back the allegiance of his people by force—for Malpha had turned the hearts of the people away from King Zenith, telling them that there was no such king—he chose one person, his only son. To the king, the crime committed by Malpha was much worse than merely stealing the symbol of his authority. The king considers the stolen hearts of his people to be a treasure valued far above a simple golden object."

"How could the king's son accomplish such a great task?"

"Malpha discovered that the son was coming against him. He laughed at the very idea that one man could defeat him, even if he was the son of the High King.

The Prince came before Malpha, challenged his authority and demanded that the citizens of Illumah be allowed to return to their rightful ruler. That snake was furious. Angered by the King's condemning proclamation, he commanded that anyone in the kingdom who defied his position as Ultimate Ruler would likewise suffer death at his hands. Everyone waited to see if Malpha had the temerity to carry out his threat and kill the very son of the High King."

"Well? Did he?" asked Tofar, begging Ameth to go on with the story.

"The Prince confronted Malpha on his rule of death. He said to him, 'Only my father has the authority to punish for the wrong that has been done. You cannot kill me unless my father allows it. If I die, it is for the sake of the people. For believing your lies, you and they will suffer a similar fate. There is only one way you can kill me, and

28

that is if I take their punishment for them. As for you, you must take your own punishment from the High King on the day he has set. Indeed, he has set a day for you to die and you will see that day. The day that I die will begin the countdown for your own day of reckoning.'"

"This is very confusing. Why would the Prince allow himself to be killed?"

"Yes, it is hard to understand. It certainly is not the way most of us would handle the problem. Malpha was furious and gave orders for the Prince to be killed. What he did not understand that this was the beginning of his demise. Malpha had no intention of giving up his power. Once the Prince was out of the way, he thought he could reign supreme without a care. You see, the High King only had one son, so there were no more siblings to bother him."

"I do not understand. How could the Prince still be here if he was killed?"

"That is the amazing part, Tofar. The Prince did not stay dead. He is the son of his father, the eternal High King.

Shortly after the so-called execution, he began to appear to people around the kingdom. It seems that his new life had unleashed a power that was greater than Malpha—one that he could not comprehend or oppose."

"What did Malpha do when he realized that the Prince was alive?" the young man continued to question, and Ameth patiently responded.

"A command was issued that no mention of the Prince be made in the kingdom. They simply pretended that he did not exist. They denied that the person they killed was even the son of the High King, insisting that he was a mentally-disturbed vagrant of no consequence. Malpha fought the rumors of his appearances, but he was not successful. Many have seen and believed that he is powerfully working within the kingdom to achieve the goal of winning back his people.

But listen to this important truth, for it is verified by my secret informants. Malpha has not been able to carry out his original command to put anyone to death for their allegiance to the High King ever since. Oh, yes. He has sentenced various ones to death, but he has not been able to carry out the sentence, not once, ever since the Prince reappeared."

"How long ago did all this happen?" asked Tofar, still digesting the amazing story.

"It has been many years. Malpha is now very old, but I am told that he attempts to renew his youth each day by drinking the juice of the koma fruit to regain strength and vitality. The koma fruit had only been used for good before Malpha used it for evil. He lives in the lie that he will not die, that he is in control of the kingdom.

The Prince, on the other hand, remains powerful and active with the strength his father gave him. He wears the golden Aram which is an arm circlet signifying his submission to the High King. He is able to appear and come to the aid of those who cry out to him. Many have seen him and believed in him, despite the threats from Malpha."

"This is all so new and incredible. Why have I not heard about this before today? Has the fear of this man been so great that no one else will oppose him? And what does it have to do with me?"

"When Malpha forcefully took over towns and villages one by one, many suffered and were imprisoned, or fled before his armies. Many were dispersed to faraway places over the years. I believe that your family may have been ones fleeing before this false ruler when you were very young. The father you seek may be one of those who fled, or was imprisoned for resisting Malpha's evil plan."

"No wonder my people have spoken of nothing else but fear and danger all my life. Do you know the place where my family may have lived?"

"I do. Long ago, the small kingdom was known as Abundant, named for the wealth and happiness of its people. Now it has been renamed Tenebrose, the Dark, and it is the place where Malpha makes his current home."

"That explains much. Now I wonder what suffering my mother must have endured during this time you speak of. She could never tell me. Even when I announced my plans to leave, no one would speak of the events of the past."

"It has been many years since this happened. Perhaps they thought that living far out of reach of Malpha would assure their freedom. Part of the struggle is that one never knows how far to go to be out of his reach. They know that your departure from a safe haven puts you in danger of falling prey to the evil ruler's grasp once again."

"What about you and Barth? Aren't you within his grasp?"

"Betwixt is on the very edge of his domain. I have eluded him thus far, though I travel in and out of the kingdom. I believe that the Prince has protected me.

Tofar held the amulet in his hand and stared at the flower symbol. "Do you believe my father was an important man in the kingdom of Abundant? Is that why the Ruler might have sought to kill him?"

"I do not want to conjecture without more evidence. But you may be sure that you did come from that small kingdom, and your family knows more about who your father was than they have revealed. The innkeeper recognized this amulet. It would be wise to make sure it never falls into the wrong hands again."

"When I was attacked by those men, I hardly had the presence of mind to cry out for help. But in my heart, I did. The attack was vicious, but it stopped as soon as the vision of the man appeared. Do you think that I saw a vision of the Prince because I was in need?"

"I do. And I believe he stopped the robbers from making sure you would not come back to Betwixt alive," concluded Ameth. Tofar was quiet, letting the implications of the story connect.

The old man continued, "You are important to the Prince. He has given you a chance to become part of his Kingdom of Light— Illumah. To those who choose to follow him, he gives a special name; the name of something highly valuable."

"Do you follow him? Has he given you a special name?"

"Yes, Tofar. My name is Amethyst. I go by Ameth, as it arouses less suspicion."

"Amethyst. My mother has several of those precious stones in her small trove of treasures."

"It is my hope for you, Tofar, that you will meet the Prince and follow him as we have done. You must realize that by joining him in his quest to take back the kingdom, you put yourself in the way of risk. It will not be easy, but it will be rewarded."

"I wonder how the kingdom will ultimately be restored to the High King. How can the so-called Ultimate Ruler be defeated?" asked Tofar.

"I do not know for sure, but I believe the time is drawing near."

"Do you think the Prince wants me to follow him?"

"I do," said Ameth.

"Will I see him again?" asked Tofar.

"I believe you will," replied the old man.

CHAPTER 5

THE PRINCE

"Look to the south, Tofar."

Ameth and his student had wandered beyond the garden and found themselves at the top of a hill overlooking the sea far below.

"The islands of Metfall, Similon, and Engnar are just beyond the horizon. Your island home is to the southeast, is it not? I have travelled in that direction, but I do not know the exact location of that island."

"It took several weeks journey by ship to reach Betwixt, with few stops."

" You mother and her people must have wanted to be very sure they would not be found, to have traveled so far." Ameth's mind seemed to wander as he imagined the distant island. "I would love to meet your mother someday. Perhaps I will," he said with a wink and sly smile. Tofar tried to imagine such an event, but the possibility remained remote.

"You are very learned, Ameth. It seems that any question I ask of you, the answer comes quickly and thoroughly. The teachers of my youth did not know nearly so much; or perhaps they did not wish to reveal the information. Was I the only one who did not know the story of my family?"

"Both of those observations may be true. Know this, my son. Great knowledge can be a heavy burden to bear. In the next days and weeks, you will learn, and with the help of the Lord Prince, you will become wise."

"This is all so new to me. My formal schooling consisted of reading and writing, storytelling, fencing, and horsemanship, but nothing about history, geography, or the larger world. I have been taught nothing of the conflicts of the larger kingdom."

"You have much to learn. I will tell you as much as I think you can understand. In time, my son. In time."

"I have so many questions now," said Tofar. "The greatest of which is about the people of my family. Who are they?"

"Patience, my son. In time, you will know. I am old, and no longer as strong as I once was. However, I still have a strong heart and great concern for the kingdom. I sense that something powerful is afoot, and you and your family may play a part."

Try as he might, Tofar could not imagine how this was true, or how he or Ameth could be part of anything powerful enough to affect the entire kingdom.

The two men turned to amble down the hill towards the cottage.

"Tell me more about the Prince," the young man begged. "How did you meet him?" A look of painful sentimentality came over Ameth's face.

"Many years ago, when I was a much younger man, I lived with my brother in the house that we inherited from our parents. They died young. My brother was a wild youth and did not take his role as oldest son very seriously. I, on the other hand, was more of a scholar and did not pay attention to his unwise actions. I secluded myself in my study—keeping it quite secret—reading and accumulating knowledge of this and that. I decided to write a book on the history of the region of my birth, and so began to travel and conduct my research. It was then that I heard tales of the Prince and the story of Malpha. Marveling at this information, I told my brother of my discoveries. He mocked it all and was convinced I had lost my mind.

One night I was returning from one of my travels when I was surrounded by a group of men who threatened to kill me. I did not even have time to think. I cried out loud, 'Help me, Lord Prince!' There was a flash of light so bright it blinded the men and caused them to fall to the ground. They crawled away and I never saw them again."

"Did the Prince appear to you then?" asked Tofar.

"After that, there were many times that he rescued me. Each time, I learned more of his character and intentions for me. Naming me Amethyst, he commissioned me to be a soldier in his kind of army. The weapons of this warfare are not swords or knives, but they are truth and wisdom. It is with these that he plans to overthrow the evil ruler, Malpha.

"How did you come to leave your home?"

"My brother chose to follow the dragon. I chose to follow the Prince. Through some faithful servants, I learned that my brother planned to have me imprisoned. Just as he was about to carry out that plan, I escaped. I never returned, though I heard that he lost his home through his careless and irresponsible living."

"I am sorry to make you recall such an unhappy event. I only asked because you have told me so little of your own life in the past."

"My dear Tofar, I have had many close friends over the years who were a great comfort to me after I left the far country of my origin. And you have been like a son to me in these few days," Ameth said with grave conviction. "I have received much, and you too will have a future. I see that you will have many opportunities and choices ahead of you. You are very young yet. Great things lie in store."

At these words, Tofar's whole body tingled with excitement at the thought of what may lay ahead, despite the voices of danger and fear that never seemed far away. He wondered if Ameth was some kind of prophet who could see the future. Would there really be a day when he could leave his fears behind and be the man he wished to become?

*

In the dark of night, Tofar awoke and snapped involuntarily to an upright position. He had been dreaming again, reliving the attack in the forest, and feeling the strong presence of the one on the white horse. Had it been a dream, or was the Prince coming to him again? He longed to reach out and grasp the vision.

"Here I am," Tofar whispered. The mellow cooing of the evening dove drifted into the room from the garden.

"I am with you."

Was that a sound, or just a gentle breeze brushing past his ears? Tofar felt a dizzying joy overpower his senses. Safety and protection settled on his shoulders. His spirit was light and free. Closing his eyes, he saw the mighty horse and its rider casting a spray of sparkling points of light over him. As the light came to rest, a surge of strength came over his body. He wanted to cry out in celebration. Looking down at his chest, he saw shackles fall from his own heart, and dark shadows fled in terror from his presence.

"Topaz!" the rider shouted. "You are mine. Fear is gone."

*

The light of early morning met Tofar's eyes when at last he awoke. The visions of the night were still fresh and vibrant, as if they had only occurred moments before. He felt stunned and lay still for some time before realizing that he was indeed free of his debilitating fear. No voices rose up to dampen his joy.

Barth appeared to begin the morning ritual of fire and food.

"Barth," he called out. Before he could continue with his good news, Barth spoke in reply.

"You have met him, haven't you? I knew it. He has changed you. I see it in your face." He reached Tofar's side in a single bound, embraced him, and loudly slapped him on the back. Tofar grimaced momentarily, as the air seemed to be forced from his lungs by the exuberant show of affection and mutual joy.

When Ameth appeared, he immediately entered into the atmosphere of rejoicing and freedom. He hugged Tofar—with far less crushing effect—knowing exactly what had taken place.

"My son, he has freed you. You are now Topaz, the Light, for I see that light in your eyes."

"How did you know that he called me Topaz?"

"Ah, my boy, I know. I know."

"I'm not afraid." The newly-named youth leaped in the air. There was no pain. Retrieving the amulet from inside his shirt, he kissed it and sensed a new purpose for his suffering.

"Let us rejoice in this day of healing. A celebration is in order. What would be more fitting than to reflect on the greatness of the High King and his son." Ameth rummaged about in a pile of documents. Finding just the one he wanted, he began to read:

A day is coming when Malpha will be no more. The Prince will reclaim his rightful place as son of the High King and restore rule over his people. When that day has come, there will be such joy and such blessing, that the whole kingdom will celebrate together. The lights of all will shine at last.

"I wrote this years ago, not having any idea how this was to take place. I begin to see the signs that the day is closer than ever before."

The words did not dampen their spirits, but they did interject a note of the serious nature of what was unfolding before them.

"I hope there will be a day when I may travel back to my island home and tell them good news."

"Many adventures lie before us yet, my son. Be patient," admonished Ameth.

*

"Today we have some important matters to reflect upon," continued Ameth after they had eaten and discussed again the story of the Prince. "Come let us walk."

The youth and the old man walked slowly down what had become a familiar path, Ameth holding tight to Topaz's arm.

"You have grown stronger over these last days, which are quickly passing into weeks. I have been planning a journey for some time now.

I am old and not strong, so this journey may be my last. It is very important. I see now that you are to come with me. We must do this together. Your arrival here is a sign. I do not mean to bring you fear once again, but you will have a vital part in the success of this venture. It will be dangerous. There are many unknowns and risks awaiting. I will try to prepare you as best I can. What do you say?"

"I do not know what to say. I cannot imagine that I would be of value to you, as I am an ignorant youth. My life has been lived in a bubble, as one floating in the air, that now seems so distant and unconnected. Do you think the Prince has something important for me to do?"

"I do. And, I think you are ready. Right before you arrived at my door, word came that Malpha is planning to extend his claims even as far as Betwixt and beyond." exclaimed Ameth. "We have no time to lose!"

*

"I have a very great task to put before you, Topaz."

Surprised at the intensity with which Ameth spoke, he looked into the old man's face. He had no doubt been thinking of the task for some time and waiting for the right moment to talk about it.

"I will do it, Ameth. Whatever it is. You have done so much for me, I could never repay your kindness and care."

Ameth began to explain, "You will think this is a very strange request. You will help me and many other people if you are successful. You and I are going to go on a journey together. I would go alone, but there is a part of the task that only you can accomplish. Topaz, you have been sent here for this purpose. It may be to find the truth about your lost father, or it may be much more important than that."

Topaz shivered with tension and excitement. His world had turned upside down in only a matter of hours.

CHAPTER 6

TENEBROSE

In the next two days, Ameth began preparing for the journey. Barth and he conferred on the care and keeping of the house and garden.

"The task ahead of us is great. We are in the Prince's hands. Barth, you do your job well. If for some reason I do not return, you know what to do. I leave my home to you for your future."

"I hope you will return, Master Ameth. The time is right. The sign has been given," and here Barth turned to look intently at Topaz who stood observing the two.

Though Ameth had warned Topaz of the danger, hearing them talk this way brought a sobering solemnity to their interactions.

"Now I must turn my attention to you, my boy," Ameth said. "We must get you ready. You have to look like you belong to the city where I am taking you. I'm afraid we must cut your hair and give you some new clothes. You would stand out far too much in your present state."

Topaz did not savor these changes, but recognized that it was necessary. Ameth brought out a pair of large scissors and made the initial cut. The thick braid that had hung down Topaz's back all his life, was gone. Immediately, the remaining hair began to spring out in all directions. "Well, I can see why your people chose the braid over the shoulder-length cut," confessed Ameth. He continued to chop until most of the hair was cropped close to Topaz's head. "It may not look as you would like now, but it will grow again in time."

Topaz held out his few belongings for Ameth to scrutinize. "These clothes you arrived in will look too foreign. You will leave them behind."

Topaz looked down at the clothes that had been provided by Ameth. He had been wearing some of Barth's extras—a pair of baggy trousers and long, plain shirt. They felt strange enough, but now he must wear clothes even more strange and uncomfortable. The final touch of hat, coat, and gloves created a whole new look of maturity that made the strangeness worth it.

"I have made the arrangements. We will sail next week to the mainland and there travel to Tenebrose." Topaz's heart skipped a beat at the name of their destination. It was the city from which his ancestors originated. He did not relish another sea voyage, but this time would be different. He had someone to travel with him who knew how to make his way around the kingdom. And he would be one step closer to his mysterious beginnings.

*

Two men walked slowly down a well-kept path in the distance. One was tall and dark, the other old and bent. From behind low-hanging, leafy branches of a nubbly tree, Mouse and Butch cautiously observed the pair.

"That must be him—tall and thin, dark, young," said the one.

"How did he get here? He was in no shape to walk. That old man could not have brought him," said the other.

"Do we go back and tell Archy or do we take him now?"

"Not so fast. Shouldn't we be sure first?"

"It has to be him. Lose the hair and the funny clothes and what do you think?"

"Someone clever stole that trinket from Archy. I don't think it was either of them."

"I say we go back and make a plan. We come back tonight and grab him."

"I can feel those coins in my fingers already. This boy must be worth a pile of gold to someone."

Retreating from the bush, the movement of the two men caught the eye of Barth. He carried two rabbits hunted from the forest and wild herbs for the evening meal. Stooping low behind a bush, he watched as they headed towards Betwixt. Once they were out of sight, he hurried to Ameth and Topaz.

"I saw the two men from the inn spying on you as you walked. They left in the direction of the town. This cannot be a good sign," warned Barth

"They were the men who robbed you. If they recognized you, they may be planning to come back. We must change our plans," returned Ameth. "We must leave tonight!"

*

By the dim light of a new moon, Barth pulled the donkey cart to a stop. At the outskirts of Betwixt, the three men quietly unloaded tied bundles and prepared to walk the final stretch to the shore where a small sailing boat waited. Ameth wore a long coat, boots, and broad-brimmed hat. The unfamiliar attire hampered his descent from the cart, but Topaz, who had walked the distance from Ameth's cottage, was there to help him down. After loading the pack with their belongings onto the younger man's back, the two bade their friend and helper goodbye and set off to enter the town.

"If the men do come back, will Barth be able to fend them off?" asked Topaz.

"Do not worry about Barth," laughed Ameth. "He will not only be ready for them, he will have a very unpleasant surprise for them if they try to break into the house."

Topaz felt a rush of courage. The anticipation of arriving in the place of his misfortune had tempted him to be afraid. Thinking about

Barth setting a trap for the robbers that very night brought a giddiness to his spirit. He was relieved to find that he could stealthily march down the narrow lanes again without fear. Ameth led him to the beach, out of sight of the familiar buildings. Two smiling fishermen noiselessly greeted them and hoisted them aboard the vessel.

"Master Ameth, it's been a long time." whispered the shorter of the two. "Must be mighty important, you and this upstart heading off to the big city, and in the middle of the night."

"It is. Shoal and Brake, this is my friend." Brake raised an eyebrow at the nameless introduction. "You must say nothing to anyone about our departure." Ameth nodded to the two in gratitude for their time and skill on a very short notice.

"This is not what I expected," said Topaz.

"I know, my son. We cannot risk being seen traveling to Tenebrose. These men are trustworthy. Alright men, we are ready."

*

As the boat sailed up the coastline in the dark, only the outline of mountains in the distance could be seen. The two men slept as best they could and woke to a brilliant sunrise.

After a while, another island came into view. Topaz drank in the beauty of the rugged mountains beyond dramatic cliff formations, interspersed with sleepy fishing villages. The journey was long and slow and required several stops for food and sleep. There was no hurry, having left Betwixt several days before they had intended.

The distance between islands was sometimes great and lacked the sight of land to break the monotony of endless seascapes. The weather held out for the most part, interrupted by a brief squall for one leg of the voyage. Ameth pulled a covering over their heads and endured the wind and waves like a well-trained soldier.

*

"Today is the day," remarked Ameth as they began the final day of sailing. Their destination grew near and at last was in sight. The port bustled with sailing vessels of all sizes and descriptions. The tiny sail

42

boat melted into the frenzied flow of marine traffic and headed for a space on the shoreline. Like a busy ant colony, cargo and passengers streamed on and off the ships as Ameth and Topaz looked away toward the docks.

"My deepest gratitude to you both," said Ameth to the sailors as he handed them a small bag of coins. The men accepted the payment with words of affection and care for their old friend. They shoved off and waved. "Goodbye and safe journey to you."

"Come, Topaz. We must find our way to the place where our arrival is expected." Ameth pointed to a large ship at the end of the wharf. "I hope we are not late."

The constant activity overwhelmed Topaz at first as he tried to take it all in and understand its complexity. He had never seen so many people all at the same time.

"I must ask something of you, Topaz," said Ameth. "You need to allow me to carry the amulet on my person from here on. It is not safe for you to have it, lest someone recognize the symbol."

"Of course, you may. Is the symbol that well known?" asked Topaz as he handed it over.

"More so than I thought. The innkeeper knew what it meant as far away as Betwixt."

"And here I thought it was an original—one of my mother's favorite necklaces. I do wonder what it means, and why would it be of value to anyone but me?"

Ameth made no comment. After a time, he warned, "We must hurry along with the crowd." He searched in all directions for potential danger, noting the presence of armed guards at various intervals along the quay. Plotting a course to avoid them, he directed Topaz toward the ship he had pointed out. Hordes of people were arriving, leaving, selling, carrying, waving, yelling. It was all so extraordinary and new. Being pulled along through the crowds, past bundles, boxes, and stacks of strange objects, Topaz felt dizzy. As they hustled along, he could not help but notice that there were people—many of them—whose skin color matched his own. In fact, the shades varied more than he ever could have imagined. He slowed his pace to get a better look.

"Come. We cannot waste any time."

Before he knew what was happening, he was being hoisted up into a carriage and shoved onto a hard wooden seat. The door was closed and, without a pause, the vehicle was in motion.

Looking to his left, Topaz saw that Ameth breathed heavily and looked exhausted. Sensing that there was another present, he looked to his right. Seated next to him in the tight space in which they found themselves, the face of a middle-aged man stared back at very close range. His deep brown eyes met Topaz's with a look of concern and urgency. Everything about him was neat, clean, and well-appointed, though not in a manner that suggested wealth. Topaz nodded towards him, acknowledging his presence.

"Jasper, this is my new friend who has recently become Topaz. For the sake of safety, and lest anyone recognize his former name, we will continue to call him Topaz. Topaz, meet my friend Jasper. You will pardon if we do not use family names. Dangerous habit even for us." The two strangers greeted one another.

"Are you alright? You look very tired. Was it a long journey?"

Ameth raised a hand to wave and smiled. "I will recover. We arrived in a small sail boat instead of the galleon yonder."

"Master Ameth, did something go amiss with the plan?" asked Jasper.

"My young friend attracted a little too much attention from the local thugs. I fear something about his foreignness aroused suspicion."

"Ah," he replied. "I understand. If I have the story straight, this young man appeared as one from the past. Yes, times have changed in the last twenty years. But never mind. My dear friends, it is such a pleasure to see you both. Master Ameth, we have missed you. I bring greetings to you from all those who serve the Prince." Ameth nodded in approval. Topaz pondered the man's calling him "master." Surely, Jasper was not also a servant of Ameth's.

"No doubt you are hungry and tired. We will arrive at our destination shortly. On our way, I thought it best to introduce Topaz to some of the sights of Tenebrose. Topaz," Jasper paused carefully framing his next question. "How much do you know about Tenebrose? Has Master Ameth told you much about the city?"

"Yes, sir, I have learned some. Master Ameth has told me that it is a great city and considered the center of the kingdom. I know so little of political and geographical matters that I hardly have any concept for all that is here. My upbringing and education have been poor in these things."

"I am aware of your background. Master Ameth wrote to me about you. We believe you have come at just the right time." Jasper's words made the flesh on Topaz's arms tingle.

"Pay close attention, Topaz. Master Ameth and I will introduce you to all that is important. As he told you already, a great task awaits you. It is difficult; we do not ask it without thought and consideration. Once we explain all to you, we give you the opportunity to refuse. You must choose to do this."

CHAPTER 7

THE TASK

"Let us begin here at the waterfront area." Jasper tapped the roof of the carriage to signal the driver to proceed with the prearranged tour. Topaz was impressed and curious to find out what was the purpose behind all the planning and care that had gone into his current adventure.

The first leg of the trip took them through slums whose appalling poverty distressed him to no small degree.

"Everyone looks so sad and hopeless," observed Topaz of the people wandering the muddy streets lined with rundown buildings. "There are many varieties of color here. I have never seen this before in my life."

The two other passengers nodded in agreement.

"My people are wealthy. Here, poverty binds many in despair. Only the armed guards I see everywhere are well dressed."

In stark contrast to the poor neighborhood, the next area revealed stone-paved streets lined with rows of richly ornamented dwellings. Those who walked to their homes stared suspiciously at the strangers in the carriage and disappeared behind heavy doors. A frequent motif at each entrance was a dragonish figure. Varying by size and pose, each dragon threatened with open mouth and jagged teeth. Green was the predominant color, though some were merely carved in bas-relief on unpainted wood. As Topaz pondered the dragon symbol, he realized he had seen it in on the side of some buildings they had passed.

"Why is the dragon image carved into doors?" he asked Jasper. Their new companion and guide turned and nodded knowingly to Ameth.

"Topaz, your friend and mentor, Master Ameth, has taught you much about the world as it exists today. Perhaps he has even taught you about history." At the mention of history, Jasper lowered his voice, though not a soul could hear beyond the confines of the carriage.

"You will learn soon that the times in which we live have changed from the ways of the past. Tenebrose and its surrounding villages, and small kingdoms of the world as we know it, were originally ruled by the Great High King who rules from Illumah, the City of Light. We knew nothing but peace and safety under that rule. That was long ago. But, as you have been instructed, a harsh and violent man overthrew that rule. He has stolen by force the kingdoms of this world."

Jasper stopped. Leaning forward, Topaz anticipated the story he had heard from Ameth now to take on more substance.

"I have told Topaz of the rise of Malpha and the dragonish creature he uses to bring fear. He also is aware of the Prince and his mission to bring the citizens back to the High King." A reverent pause in the narrative ensued. "Topaz has seen the Prince."

Jasper responded with a hopeful smile. "Excellent!" he exclaimed.

*

The carriage drew to a halt, and the three looked up from their intense conversation. A high wall was before them, interrupted by an enormous ornate iron gate. Armed guards in full uniform stood at attention on either side. Topaz's attention was drawn to the gate and what lay beyond.

"This is what I wanted you to see first, Topaz." Jasper pointed to the walls beside the gate. They were decorated with murals depicting the history of the city. The young man's eyes traveled over the painting, noting how the dragon breathed fire and rained down sharp swords from its claws. A startling image emerged from the scene that caught his gaze. Underneath the fierce dragon lay a dark-skinned warrior. He had tattoos on his arms and legs, and down his back was a long braid of black hair. Colorful bands were woven into the hair. As shocking as this was to Topaz, Jasper instructed him saying, "Look closer. Look at the tattoos." Topaz looked and beheld the now familiar flower pattern that matched his own amulet.

"Who was that man?" asked Topaz.

"He represents the defeat of the kingdom of Abundance, now renamed Tenebrose. Each of the people in the mural represent a defeated people who now serve the dragon, or no longer exist," said Jasper. "You can see why Master Ameth had you cut your hair."

"The tattoo symbol; does it mean anything?"

"We are not sure of the meaning. It may be a symbol representing the former kingdom. A wondrous tree called koma grew only in the kingdom of Abundant. It's fruit was said to have amazing powers to heal, strengthen, and give rest to those who ate its fruit. I believe the blossom of that tree may be that symbol." Jasper watched closely to see Topaz's reaction to the scene. "What does this flower mean to you?"

"Only this." He held out his hand to Ameth who pulled the leather tie from his coat and showed the amulet to Jasper. "Does the tree still grow in Tenebrose?" Topaz noted the look of surprise on Jasper's face, and the quick and knowing glance to Ameth.

"The fruit of the tree is very valuable here; so much so that Malpha has ordered all trees to be cut down. The only remaining ones are planted within the walls of his estate which surrounds the palace. The fruit now is said to have magical powers, but we think that was only a rumor created to explain why Malpha restricted access to it. Where did you obtain the amulet?"

"It was sent to me from my mother's chief adviser. I had not intended to bring it with me. I am not sure why he thought I should carry it. He said it had been important to my family and he wanted me to have it to remind me of them."

Ameth replaced the amulet in his coat. "I will keep it for now. It may be dangerous for Topaz to wear it."

"There is no doubt that my family came from this place. I wonder now if any of them survived when Malpha overthrew Abundance."

"Some hide. Some have risen in the ranks of Malpha, for he enjoys promoting former Abundanites to power as a sign of his superiority over them. Some may be in prison. We do not know. As you will see, what matters most here is to whom one pays allegiance. But let us continue our tour."

Topaz was painfully aware that what lay behind the secrets of his past had been caused by the evil ruler he had been hearing about. Everything he had learned drew him further into the very world he was warned to avoid. But he knew he could not turn back.

*

"This is the palace of Malpha, who calls himself the Ultimate Ruler." Jasper pointed to the large building behind the wall. It was surrounded by empty fields growing a mixture of grass and small shrubs. In the distance, he could see orchards of stately trees. Workers could be seen tending the grounds, though no results of their work were in evidence.

The palace itself was drab and uninviting. Pillars, parapets, and partitions formed its most notable characteristics. Completely lacking in artistic beauty, it exhibited power and protection, rather than wealth and wise design.

"Make way! Make way!" shouted the driver of an approaching carriage drawn by matching black horses. Jasper tapped the roof again and his driver moved the offending carriage out of the way. Iron gates opened as if by magic before the carriage and driver. Shouting curses, he whipped the horses through the gateway. Topaz tried to get a glimpse of who was in the fast moving vehicle, but saw only flashes of bright red before it sped down the long driveway to the palace.

"Malpha seldom leaves his palace home. We try to keep track of those who come and go to learn what he may be planning. As you can see, it is difficult to find out who comes and goes," Jasper said as they turned the carriage around and headed to their next stop.

The three men drove slowly through winding streets and jagged lanes. The carriage slowed again, and Topaz looked out the window. Another kind of wall was before them, this one cold, dark, dirty and very high. A large gate was built into this wall as well, but it bore no signs of wealth. Beyond the gate was a stark building that was unmistakably a prison. Heavy iron bars built into craggy stones with long narrow windows high in the walls characterized this building. It was enormous, dark and foreboding.

"Yes, Topaz, this is a prison. No one knows for sure who is in the prison or why they are there. Some of our people who have been accused of serving the Prince are imprisoned here," Ameth whispered.

The carriage started again. Topaz continued to observe the buildings as they rode along. It appeared that the city was built from a ruin of the former kingdom. Older buildings were single story and constructed of sawn timbers with neat roofs woven from long reeds or a thick type of grass. Many had been burned to the ground. Upon the charred remains, stone buildings had been raised up, some artfully done and others hastily built. The high-pitched roofs were made of slender logs cemented together with a strong, dried mud. Topaz wondered if the logs were the remains of the koma fruit trees that had been cut down at the command of Malpha.

*

When they reached their final destination, the three men stepped down before a building unique in style. It combined the elements of the original timber and grass—the remains of a partially destroyed home—with neatly-laid stones and well-matched log and mortar roof.

Similar buildings were dotted around a small court yard. Flowering plants and shrubs completed the warm, welcoming home. Passing through the plain, wooden doors of the original timber wing, a tidy kitchen with a plastered brick fireplace could be seen through a large, arched entryway. Piles of vegetables from the garden lay on a heavy, wooden chopping block in the center of the room.

The newer section of the house was cool and shadowy. A narrow staircase wound up into the dark. Ameth climbed very slowly up each stone step. Jasper opened the door at the top and showed the visitors into a bright room. To Topaz's surprise, there were ten people already present in the tiny space, seated on small wooden chairs, some on the hard uneven floor, but all patiently waiting for the three to get settled.

Jasper was not at all surprised to see his guests. At the sight of Master Ameth, the visitors bowed low and sought the old man's hand. Topaz saw that some had tears in their eyes, and others gently, but firmly, gave warm hugs. They all knew and respected Master Ameth. He began to realize that he had underestimated the stature of his friend and mentor.

"Fellow followers of our Lord, the Prince, and his father the High King, I am very happy all of you could come today. Welcome to my home. Let me introduce you all to our new friend, Topaz," said Jasper as he waved his hand toward the young man behind him. "Aahhh," came the soft response from those assembled. Topaz bowed, as he thought appropriate, while the others nodded and smiled at him.

"Topaz, as I have told many of you already, has come from a foreign land." Here the guests whispered among themselves while observing Topaz's appearance. "He is new to our city. We have this day given him a tour and explained the customs and history of Tenebrose, formerly known as Abundant."

"He has met the Prince, for his name is Topaz, the fearless one," proclaimed one of the guests. Topaz, hearing himself referred to this way, opened his mouth in amazement and would have responded, but

51

Jasper spoke first. "He has, and for that we are most grateful. This is the sign we have been waiting for. My friends, the time is near."

"You are right! He will be perfect for the task," added another.

"Topaz, as you know by way of Master Ameth's letters, has an unusual background that qualifies him to be trusted with this task. He has come to us from a far island where he has not been privy to the events of our history. His ancestors, no doubt, came from the kingdom of Abundant. Unfortunately, the great misfortune of many surviving Abundantites has been to become slaves of the current ruler. Along with many people from other towns and kingships, Tenebrose has become a kingdom of slaves, for all must do the bidding of Malpha."

Topaz's heart began to beat a little faster as the moment to hear the details of his task grew nearer. He sat forward following Jasper's every word.

"Malpha boasts of his dominance over the entire known world, though we believe there are still some pockets of resistance. Once he has achieved his goal, his rule will become even more cruel and harsh. He must be stopped," said Jasper.

"We all know what has to be done. Our friend, Topaz, has agreed to do whatever was needed for the cause," added Ameth. "What Jasper is trying to say is, we need someone on the inside of the palace grounds. We believe Malpha is planning a celebration for his complete dominion over the kingdoms of the known world. That much we have been able to discover."

Jasper paused so that Topaz could digest the information. In a quiet voice he added, "The only way for him to claim that power is to remain in possession of The Promise—and by the way, he calls it 'The Curse'. Without that golden pome, he is powerless. Do you understand what I am saying?"

Topaz gulped. "How does one get inside the palace?" he asked sheepishly.

"The only way is to become his slave," replied Jasper.

CHAPTER 8

A LOOK IN
THE WRONG DIRECTION

Topaz sat motionless, shocked at the long-awaited revelation. How? What? So many questions clamored within him.

"A slave?" he whispered trying to overcome his reaction to the news.

"What is needed is to have someone working in the palace. Most workers there are not volunteers," continued Ameth. "I think I know a way for Topaz to be placed there."

"What do I have to do to become a slave?" asked Topaz.

"The people who are working there now are not slaves in the sense that they are owned by someone. They are slaves meaning they have not necessarily volunteered for the work and receive next to nothing for their labor. You have demonstrated your talent for working with wood. The palace is constantly under construction and in need of workers with skill," added Jasper.

"That does have the ring of risk about it. If it is as you say, I would be employed to work on the palace grounds. How do I gain such employment?"

"You will go to the wood carvers shop and ask for a reference. Few people are asking for that kind of work," said Jasper.

"And the reason for that is...."

"The task will be uncomfortable, as you will be treated like a slave is treated. You will be tempted to react to the mistreatment, but you must not. Whatever they tell you to do, do it well. Keep silent, but listen carefully. See if it is possible to locate where The Promise is kept in the palace. Find out details about the celebration."

"Why is it that you believe I am especially suited to do this?"

"For one, you are not known by anyone or associated with any particular group. For another, there are many people like you who are working inside the palace. They may trust you more than they would one of us who are not native to Tenebrose. Only do not tell anyone about your story or where you are from."

"You have been fair enough in warning me about the danger and risk involved in the task. It is for the High King's own purpose that I have been given new courage and freedom from fear as a gift from the Prince. I will need all of it." said Topaz. "How will I communicate with you if I do get into the palace grounds?"

"There will be a young boy posted outside the gate once a week. You must see if you can pass him a note of some kind. If you believe you are in danger of being intercepted, write something meaningless to pass along. Then we will have to find some other way."

Topaz found it difficult to sleep that night. Pondering all he had heard and all that lay ahead of him was heavy indeed. Excitement had replaced fear, and anticipation had overcome what he would normally dread. Perhaps in all of this, he would find out more about his family. The last conscious moments before sleep were spent imagining a homecoming, telling his mother of his adventures, and finding news of his father at last.

*

Walking between dilapidated, wooden buildings, Topaz smelled rancid mud and decay. Overnight rain had softened the ground, wafting up unpleasant odors. His boots kicked through discarded trash that was strewn about in the road. Standing nearby were the dreaded soldiers keeping watch on the citizenry. Topaz kept his head down so as to draw as little attention as possible. A short distance behind him, a young boy appointed by Jasper and instructed never to let the young man out of his sight, strolled along trying to appear aimless.

After an hour of walking slowly along the lane, Topaz came upon the small, woodcarver's shop he had been directed to find. A large dragon image hung above the open door. On the path near the shop entrance were samples of carved dragons of varying sizes for sale. He bent over to examine them. The work was not expertly done. Though it would gall him to be required to carve such images, he knew he could do much better.

He gently picked up a wooden creature, stood up and turned to a balding, older man he assumed to be the shop owner. Wondering how he would broach the subject of his desire to find employment, he decided to begin the conversation by asking the price of such a work of art.

"This is a fine piece," he began with a nervous rasp in his throat.

"Indeed it is. But I have others inside, carved with greater skill. Come, let me show you." The shop owner had a glint in his eyes that reminded Topaz of the innkeeper of Betwixt. An immediate distrust was aroused, and he hesitated before entering the dark cave-like shop interior.

"Can you tell me what the price is for such a piece? You see, I don't have much money."

"Don't waste it on this. Come, you must see what I have inside."

"Well, in truth, I am a wood carver. I am looking for work," said Topaz with a sheepish grin.

"All the more reason for you to come inside, my boy." Topaz suspected that once inside, he might be introduced to the involuntary part of his new employment. He glanced backward casually hoping to see his lookout standing at a distance.

He took a step closer when something drew his attention in the opposite direction. Like a magnet, his eyes were drawn to a slender form passing the periphery of his vision. There they were fixed on a pair of women passing the shop. One was stout and elderly; the other was slender and dressed in a long flowing gown that swished from side to side with each step. Having seen very few such sights in his life, he found he could not tear his gaze from the younger woman's mesmerizing figure. A brief turn of her head in Topaz's direction and a coy smile sealed his fate. He took another step, then tripped and momentarily lost his balance. A crunching sound reached his ears. He had stomped upon one of the dragons. The carving was crushed and broken into several pieces under his booted foot.

"What have you done, you silly oaf?" yelled the shop owner. "Don't you know that you have committed a capital crime? Help! Police!"

A uniformed guard appeared, as if from nowhere, in response to the call. As he approached, Topaz cried out apologetically, "Oh, blast it, anyway. It was an accident. I'm sorry. I will pay for it."

With eyes wide in alarm, the guard quickly grabbed Topaz and held him firmly.

"What have you done? You not only destroyed the sacred image, but you have cursed it as well. Do you not know who the ruler of this land is? You are not a foreigner. You must know that this is a crime punishable by imprisonment," the guard yelled.

"I can explain. I tripped. I…, I…, I wasn't trying to break it." It was no use. The guard would not listen to excuses.

"Right then. To prison you will go!"

"Prison? Can't you just send me to do labor somewhere, like the palace for instance?"

"Listen to this one! He thinks he can go to the palace to work. What is this some kind of plot against the Ultimate Ruler? A traitor! A spy! That is what you are."

56

The guard signaled to others, who must have been watching the spectacle, and between them, they shoved Topaz roughly down the street. The prisoner tried to look back to see if his arrest had been observed, but the young spy was nowhere to be seen.

*

Hands bound behind his back as he walked the muddy streets had resulted in more than one fall. By the time Topaz walked the distance, pushed along by impatient soldiers, he was tired and more dirty than he could remember ever being in his life. Humiliated and hungry, he arrived at the dark entrance with a sinking sensation in his stomach. The plan was ruined. Doubts began to creep into his thoughts as he wondered how he would escape. Jasper's words about few ever being seen again once entering the prison blasted his thoughts into tiny specks of dust.

"Help!" he cried out in his mind, afraid to actually utter that word before the men who shoved him before the Prison Master.

A bespectacled, gray-haired man clothed in a dirty, dark green robe appeared behind a high desk. He wore a hat of matching green that looked like a large mushroom. Frowning and blustering, he looked up from his ledger to show a reddened, puffy face. "What is the charge?"

"Treason, Chief Master Your Honor Sir," grunted the highest ranking guard.

"Treason? I haven't had a good case of treason all day. What did he do?" The Prison Master turned aside and sipped from a small bottle of liquid he had taken from inside his robe.

"He willfully crushed a dragon image and called down curses upon it," the guard reported with a gleeful smirk.

"Ho! Subversion, treachery, sedition! This is serious, indeed." He sipped again, as if no one could see him when he wasn't facing forward.

"And get this, he wanted to be sent to the palace to work as a punishment," added the guard.

"Oh, my. What have we here? A spy? A conspiracy is afoot. I can always smell a conspiracy. Away with him." A loud hiccup erupted with

57

the last word, punctuating the command and adding comical finality.

A new set of prison guards took hold of Topaz and shoved him into the dank and desolate building. All hopes he had imagined that these crimes were the kind satisfied with a fine were dashed. The words spy and conspiracy confirmed his cruel fate. What kind of punishment awaited him?

*

The guards led Topaz away through a corridor into a large room. As they drew nearer, a foul smell met his nostrils. Angry shouts reverberated and echoed through the stone halls. Iron rings pegged into cracks between the building blocks held chains, and on each chain was a prisoner attached at the ankles with fetters. Behind him, a heavy iron door creaked shut with a thud.

The plan has gone terribly wrong. Prison! Will Ameth and Jasper know what has happened to me? Is there any chance of rescue? Help!

CHAPTER 9

GAZRAK

Caw, caw, caw. Unseen crows flapped their wings, called to one another and settled into dense forest branches against the approach of night. In the stillness sat four cold and weary strangers huddled together, waiting.

"Where do you think we are?" a weak voice ventured to ask any of the three others who had the strength and mental awareness to answer. A male voice replied, "If I said 'In a forest' you probably would not be at all amused." A slender foot kicked the speaker. "You are right! This is not the time or place, but we need something to cheer us up."

"We need shelter for the night," came a different female voice, "not to mention food! I am starving!"

Shabby and dirty from their journey, the four looked nothing like the four who had set out days before. Bright green, crimson, and blue had turned to brown, having gone unwashed on their journey; up mountains, down valleys, through caves, up through the long tunnel, over streams and hills, and now, into a deep forest of mud, roots, and tree branches that grabbed and tore at them.

"It is hard to believe that only days ago, we saw the Prince himself and had our hopes lifted," said Jewel.

"And we thought that the next stop was going to be the City of Light. This is a far cry from that reality," added Ruby.

"We have to think about what he said—what the diary says— that ultimately we will get there. In the meantime, he told us to tell others about him. I am not sure who that will be, but this must be part of what he wants us to do," Diamond said authoritatively. Gem looked doubtful and responded, "How could this be part of some grand plan? We are lost. We have no food or shelter. We have no idea which way to go."

"Think of the ways the writer of the diary related, how each time he confronted danger, some purpose always came to light," retorted Diamond.

"Then think about how the diary ended—very suddenly—saying that he was in danger of being found out. His life was threatened and we don't even know if he escaped! Jewel told us that the secret study was ransacked. The books were thrown about on the floor. The tapestry of a dragon image hung over the words about crying out to 'The One' for help. Suppose he did cry out for help? We don't know if he received that help," countered Ruby.

"We have seen the Prince. He will not leave us out here to die. He will bring the help that we need." Diamond turned to raise his hands to the sky, "Help us, Lord Prince! We cry out to you!"

The four sat in the stillness listening for anything to stir. Crickets chirped. The crows flew away and were replaced by cooing birds that fluttered above their heads. Diamond moved closer to Jewel and held her hand. "I know this is not the perfect moment to bring this up, but, Jewel, I want you to be my wife. It seems we are meant to be on this journey together. I love you."

"This is a strange time to propose. How do you think a marriage can take place when we are lost in the forest?" asked Ruby who sat on the other side of Jewel.

"I love you too. We are from different worlds. You are wealthy and educated. I am orphaned, poor, and lowly of class. Are you sure that you will not regret being wed to someone like me?

"It makes no difference now. I have left that life behind. All of us, we are no longer the people that we were." All four agreed on this point.

"I will marry you. We may not have the luxury of a grand ceremony, but that is alright with me. Perhaps when we get to a town, we can arrange for a wedding."

"She assumes we will arrive at a town at some point in the future," said Ruby to Gem. "Optimistic, I dare say."

"I want for us always to be together no matter what may come." Diamond put his arm around Jewel's shoulders as the chill of evening crept upon them.

"Well, congratulations, you two. May all your dreams come true. For now, can we find a way out of this forest?" Ruby reminded them.

"What is that sound?" asked Gem.

"Birds, of course," said Ruby. "That is all we have heard for hours."

"No. I hear something else. Shh. Don't make a sound."

"I hear it too. The breaking of twigs just ahead. It could be a wild animal. Duck down behind these rocks. Be quiet and listen." The others obeyed and hoped for a deliverer to appear and not a wild creature of the forest.

Squishing mud under foot, heavy breathing, and the crackle of broken twigs broke the stillness. They did not know if they should be alarmed by the sudden intrusion on their lost, isolated state, or relieved that other beings existed in this wild, forsaken place. All eyes searched through the fading dusk, not only for the familiar shapes of human beings, but sympathetic ones who could direct their path to some hospitable shelter.

The forest had become animated. The trees and branches were moving, swaying, coming closer and were almost upon the little band of lost wayfarers. Large, hulking figures like walking piles of brush moved in their direction. Was the forest they had stumbled into enchanted? Did trees really walk around? The four froze, afraid to move or speak.

"Ahhh," cried Jewel softly as the approaching trees brushed past her exposed foot. She buried her face in Diamond's chest.

A grizzled, bearded face instantly shot out from the cover of camouflage, glared at the four, and croaked an unintelligible command to the others. Before they could react defensively, the creatures surrounded the tiny group with knives drawn.

"Ya de?" barked the largest of the figures. The four stared in disbelief at the bedraggled, cruel face. In the last light of day, it was difficult to see the features well, but it was clear that these were indeed humans. They did not look like anyone or anything the four had seen before in the woods. Each was wearing an enormous, hooded cloak made from ragged strips of cloth dyed in various shades of greenish-brown and brownish-green, then patched over with material that looked just like trees and branches. It was difficult to see a firm outline where clothing stopped and trees began. Each carried bulky cargo beneath their forest-like coverings, making them well-disguised and hidden.

The leader's lips twisted into snarling contortions showing uneven teeth with one prominent gap as he confronted the unexpected strangers. A shaggy beard and tangled strands of orange hair framed his rough face.

The young, fair-haired Diamond spoke up first. "Greetings." The figures conferred with one another in a strange language and one quickly replied. "Who you?"

"My name is Diamond," he stammered. "We mean you no harm. We are just hopelessly lost!" Immediately Diamond realized what a strange thing it was to tell these men they meant them no harm, when it appeared that the travelers had greater potential for doing harm to him and his companions.

"Please. There is no need for alarm." *Another stupid remark*, thought Diamond.

62

"I don't think he understands what you are saying," came a weak, whispering voice from behind. With the weapons pointed inches from his face, Diamond became distracted by the look of the knives, wanting to know how they were made. His fascination with blades had not left him, despite his leaving the family business at home.

"What she say?" demanded the leader lunging forward with his knife. "No. No. Don't worry. This is my….ah, my wife-to-be, Jewel." Diamond slowly brought Jewel forward and continued introducing the other two companions. "This is Ruby and this is Gem."

"Who you?" he repeated. He beat his chest in anger and thrust his arm around in a circle. "My land. We hunt. You go!" The four shrunk back in dismay and fear. One of the men spoke to the leader drawing his attention away. There was a momentary retreat as the travelers huddled and growled at one another angrily; hands flailing, random shoving and threats between them, breaking the monotony of their conference.

"I think he is saying they are hunting. Perhaps they think we will scare the game away," offered Jewel.

"With all they are carrying, it looks like they are finished with the hunt for today," Diamond responded. "Here they come."

"You, you, you, you," yelled the leader motioning to each of the four, as the huddle dissolved into a threatening circle. "Come! Go!" He waved a hand in the air gesturing for the four to follow him. As they began to comply, the silent company fell in behind.

"Where are we going? whispered Ruby. "I didn't think anything could get worse than what we have already been through. Maybe I was wrong!"

It was now almost completely dark. They could not see where they were going; they could only follow the one ahead feeling for trees, bushes, logs, stones, or other obstructions in the path that could cause a fall.

"I'm sorry for all this," whispered Diamond loudly, turning to Jewel as she tried to keep pace with him. She could not see his face, but she reached forward and stroked his hand. The leader growled something in his language that Diamond understood as "keep quiet", so he attempted no further communication.

The journey was long and, despite the unpleasantness of trudging through oozing mud, gave Diamond time to think. How had they gotten themselves in such a fix as this? When they emerged from the long tunnel, after their harrowing escape from near death at the hands of Chief Legerdemain, they felt a sense of victory and optimism. Exhaustion had left them drained of all energy, but reflecting on the events of the last days produced an exhilaration and joy that temporarily eclipsed the need for rest and food.

Then, like a dream or a ghostly apparition, the One who had brought their lives together had appeared before their eyes. At last, to see the Prince—the man behind all the strange and wonderful events that in the present seemed to be a hazy, impossible dream—filled them with strength and courage. Before they could even fully register the realization of his wonderful presence, the Prince galloped away and disappeared leaving them with a promise of his return and a future in his Kingdom of Light.

Stunned, and disoriented, they had pondered the meaning of his words. Not knowing what else to do, the four rested and spent time reading the diary Jewel had taken from the secret room. Diamond remembered that he was the first one to read it. Its contents were so important, he knew the others should hear what the diarist recorded. They had sat together just days before. Diamond read aloud savoring every word, trying to understand what this unknown man had written so they could put the pieces of the puzzle together to make sense. Still there were questions, but they knew so much more than they had before.

Diamond strained his mind to recall the words and the story that had helped them understand more of the world that they lived in. It was a world of conflicts and struggle for power. The man who wrote the diary many years before uncovered a plot to subjugate the whole of civilization under the rule of a cruel and heartless beast of a man. Rumor had it that not only was he beastly in behavior, but he had the power to turn himself into a beast and devour his enemies. The threat of his plan for dominion spread like gangrene through the land. One, and only one person was able to thwart those plans. It had to be none other than the Prince himself, even though his appearance would have been many years before. Had it all been real? Slogging through the night, wet, bedraggled, hungry, and confused, made their journey into a miserable fantasy.

*

The trail led through a maze of boulders and then what felt like a tunnel before a light appeared and grew brighter. It was a fire—warm and beckoning. Ruby collapsed in an exhausted heap, followed by Jewel. Gem and Diamond remained standing, wary of the company they had come upon. Faces draped in rough, drab clothing appeared out of the night, looking just as wary of the strangers. Excited, unintelligible utterances ensued. Diamond tried to make sense of it and felt sure that the families of the men were alarmed to have visitors thrust upon them. From the gestures and tone of voice, it appeared that the hunters explained how they discovered the four. Several women complained loudly and waved their arms in dismissal of the intruders.

"What do you think they are saying?" asked Jewel as she hung onto Diamond's arm for comfort.

"Please let there be some food and sleep somewhere in the solution, cried Ruby. "I cannot move from this spot."

The crowd suddenly grew quiet. From between two arguing women, a small, old man appeared and stood before them. His loosely-fitting, tailored coat and breeches gave him an air of distinction as he leaned heavily upon an ornate cane. His white beard had been rolled up and fastened into a knot under his chin. With narrowed eyes and an angry grimace, he spoke first to the returning hunters. They sheepishly answered him in like, unintelligible syllables.

Turning to the strangers, he asked in a language the four understood, and with far less malice, "We have not been introduced. I am King Furcula. May I know who you are?

65

Diamond, who felt himself to be responsible for the group, spoke. "My name is Diamond. This is Gem, my brother, and his mother Ruby." Diamond paused, not knowing how to introduce Jewel. Ruby broke into the conversation, "This is Jewel, my servant." Jewel raised her eyebrows and smirked in annoyance. Diamond found his senses and added, "We are to be married."

A sudden knowing look of amusement passed briefly over King Furcula's face. "You do not answer my question. Who are you?" he repeated. "Are you from Wanderdown?"

"King Furcula, we are not from Wanderdown, wherever that may be. We were traveling through the country and we got lost in the forest," explained Diamond.

"Come now, you must do better than that. Lost? In the forest of Gazrak? And Wanderdown is not your home?" The puzzled looks on the faces of the four answered his question.

"We left our home permanently, and not being familiar with the surrounding country, found ourselves in the forest." Diamond looked at the others to see if they had anything better to contribute.

"We escaped," Gem blurted out in a blunt confession. Ruby and Jewel both winced at the frankness of his words, imagining the jeopardy this admission might bring.

"You escaped? From your rulers? Are you criminals?" the old man asked pointedly. Diamond thought for a moment and then replied, "Yes. We did escape from our ruler. He is a man with an evil intent to punish these three for crimes that did not warrant prison, let alone death by hanging." The old man quickly translated for the small crowd who responded with a communal murmur.

"An evil ruler, you say? Why is it that people always think rulers are evil?" King Furcula shook his head in disbelief. "Do I understand correctly that you do not know where you are? How can that be?" Furcula continued to scrutinize the travelers disheveled appearance, coming to the conclusion that they had indeed been traveling in the woods for some time.

Diamond's honesty had gotten him into trouble before, as he

well remembered. But telling the truth seemed to be the best way to find help.

"We escaped through a secret tunnel. When we reached the end, we were not even able to tell the direction we had come from. We tried to head for the cover of forest in the hope that no one would be able to track our path. We know nothing of where we are, who you are, or what language you speak."

"Delightful!" said the old one with more than a hint of sarcasm. The four waited for some explanation. "I know your world." He paused. "And I know evil rulers. And this," he said, "is the village of the Gazrak." The old man leaned with one arm on his cane and raised the other arm sweeping it toward the band of forest dwellers. "I am the 'evil ruler' in these parts," he said with a sinister chuckle. "I tell these simple people what to do, and they do it. And by the way, those who come to Gazrak never leave." He turned and began to walk away with that terrifying thought hanging in the air.

Each of the four cringed at the foreboding words, trying to understand the speaker's message. Did Furcula intend to hold them as captives? Was he really evil, or was he making fun of their story?

"You speak our language. How did you come to be here with these people?" asked Gem hoping to delay the sudden departure.

"That is a long story for some other time. I am from your world, but these people needed me, so I am here. As I said, I am their ruler. No one disobeys my command."

"We appreciate your taking us in like this. We are very hungry and tired. We would gladly repay you in any way we can for some food and shelter," Diamond begged.

Furcula laughed, "Yes, you will repay us." He turned to the others and spoke in their language. Several women scurried away and brought back bread and drink. Others brought coverings to wrap around the strangers for warmth.

A young woman, who looked to be Jewel's age, emerged from the huddle of villagers and beckoned them to follow. Her bright orange hair was tied back under a hooded cloak revealing a cheerful, freckled face. In the dark, it was difficult to see much more by the dim light of her lantern. She attempted to introduce herself once she made sure none of the others were looking.

"Rista," she whispered. Looking them all over carefully, she giggled and grabbed Gem by the arm. "Come."

The weary travelers rose, staggered along behind her, and were shown a dark wall of stone. Rista raised her lantern to reveal a shallow cave. She handed over the lantern and reluctantly departed, winking at Gem and tossing her head in a flirtatious gesture. He smiled in return, then turned to find the others laughing at his dazed appearance.

The floor of the cave had been hastily prepared with long dried grass and rough quilts. Each chose a spot and soon snuggled in forest blankets.

"What will happen now?" asked a quiet voice in the dark. Diamond reached out his hand to touch Jewel's. "Everything will turn out well. Wait and see."

CHAPTER 10

THE GODS HAVE SPOKEN

Morning was difficult to discern; the light did not quickly reach the interior of the cave where the four found themselves upon waking. Diamond crawled out and found Gem sitting on a stump eating a leftover chunk of bread. The view from the cold, damp forest floor, which they saw for the first time in the light of day, allowed just a glimpse of the sunlight touching the tops of the trees. The two men waited impatiently for its warmth to descend down the steep, rocky cliffs that formed a boundary for the Gazrak camp.

Arising above the twittering of morning birds came the groan and moan of Ruby. "Aahh. I ache all over. Someone please tell me that there is a warm spring nearby and a change of clothes." Jewel had wakened, but lay quietly, denying that the day had begun.

"Come. Now!" a low, growling voice broke the morning air. The four strangers turned each in their place to see where the voice originated. A tall, young man stood before them, shaggy and unkempt.

The missing tooth gave evidence of their having met already. He had approached so quietly, no one heard any movement in the bushes. He was dressed much the same as he had been the night before, though without the forest robe. His shoulder-length hair was now exposed and hung in matted ringlets making his head appear large and wild. Diamond could just make out a long, dangerous looking knife strapped to the man's waist. He tried to get a better look.

"You come," he repeated and urged them with a hand motion to follow him.

Despite the fact that the sun had now fully risen, the camp was still cloaked in darkness. It was not far to a slow-burning fire pit that, to their amazement, emitted no smoke. Several women prepared food and shyly handed hot loaves of a primitive bread and gourd cups of a strong tasting tea to the four who received them with much gratitude.

The newcomers looked about them for signs of habitation. Trampled foot paths in all directions yielded no clues to the lifestyle of the forest tribe. Although people began to gather around the fires, their appearance from behind trees and bushes mystified the four.

Something heavy dropped from above and landed on the ground in front of Gem, startling him so that he jumped backwards. It was a crudely made boot. Gem and the others looked up into the dark branches above but could see nothing unusual. "Kapato," said a muffled voice. A female voice scolded something in return. Though they could not discern where tree ended and dwelling began, they realized that the entire village was woven invisibly into the branches of the enormous deciduous trees that surrounded them.

"Ah," said Furcula mysteriously appearing, as the others had done. He raised a hand, touching the edge of his forefinger to his forehead in a kind of salute. "Pardon our careless friend." He motioned to a child to pick up the boot and return it to its owner. "We do not welcome guests to our forest for the most part, so you will have to forgive us for not having more comfortable arrangements to offer."

Diamond held out a hand to the old leader, but the latter's hand did not reach back. He realized that the salute must be the local greeting, so he raised his hand to do as the old one had done. Furcula nodded gratefully.

Ruby sat down on the ground and savored the bread and tea. Jewel ate with enthusiasm and a great many facial gestures, trying to show the women how much she was enjoying their creation, and knowing that her words would mean little to them.

"We do not wish to stay and expect you to feed us. We will move on as soon as we can determine which way we should go. Perhaps you can advise us on that matter," offered Diamond in hopes that Furcula's warning had not been in earnest.

"Oh, my. Maybe I've forgotten how to speak my native language. Diamond—that is your name, is it not? No one who comes into our forest leaves again. Didn't I say that? I'm sure I did." Fucula chuckled under his breath, annoyed at having to repeat himself, and continued, "My men brought you here because they did not know what else to do. You see, no one ever ventures into this forest as you have done. People on the outside know that it is not, how shall I say, advisable. Now you are here and we will all have to make the best of it."

The four were stunned at what they heard. They tried to imagine the implications of such a consequence. What of their plans? Dreams of arriving at the Kingdom of Light had spurred them on. Visions of serving the Prince in the challenge they imagined burned a fiery brand of commitment and welded a bond between them.

Gem leaped forward prepared to challenge Furcula's declaration. He was jerked back by Diamond who grabbed his shirt and stopped him. The two looked around and saw the tall, threatening presence of frowning men closing the distance between them.

"Wait," cried Diamond. "We do not want to bring trouble. We will do as you say." Gem, Ruby, and Jewel stared at Diamond in alarm and amazement, wondering why he was giving in to Furcula's demands. Diamond turned to them and whispered, "It will be alright. I'm almost sure. Just trust me right now." The three stood frozen in silence, each imagining a future as part of this wild group and submitting to Furcula.

"What tasks would you have us do? I am very handy sharpening knives," Diamond offered. Gem fumed and bit his lip. Jewel and Ruby stiffened with apprehension.

"You can see that our ways are simple. We subsist by foraging for the things we need," said Furcula in tones that Diamond felt held some additional meaning. "My people do not speak the language of the outsiders. You may start by learning our ways." The four wondered in what primitive customs they would be required to participate. "We will begin tonight. Gazago!" he shouted for all to hear.

"What is gazago?"

"That is our word for wedding." said Furcula.

"Who is getting married?" asked Ruby.

"You are," said the king to Diamond.

"Wait a minute. We have not prepared. Can there really be a wedding on such short notice?"

"Were you telling the truth about your engagement? Are you lying to me about this woman?" asked Furcula.

"I am telling the truth. We do want to marry. I was thinking that we would not have an opportunity so soon."

"We will welcome you to our community with a celebration. We will have gazago and kill all our pigs with one trap." The four looked around and did not see any pigs. "Two events, one ceremony," Furcula added shaking his head at their ignorance.

The king translated his announcement to the crowd and a whoop and holler went up in excitement for the evening celebration. He finished his remarks with instructions to the women. They hastened away and soon returned with piles of clothing from which the four could choose clean outfits. Picking through the odd pieces finally yielded adequate changes so that their soiled clothes could be taken and washed. Rista did not miss her chance to grab Jewel's muddy green dress for her personal attention.

The rest of the day, Ruby and Gem busied themselves attempting to help prepare the food, gather firewood, and clear the forest space, all the while listening intently to the strange sounding language. Several young women escorted Jewel to a shady natural pool on the other side of the tunnel into the camp. The cold water was refreshing after days of tramping through hill and dale. The women chatted while putting wild flowers in Jewel's hair. She tried to imagine what they were asking her, but she could understand nothing of their language.

A group of men brought Diamond to a clearing at the edge of the camp and proceeded to build a temporary shelter. Furcula appeared late in the day to explain that the hut was the customary way of housing a new couple until a more permanent tree house was built. Some of the men spoke to the leader who then turned to Diamond with their question. "They want to know how much you paid Jewel's family for her hand in marriage."

"I paid no price. She has no family. She is an orphan," confessed Diamond.

"And you? Do you have a family? Do they agree with this marriage?"

"I do have a family," Diamond answered imagining his mother's displeasure with his choice of bride. "My family will never see me again, so it does not concern them anymore."

Furcula nodded in agreement and translated for the men who mumbled to one another in surprise.

That night, gathered closely together around the fire, the band of forest people swayed together like a wave on the sea in time to the music of wooden flute and log drum. Jewel sat in quiet remembrance of similar celebrations of her recent past, though with a crowd of people who, in appearance, were far different. Men were dressed in an odd mix of items from the ill-fitting trousers of a farmer to formal buskins and breeches, and women showed up in lace-covered skirts with varying sizes of shawls and head scarves. The villagers enjoyed the occasion to the fullest extent, however bizarre their appearance.

How far they had come since the days when a different group of villagers thought she was a goddess, celebrating Ruby's and her arrival.

Thinking back brought a smile to Jewel's face. Wondering what their lives would be like in the future if the forest village was to become their permanent home changed her smile to a look of worry.

Furcula raised his arms to bring everyone's attention to himself. He gave a brief speech to the crowd before calling Jewel and Diamond to his side. As he spoke, he tied a colorful ribbon around each of their wrists. The final gesture was to bring the two ribbons together and tie a firm knot. The couple did not understand anything he said, but they understood the symbolism of the ceremony.

The Gazrak people stood to cheer the newlyweds and the music resumed. Rista leaped to her feet. Casting aside her outer cloak, she revealed her very best full-skirted dress. She whirled and twirled tantalizingly, displaying all her best feminine charms, all the while keeping eye contact with Gem. With one hand over her head and one on her hip, she jumped gracefully to the beat and the light clapping of hands of those gathered. Subdued woops and yells combined with exuberant body motions created a feeling of quiet celebration.

Furcula stepped forward bringing the music to an immediate halt. Crouching down, he pulled a rough leather bag from his coat and carefully dumped a pile of small animal bones on the ground in front of them. He took hold of a wooden stick wrapped with a pitch-like substance and thrust it into the fire until it burned brightly. Fascinated, the four strangers watched him wave it over their heads three times while chanting a hypnotizing tune. He stared down at the bones and grunted to himself. All eyes were on the bones trying to decipher their hidden message. In the strange language, Furcula stood and made an announcement. Then he repeated in the language of the four, "The gods have spoken. The strangers are welcome and will stay! Long life to Diamond and Jewel!" Jewel felt a shudder ripple through her body hearing the emphasis on the word 'stay'. Shouts of agreement went up from the group.

"I will introduce you so we may know who is living among us," said Furcula. He spoke in the Gazrak language and gave a short sentence for each of their names. Something about the way he said their names seemed to include a snarl of contempt. It was slight and barely noticeable. But notice it, they did.

A buzz of whispered conversation arose from the women; each one speculating on the story that brought the strangers to their camp. Rumors jumped from group to group like grasshoppers on a summer day.

Rista stood waiting to begin the dance again. Behind her, Agafa tugged at her arm. She shrugged off his attentions and came forward to where Furcula spoke with the four. The young suitor bristled at the slight, staring at Gem with furrowed brow.

"You have met my granddaughter, Rista," remarked Furcula. "She is promised to Agafa when she comes of age. Which, by the way, is soon." The small ruler turned his gaze to Gem and paused for effect. Agafa smiled, squared his shoulders, and gave a haughty look of distain for the intruders.

"King Furcula, I thought you said you are not from here. How is it you have a granddaughter?" asked Gem.

"I adopted her when her parents were lost to the outsiders." Furcula reached up and patted the young woman on her head. "I am the only parent she remembers now. Rista, you have work to do. Go! Gazago is finished. Everyone to the trees." Rista obeyed, but not before giving Gem one last flirtatious glance.

Gem stepped back and melted into the group. He turned to his companions and said with an embarrassed smile, "She likes me. What can I say?"

"You don't have to say much. I think you like her too," added Jewel.

"Be careful, brother. Looks like she's taken," Diamond warned.

*

The area cleared of people, the fire died down and the piercing chirp of crickets dominated the night. Diamond and Jewel were escorted to the new bridal hut.

"So are we really married? It feels like there should be more to it than that. I did not understand a word of what Furcula said."

"We can say our own promises. The one who brought our hearts together will hear them and truly "tie" our lives together."

Gem and Ruby found their way by dim lamp light to the cave and were soon wrapped in their rough blankets against the chill of midnight.

*

The next morning the Gazrakites returned to a normal routine. Celebrations were in the past, and daily chores awaited. Mealtime brought the four together again in the shade of the trees.

"What is to become of us?" asked Ruby. "Today we begin to be part of the Gazrak tribe. Is it possible to imagine that we can escape through the forest? I do not want to be here."

"Every time he hears our names, Furcula gets such a look on his face. Is there something about us he fears?" asked Jewel.

"Or hates!" commented Diamond in deep thought. "We are the treasured ones of the High King and our names reflect that reality. He may know of the Prince. It would not surprise me to find him to be an enemy. Perhaps he knows more of the outside world than we are aware."

"What if he overhears us talking and finds out who we are?" asked Ruby.

"That is a chance we have to take. We cannot forsake our purpose and who we are."

*

That night, the four sat together at the opening of the cave before Diamond and Jewel departed for their own quarters.

"What can be the purpose of our being here like this?"

"We have not used our treasures since we have been here. Maybe they can help us. Diamond, your great white stone can cut through bars of iron. My green stone can shine like the sun bringing light and promises of truth."

"My blue stone and key can open doors long locked and deliver from the darkest dungeon," reminded Gem.

"My song can bring peace to the weary and light up the night with comfort and joy." There was a rustling sound as they located the precious gifts they each carried with them. Diamond held out his clear stone. Jewel held out her necklace, and Gem brought forth his key with the blue stone embedded in it.

Jewel's thin voice spoke into the darkness, "Ruby, sing for us the words of the diarist. We need to gather close and remember who holds our lives and future."

Ruby hummed a gentle, emotive tune. Jewel rubbed the green stone and dancing words of truth appeared in the air. They all repeated the lines and a warm, bubbling mixture of lights circled just above their heads illuminating the interior of the cave.

I know the one in whom I have believed.
I know that he is able to bring me all the way
to his wonderful Kingdom of Light.

In the pitch black of the forest, a lone figure watched and listened in amazement, then quietly slipped away.

77

CHAPTER 11

SUSPICIONS

'*Bazako*', said Rista, articulating each syllable with care. "*Yano balop bazakomo birizapo.*" said Jewel slowly. Rista nodded and said "Yes, I cook in pot balop." Both women laughed as they learned together. "No, no. I am cooking balop in the pot." Jewel corrected, and both women laughed in triumph at their language accomplishment.

Rista paused and flashed a huge smile. She raised her hand up as if to call a halt to the lesson. Reaching behind, she produced a bundle wrapped in a rough cloth and presented it to Jewel. The curious receiver carefully pushed aside the wrapping to reveal a clean and bright green gown. Rista clapped with excitement bouncing up and down on her toes. Jewel stared, amazed at the restoration wrought by the hands of her young friend.

"Wonderful!" cried Jewel.

"Wonderful!" mimicked Rista.

"Thank you, thank you. How did you get it so clean? It was a ruin a few days ago." Jewel grabbed Rista and gave her a vigorous hug practically lifting the petite girl off the ground.

"Thank you, wonderful," Rista continued to practice her new words.

"Yes, wonderful, thank you. Now you two finish!" mocked Ruby. "We be in big trouble if no finish."

"Don't talk like that. How will she learn our language properly?"

"Why would she want to learn our language? Oh, I forgot. She has plans for a certain young man." replied Ruby looking into Rista's face. "Rista has plan, no? Yes?"

Rista listened intently to the banter trying to understand the humor.

"*Hapaze!*" scolded an older women who worked next to the three. They all understood that the men would soon be arriving for their meal and haste was required.

*

Rista stood behind the cauldron and dipped a heavy ladle into the stew. Diamond was next in line. Bringing up the steaming broth and serving into the primitive bowls required skill. She made sure she applied that skill in seeing that the bowls of the newcomers were filled with the best of the meat. Jewel saw that this time Gem winked back at Rista and smiled. The young woman shivered with excitement at his gesture.

*

As they sat together on the log bench, Jewel asked, "How is the work going up there in the trees? Are you learning how the Gazraks make invisible homes from branches and leaves?"

"You will not believe your eyes. Up there, a most complicated and ingenious series of dwellings have been created. The place they are preparing—I should say, we are preparing—will amaze you. You and Diamond should find it much more comfortable than the hut. Mother will have her own place as well."

"Why don't you want to sleep in the trees like the rest of us?" asked Jewel.

"I like the feeling of being able to get out quickly. The tree houses seem so closed in. Maybe they remind me of a prison cell," said Gem.

79

"How do they get up there? I have never seen a ladder or stairway," Jewel asked.

"Behind those large trees is a false tree with a circular stairway inside. You would not find it unless you knew it was there. With their knack for camouflage and disguise, the Gazrak people feel safe here."

"How do they make it so invisible?" Jewel continued. "Someone wandering in the forest would never guess that a whole village is above their head."

"The Gazrak people may be short on gardening skills, but they are geniuses when it comes to not being seen or heard," added Gem.

Jewel waited for the right moment and then asked, "Gem, how do you feel about Rista? I can tell she has made up her mind that she will marry you some day. That is most unfortunate because Agafa grows more and more jealous. Do you worry that he may try to hurt you?"

"I know what Furcula said about her being promised to Agafa. I can tell she does not regard him well. I do not want to aggravate that brute though. Rista should be able to decide on her own who she wants to marry."

Before Gem could finish his thought, Rista appeared and sat down with them. She rattled off a rapid series of words that left Jewel startled. "Oh, I'm sorry I don't understand you. Say it again." Both felt the frustration of wanting to communicate.

"Oh, where is your grandfather? He could help translate."

"Grandfather go," stammered Rista.

"Where did he go?" asked Jewel. "Did he leave the camp?" Rista nodded her head and tried again. She held up three fingers and motioned that he would return in, what they assumed, was three days.

"That is strange," said Gem. "Why would he leave for several days? He can barely get around here with that cane, let alone go on a journey through the dense forest."

Diamond joined the group but was quiet. After a short pause and while staring at Rista, Gem spoke in a low voice, "Have any of you thought that it might not be so bad to stay here?" Rista returned his stare and smiled as if she understood the strange words.

"Are you serious? This is not where we are meant to be. I am sure of it. We must not forget where we belong." Diamond reasoned. "We must encourage one another and stay strong. Perhaps there is some reason to be here. Something good will come of this. I believe that. But this is not our final destination. I am just saying that there might be a purpose in our being captured. These people need to hear about the Prince. This place too must be part of the larger kingdom of King Zenith."

"Prince. Who is Prince?" interrupted Rista. The four turned to look at her, contemplating the possibility that she could understand if they tried to explain.

"We must work harder at learning this language," concluded Jewel.

*

Several days passed. Jewel and Ruby wandered among the knots of women who were seated on the ground, accompanied by their small children playing in and around them. Curious as to what they were making, the two seated themselves in one group after another, watching the women tear patches of cloth. They carefully worked each one into the coverings that the hunters wore to hide their nocturnal activities. Choosing colors and textures that could not be distinguished from real vegetation, they knew exactly how to create the appearance of underbrush. Other groups mended quilts from scraps of more vivid colors that could not be used for disguise. Still others reshaped clothing to fit whomever was in need of a new outfit.

"Apey!" urged one of the seamstresses, patting the ground to show the two where to sit. Another held up a piece of cloth along with slender, wooden needles and coarse, handmade thread.

"They want us to join them."

"Why not? It looks like a way to be helpful."

*

The never-changing meal time saw everyone gathered under the trees at mid-day. A hunting party had returned from the forest hours before with fresh meat. Women and older children dished out the stew, the pattern the four had observed each and every day.

"We have not seen the King for more than three days. Where could he have gone?" asked Diamond. Jewel recounted her conversation again with Rista predicting his absence of three days. "He should be back from wherever he has been."

Diamond found Jewel's hands and held them affectionately. "We will find a way. Do not give up. There is a future for us, I know."

"Cut the lovey stuff and eat your food," Gem said with a smirk spooning the meal greedily into his mouth.

"I've tasted better from a scrap heap at the slave market," complained Ruby.

"Come now, just look what they have to work with. Meat, simple vegetables, bread. What would you expect?" Diamond encouraged.

"I see no gardens. They raise no animals and yet they always have bread and meat to eat. Where do they get their food?" asked Jewel.

"And clothes!" added Ruby.

"I have asked myself that and many other questions," commented Gem. "Where do they get all the things they have? When the men returned from their hunting trip new things appeared in the village."

Just then, a small loaf of fresh bread appeared in front of Gem's face. The conversation ceased and all four looked up to see the smiling, freckled face of Rista.

"For you!" she said with excitement and suspense as she waited for a response from her new interest. Gem received the gift and smiled in return. Their fingers touched causing Rista to giggle before she ran off and disappeared into the crowd. Gem ducked a little lower where he sat and turned red with self-consciousness. "I hope Agafa didn't see that."

*

"Jemi, Damoni, kom," a village man yelled and beckoned them with an arm pulling gesture.

"It is back to work for us. Looks like we are needed to finish up

82

the tree house. I think we are getting fairly proficient at hidden tree dwellings now." Gem and Diamond jumped up and walked toward the waiting men.

"Every time the hunters return from a trip I have an awful feeling about this place, Ruby."

"What do you mean?"

"I suspect that we are living with a gang of thieves. How else do you explain all this?" Jewel's voice trembled.

"How do they get away with it?" Ruby continued her questioning. "Where are they going to steal, if that's what they do? Why hasn't someone found their hideaway and broken up this band?"

"It can't be long before we find out the answers. They must know we suspect them of something," said Jewel.

"You are right. What can we do about it? We can't stay here forever. We are nothing more than slaves again in this camp."

*

In the shadows of giant, leafy trees, Gem craned his neck to hear any meaningful words. Before him, the hunters prepared to leave for a trip into the forest. Gem watched as Furcula gave them instructions and tried to listen in on the conversation. The words were spoken so quickly, he could not get a sense of the meaning despite all his work at learning the language.

The old leader had returned the day before. He did not look any worse for having trekked in the forest for almost a week. Upon his return, he called a meeting with Agafa and his primary hunters. Judging by the reactions of the men, Gem realized that information Furcula passed on to them affected the strategy of this upcoming, hunting venture.

The men rubbed a lotion smelling of tree pitch on their skin before donning empty backpacks, and finally their woodsy, hooded robes. He expected to see bow and arrows or spears, but there were none that he could observe. Instead, they carried knives honed to deathly sharpness by none other than Diamond, whose skill in this was unsurpassed. One hunter bore a shovel, another a large digging fork.

Eyeing Gem, Furcula approached and spoke. "You are a smart one, aren't you?"

"What do you mean? I am learning how the men get ready for a hunt."

"Perhaps you are ready to join them?" said Furcula. "I think it is time you began to be one of us."

"I will have to know how to prepare." Gem did not mean to sound like he was volunteering, but now it was out of his mouth.

"That is right. Soon you will go with the men and do your part to support our fine community. You and Diamond both will be very helpful." Furcula looked at Gem with the same partly closed eyes, trying to read his mind.

"I guess you are no stranger to the difficulties of walking in those woods. You have been gone for days. What do you do when you leave here like that?" Gem realized he was being very brash in asking such a question.

"A poor, blind beggar is still welcome in most parts of the country. A poor, blind beggar sees and hears a great many stories as he roams the streets." Furcula winked at Gem and laughed out loud. Gem laughed with him, trying to digest the meaning of Furcula's words.

*

The men arrived back from their hunting trip the next evening, trudging slowly and wearily past Diamond and Gem. Each man slid his cloak to the ground and lowered the catch from woven bags to waiting tables. Looking exhausted and filthy from a long night and day of work, each slunk away to find a bed.

Large chunks of raw meat lay in the open as the women set about cutting, smoking, and cooking portions over an open fire. Jewel and the others wondered what animal they had hunted down to provide such a great quantity of meat. It was impossible to determine from the resulting hunks that now roasted on the fire. The smell was tantalizing and they could hardly wait until it was time to eat.

"Get busy, you two!" Furcula demanded trying to sound light and merry. Jewel and Ruby found knives and began to help.

*

Late in the evening the forest people gathered around the fire to share their food. Before long, someone began to beat a soft rhythm on the side of the log upon which he sat. A flute player joined in and suddenly a celebratory mood was in the air. The hunters appeared looking rested. The odd shirts and strange-looking trousers had replaced the soiled camouflage garments. Diamond and Jewel began to clap softly along with the others. Soon Ruby began to hum and then to sing along, catching a tune she could follow.

His mood suddenly stirred by the music, Agafa stood and walked over to Ruby, flung one arm into the air, and with the other grabbed her by the waist and swung her around. Ruby was delighted. Everyone smiled and laughed to see the tiny woman being flung about by the young hunter.

An incredulous smile beamed from Ruby's face as she sailed by her companions. Gem clapped and waved at the novel scene of his mother enjoying herself as he had never seen until now. Agafa sneered at Gem each time they whirled by, sending a chill of fear over him when he realized the power these men had over their lives and future. It could be good, or it could be very bad.

Acting as sorcerer, Furcula once again took center stage. He threw the animal bones on the ground while waving his cane about and shouted, "This is good!"

Diamond watched and wondered what significance there might be to the obvious sign of approval. In the meantime, Agafa whirled Ruby into the crowd where she collapsed into a joyful state of exhaustion. Having already targeted his next partner, he caught Rista by the hand and pulled her into the circle. She reluctantly complied, but her gaze was fixed on someone else.

Gem watched and admired the energy of the dancing couple. Agafa wasn't exactly light on his feet, but he made up for it in sheer strength. Picturing himself whirling around with Rista formed a pleasant thought, but the evening was getting late. Gem turned to go when someone caught his hand and yanked hard. Agafa stepped back as Rista forced Gem into position to continue the dance. He stood feeling foolish, as he had never danced before as the Gazraks did. A look of shock came over Agafa seeing his rival being brought by his intended bride into the center of the gathering. He turned and stalked angrily away from the circle.

Slipping one arm around Gem's waist, Rista encouraged him to jump in time to the music. He looked into her eyes and suddenly they were off, flying through the air. The crowd clapped and cheered louder. Even Furcula smiled his sly, conniving grin.

The music stopped. One by one the crowd fell back into the dark. Rista held onto Gem's arm and said something in her language. Gem shook his head. "I do not understand what you are saying. Two words! That is all I know—'you' and 'me'—what about you and me?"

Rista looked at Gem and tried again. "You, me," More unintelligible words ensued. She took one of his hands and held it tightly in her own. With her second hand, she took a scarf and wound it around their bound hands. "You mine," she said emphatically.

"Rista, are you saying we should get married? We cannot do that. Your people would never have it. I cannot stay here forever." Rista's eyes pierced his own with a look of disdain.

"You stay. Furcula say this!"

"You don't understand. I wish I could explain, but you will not know what I am talking about. I have to go to another place far away. It is called the City of Light. You could go too, but you don't know the Prince."

"Who is Prince?" asked Rista. "Where 'City Light? Me you go."

Gem looked around nervously wondering if anyone was overhearing their conversation. The firelight was very dim. What would Rista's grandfather think if he was talking to her alone in this now abandoned place?

"We can talk about this tomorrow. You go now," Gem touched her forehead brushing back a tangle of orange waves. For a moment they looked into each other's eyes before the spell broke.

86

"Go. You know that word. Go now." Gem pointed to the trees as he backed away toward his cave dwelling. Rista lowered her head and pouted before complying with his instruction.

CHAPTER 12

THE HUNT

"The men will hunt tonight. We will take you as well. Be ready early. It is a long way to the hunting ground." commanded Furcula. Before Gem and Diamond had a chance to reply, he walked away and was gone.

"Yes!" Gem replied to the empty space where the old leader had stood. Anxious for something to do after days of inactivity, he bristled with excitement.

"Wait. I think I should stay here. You go without me." Diamond had a great unease about going on the hunting trips. The time had come to take a stand on his unwillingness to participate.

"What? Why? Are you out of your mind?" asked Gem in utter frustration. "What will happen to us if we don't go with them? We have to go."

"You go ahead, Gem. I'm staying with Jewel and Ruby." Diamond lowered his voice to barely above a whisper and continued. "Aren't you a little suspicious by now that the meat we have been eating tastes very much like cow? These people are not raising cattle.

They are stealing from the villages out there somewhere. What they are doing at night is dangerous and could mean imprisonment or worse if we are caught."

"What choice do we have? They have taken us in. Where would we go if we left here? We do not know this country. We do not know the way out of this forest."

"This was never meant to be our final destination, you know that. The Prince said he would lead us and we would discover what it was we are supposed to do and where we should be heading. So far we haven't had any clues to where and how that is to happen. But we have to believe that it will happen," Diamond pleaded with Gem.

"I'm going. That's it and ….."

"And what? What is it you aren't telling me?" asked Diamond.

"And Agafa keeps following me around. Won't let me out of his sight. He challenged me to go in front of the others. Said I was probably a coward." Gem lowered his head and frowned in disgust.

"Well, be brave and be smart. Don't risk going back to prison because of some girl."

"What do you mean, some girl?" asked Gem angrily.

"I know what's going on, brother. I see Rista also following you around and taking every opportunity to talk and flirt. She likes you, and Agafa doesn't like you because of it. Watch out for him. He is out to get you."

"Sure I like Rista. I like her a lot. But you let me worry about that. You cannot tell me what to do. I am your older brother, after all. Why do you always think you are in charge? You are always the one who directs and leads. Do you think you are so much better than we are?" Gem was angry and, for the first time, he blurted out his thoughts.

"I know you are older. I love you as my own brother, though it is only through our father's blood. Please don't misunderstand me." Here Diamond paused knowing that his revelation might cause even further pain to Gem. "I believe that I am to lead us," he said. The older brother squirmed where he stood wanting to lash out again.

"Gem, I had a dream, and it was so real I can see it still. It made an indelible mark on me. I dreamed that you and I were fighting a great battle against a strong enemy. We were in a castle far from here. The enemy was the great, green dragon." At this, Gem stood taller and almost smiled. His expression changed as Diamond continued.

"We were fighting together, Gem. But the Prince came and told me to lead the charge. I believe this was a message from the High King himself. I don't know what it means, but I am sure he intends me to be the leader, and the rest of you will follow me."

Gem could feel his face grow hot with anger. No words would come. He turned and walked away.

*

As the morning sun rose, the men quietly gathered in the center of the camp, as was their custom, smelling of tree bark and sap. The bulky capes were drawn over their net bags and hoods pulled over their heads so that in the shadows no faces could be seen. Each one examined their newly sharpened knives that glistened in the sun.

"Where Diamond?" asked Agafa with a stern face.

"He told me he's not coming. I don't know why." Gem pulled the rough hood down to hide the fear in his face and forced the halting words out knowing they would not be well received.

"Hmff," uttered Agafa, turning toward the men and motioning for them to head out of the camp. Each knew the routine so not a word was uttered as they marched out singly, forming a long, slithering snake-like line, moving in and out of the trees. Gem could not see anything and felt his way clumsily along, occasionally bumping into a bush or tree. He was amazed that the group had mastered the art of traveling silently without more than the snap of a twig being heard. He wondered as he went why they would take him along, since he was not trained in similar arts. Ruminating on Diamond's words, he mentally tried to prepare for any move that Agafa made to trip him up or give him away.

The walk was long and Gem grew weary. It was almost night when the group reached their destination. They halted and spread out.

Gem stood there not knowing what to do. He heard nothing. After a long while, one of the group bumped Gem in the dark and shoved a heavy sack of grain into his arms, whispering instructions for him to carry it. He stowed it under his cloak, as he had seen the others do. There was no sound. The men shoved and pushed Gem along; the long march back to the camp had begun. Bone weary, the troop suddenly broke into daylight and the village lay before them.

Gem was beyond tired. The sack of grain had become intolerably heavy, and once it was delivered to the waiting women in camp, his body felt light. He was faint with hunger and tiredness and could think of nothing else besides lying down to rest. The others grumbled in the dark, each heading to his shelter in the trees.

A loud voice not far away momentarily aroused his attention. Someone was unhappy, but Gem was too tired to care. As he turned to head for the cave, a chunk of bread and a wooden cup of drink was thrust into his hands. Summoning his last bit of energy, he drank and ate before falling into a deep sleep.

Gem awoke late in the afternoon. He was alone, but a rustling sound stirred his senses and signaled the presence of someone. At the entrance to the cave, Rista's wide-eyed face appeared and then beamed to find him awake.

"Rista, you are not supposed to be here. Your family will kill me if they find you here. And what about Agafa?" The muscles of Rista's face contorted into a sneer. "No. No like Agafa." She muttered something in her language and looked frustrated, not knowing how to communicate her thoughts to Gem. She reached out and grasped Gem's upper arm and stroked his bicep. Gazing into his eyes, she said softly, "Brave, strong." He flexed the muscle evoking a giggle of delight from his admirer. "You are prince," she continued. At the mention of the Prince, Gem's senses returned.

"No, I am not the Prince. Someday I will tell you about the Prince. But for now you must leave, Rista. If you like me so much, then don't get me killed!" Rista pouted and backed away out the entrance. Before she disappeared, she turned to grin and wink at Gem.

Diamond bumped into Rista scurrying away from the cave, still giggling. He entered the dark interior and looked at Gem in amazement. "What was that about?"

"She came in here to tell me she thinks I'm brave and strong. Gem confessed with a mix of amusement and pleasure. "Does that meet with your approval, Oh great leader?" he added with contempt, remembering their earlier argument.

"You are being foolish. Our stay here is getting very complicated. You are being drawn in to such an extent that it will be difficult to leave, if we ever do," Diamond observed with a scowl.

"I can take care of myself. Don't worry so much," Gem retorted, angered by his brother's caution.

Diamond could see that Gem enjoyed being admired and his feelings for Furcula's granddaughter grew daily. He mentally put aside his brothers choices and pointless anger; a more pressing matter was on his mind.

"What did you do last night? Was the party sent out to steal as we suspected?"

"I didn't see anything being stolen. My role was playing pack horse. I haven't even seen what was brought back. Have you?" .

Gem did not feel like answering his brother's questions, though he found himself replying grumpily. "I saw only food supplies—meat, vegetables, grain."

"Why do I believe that they did not find a market in operation in the middle of the night?" commented Diamond as he pondered the whole affair. "Did you find out where we are? Did you see the way in and out of this forest?"

"I didn't see anything. There is the tunnel they go through not far from the entrance to the camp," Gem said, remembering how the four had noticed it when they first entered the Gazrak village. "Other than that, I had to keep my head down and covered as we left and returned from the hunt. I know it was a long way. I am tired."

"Do you think you could find your way again? Was there a path they followed?" asked Diamond.

"No! No. Whatever took place, I have to admit that these men are expert in the art of stealth. They made not a single sound. I don't know where we were. One thing is sure, they knew where they were and exactly what they were after."

Diamond thought for a minute and replied, "I wonder now why they allowed us to stay here with them. Once we are part of this, we will not be able to leave. We will threaten their survival and safety if we leave, as we may tell someone where and how they live."

After Diamond left him, Gem sat alone in the cave trying to put it all out of his mind; choosing rather to ponder the pleasure of seeing his mother dance and sing, of Rista and her charms, her admiration of him. It felt good. And how could it be wrong to merely carry loads of food back in the dark. He did not see anything being stolen. Why would he want to leave?

*

The next day the routine began again. Diamond saw Furcula at a distance in a serious discussion with some of the older men. He concluded his talk and approached looking sullen and angry. Diamond knew that the leader was angry with him for refusing to go on the raids with the others. He sensed a showdown was coming.

"Greetings, Furcula." Diamond tried to sound friendly and lighthearted.

"Do not greet me, Diamond. I am deeply troubled with you. While you enjoy the hospitality of my people, you do nothing in return. We have a difficult life, and men are expected to provide."

"I am sorry, King Furcula." Diamond could think of no good excuse other than the truth. "Perhaps I am uncomfortable with how the forest people obtain the provisions. Is there no other way?" Furcula fumed silently as he considered his reply. "You will go with us next time. I have spoken and it will be done." Diamond gulped and had nothing to say in return. He nodded in resignation, and Furcula turned and hobbled away into the afternoon sunlight.

*

Gem, Ruby and Jewel sat dumfounded hearing of the confrontation with Furcula. Jewel moved closer to Diamond, hooked her arm through his and laid her head on his shoulder. "Diamond, I am sorry. I am afraid for you. Furcula is very angry. Maybe you should have gone with them. What do you think this means?"

"No. I do not believe I was wrong. I do not know what will happen because of my disobedience, but believe me, it was the right thing to do."

Standing motionless, Gem bristled inside at the implication of his own wrong doing. "You know I had no choice. You have no choice. These people have been living this way for a long time without being caught. So what makes him think this is all so bad?"

"Beside the fact that these supplies belong to someone else who worked hard to provide them for their families—families who must now go without, beside the fact that if you were caught along with the Gazrak men, you would spend the rest of your life in prison; beside those things, I can't think of anything wrong!" barked Diamond in return.

"I am just trying to do what we must to survive here." Gem's mind raced with jumbled thoughts. He had made a great effort to please the hunters, doing what he was told, carrying his share of the load. It was obvious that the men did not like Diamond for rejecting the role they had offered him. "Agfa is angry. The hunters are angry. They will make you pay for your disobedience. I'm sure of it. Does that not concern you?"

"I will take my chances. Like someone else I know," he added looking straight at Gem.

*

As the sun was rising, the forest men once again found their way to the camp circle. Several days had passed since the last hunt, and Diamond knew that he must go with the men this time. Furcula had made it very clear that this was his last chance to prove his loyalty. The wizened ruler surveyed the smaller than usual band assembled before

94

him, inspecting the cloaks and equipment.

"They haven't given you a very sturdy cloak. This thing barely covers you. At least it is a bit lighter in weight," remarked Gem observing the items issued to Diamond. Lowering his voice to a whisper, he continued, "Stay close to me."

"Are you ready to do your duty, Diamond?" asked King Furcula.

"I am, but you know my mind. I do not wish to steal," answered Diamond. Gem shuddered at his brother's audacity and threw him a look of distain.

"You do amaze me, young man," returned the leader with a hint of laughter in his voice. "Get out of here now before I do something rash."

Furcula waved his hand in resignation, directing the men to start marching. Turning away from them, he continued to wave as if ridding himself of a pesky mosquito.

*

With the two newcomers at the end of the line, they marched through the woods weaving in and out of trees, rocks, bushes, up hills and down, until almost dusk. Diamond faltered at every step trying to keep up with Gem, who by now, was more skilled at navigating through thickets and brambles.

When the destination was reached, Agafa's men spread out in the dark, leaving Gem and Diamond alone. "Don't worry, they will be back soon," whispered Gem. "And don't sound so downcast. You want to eat tonight, don't you?" Diamond did not respond. This irritated Gem. Inside, he knew something about this hunt was meant to be a test for Diamond, and he would likely fail. Maybe now his brother would acknowledge that Gem was the stronger and wiser one of the two.

*

In the stillness, an insistent whisper reached their ears. "Gem, come now." Gem left his position and followed the sound into the dark. There was silence for several minutes and then just ahead, a commotion of voices filtered through the trees. Yelling and glimmers

95

of torchlight flashed around Diamond. In a panic, he wondered if he should flee, but he did not know in what direction to run. Where was Gem? What was happening? Something had gone wrong. Were Agafa and his men in trouble? Diamond crouched down in place and pulled his cloak over his head hoping he would not be seen. The voices grew louder until they were practically on top of him. "They ran this way! Get them! Don't let them get away!" came voices from close-by. A flash of torchlight revealed to Diamond the fleeting vision of the forest people scurrying away into the dense bushes with Gem running with them. For just a split second Gem's glance was visible. He saw in his eyes dismay, but not panic. In a sudden burst of motion, someone grabbed the cloak from Diamond's back and whipped it away leaving him exposed there in the forest. Who? What? He did not see the culprit or understand why they had left him there.

"Here! Here! We found one of them!" shouted a gruff voice next to Diamond. In only a few seconds it was over. Two men grabbed him and jerked him upward from his squatting position.

"Shall we chase the rest of them?" yelled a voice. "No, don't bother. We will never catch them, let alone see them. This is a rare careless one. Your life is over, criminal!"

"Maybe we should hang him right here and now!" shouted a wide-eyed farmer. "No! We have plans for this fellow."

*

The hunting party returned earlier than usual. No one had yet stirred in the camp; no one except Fucula, who waited for word of the mission. Agfa looked up briefly and nodded. "It is done," he whispered in the language Gem was only now beginning to understand. The king said something in reply then quietly disappeared into the woods.

It was true. The mission had been to leave Diamond behind and make sure he was caught. Gem bit his lip and his whole body went limp realizing that Diamond would believe he had been betrayed by his own brother. What would he tell Jewel? He knew he couldn't tell her the truth.

Recalling skills from his past, Gem tried to hide his grief and fear

96

behind a face of stone. He headed in the direction of the cave. It would not be long before Jewel and Ruby appeared for their morning chores. What would he tell them?

He did not have to wait long. Jewel rushed to his side with her wide, gregarious smile. "How was the hunt? What did you bring back?" She looked at Gem and saw slumped shoulders and stony expression. "You are back early! You look very tired. Are you feeling ill?" Jewel looked behind Gem to see where Diamond was. "Where is Diamond? Is he alright?"

Gem's woeful look sent alarm through her senses. Jewel looked into Gem's eyes and knew something was terribly wrong. "What is it? Tell me."

"He was captured by the village men. He didn't make it back. I am so sorry." Gem could barely get the words out of his mouth. Jewel grabbed her mouth with both hands and screamed a muffled cry. She fell to the ground and wept bitterly, rocking back and forth.

"How did it happen? What did you see?" she begged.

"I don't know exactly. He was with me. Some village men chased us. We all ran back into the forest, but somehow Diamond did not run with us. I wasn't even sure he was missing until we were on the trail back to the camp. In the dark, it is so hard to tell what is happening."

Ruby heard the explanation. She glared at Gem and then flung herself upon Jewel in an attempt to comfort her grieving friend. "Weren't you watching out for him? You know he did not want to go!"

"It was very dark. I don't know what happened to him."

"Maybe he lost his way. Maybe he will be back later today when he finds his way back," Ruby offered, trying to console Jewel.

"It is impossible. No one finds their way back here. If they could, the villagers would have raided this place long ago. No, I am sure that he was taken by the men of that village. Do not think he will be back."

"Where is that evil ruler Furcula? I will tell him what I think of his leadership."

"You won't find him to tell him anything. I saw him heading for the forest," said Gem

97

"We must report for our duties, Jewel. I will have words with Furcula later." Ruby led Jewel away to begin the daily chores. The camp buzzed with the news of Diamond's capture. When they heard, the Gazrak women were sympathetic, though not surprised at Diamond's fate.

"What did you expect with such insolence?"

"Who will sharpen the knives now?"

"Perhaps now she will marry one of our young men."

"The gods have spoken."

*

Gem lay down to sleep, but he could not rest. He saw the whole scene before him over and over in his head. What could he have done? Nothing. It was clearly intended to be a trap for Diamond. He could not bring himself to disclose this to his mother and Jewel. And what about that dream that Diamond had about being a leader. He said he would lead them all to victory on their quest for the Prince. *What a joke that was*, he thought. Wherever Diamond ended up after this day, Gem knew they might never see each other again. Diamond may even have been executed, being blamed for all the night raids for all the years that the Gazrak people had been stealing from them. He tried not to think about what Diamond would have to suffer.

CHAPTER 13

WANDERDOWN

"Wake up!"

Diamond woke painfully. Kicked and beaten, bruised and battered, he moved in slow motion, while his captors roused him from sleep.

"I said wake up, you scoundrel! Sit up. You have a lot of talking to do." Through blurry eyes, Diamond beheld the angry faces staring down at his rumpled form. He lay on a stone floor that was cold and unforgiving of his painful, miserable state. Even the sturdy trousers and jacket provided to him by the Gazrakians couldn't soften the blows of his new captors, nor the hard surface on which he found himself.

He tried to sit up and found he did not have the strength. Looking around, he saw the gathering of citizens. Someone knelt beside him, grabbed him by the shoulders and forced him into a sitting position. Diamond's face contorted with pain, but no mercy was shown by those whose possessions had been systematically stolen over a period of years.

"Tell us where the others are. You hear me?" yelled a slender bearded man of forty.

"I can explain," Diamond tried to open his eyes fully and understand his surroundings. The cluster of men, intent on hearing firsthand from their captive, made the room look small. He could see little more than a circle of angry faces and pointing fingers.

"Explain! Explain? Is that what you are saying? What is there to explain? You and your people have ruined this town!" he yelled into Diamond's ears.

"Here, let me have a go at him," cried another, pushing the bearded man aside. "You are in a heap of trouble, young man. We want information and we want it now. You will tell us what we want to know or you haven't seen nothing yet, ya hear?"

"Let him be a spell. We beat him up good. Can't you see he is in no shape to squawk." The voice of calm reason prevailed and the men backed away. Diamond tried to remember how he came to be in the grim predicament. It was all a blur of pushing and shoving, punching and kicking.

"What is your name?" asked the calm voice. Diamond turned his head toward the sound trying his best to cooperate.

"…mond, oh, can I have a drink of water?" The words were on his tongue, but the articulation of them came out slurred and indistinct. The first syllable of his name got lost somewhere, and what came out of his mouth sounded more like "mondo. Ca hab din wat."

"I think he said his name is Mondo. That is a start," said the calm voice. "What was the rest? Anyone get that?"

"Says he wants a drink of water," offered another observer.

"So, Mondo, you want this drink of water? Eh? Then start talking!" The bearded man grew more and more impatient.

"Back off, Rickter. Give him a little more time."

Diamond tried again to speak. Opening his mouth was as much as he could manage before fainting dead away.

*

100

Diamond could not tell how much time had passed before he woke again. The crowd had diminished. One interrogator remained, sitting nearby on a short, three-legged stool. His head rested in his hands, and he appeared to be sleeping. Dressed in high boots, leggings, and a gray coat that reached the floor, the man did not appear as threatening as the mob that had been present earlier. His long legs and bony knees protruded over Diamond's face.

"I will tell you everything I know," Diamond volunteered, trying to speak as clearly as his mouth would allow. The long-legged man jerked awake in his seat and shook himself into alertness.

"What's that? You want to tell us what we want to know? Well, Mondo, my boy, I am listening. By the way, the name is Horatio Kibble. I am the Keeper of the Peace here in Wanderdown, otherwise known as the KoP. I have a lot of questions for you, and you had better have some very good answers. Is that clear?"

Diamond gathered his courage and began. "You see, Mister Kibble, sir, my friends and I were lost in the woods. We had no idea where we were…"

"Now I don't want any nonsense from you. You and your friends are monsters! How can you lie there and tell me you were lost in the woods? You better have something better than that to tell me." Kibble stood up and began to pace back and forth.

"No. I mean the four of us. We were lost and the Gazrak hunters found us."

"Gazrak? Who are they? What do you mean the four of you?" asked Kibble whose patience was becoming as exhausted as his sleep deprived body.

"It is a long story, but suffice it to say, my brother and two friends got lost in the woods when they found us. We were forced to go with them to their camp. They would not allow us to leave. We were captives. They forced me to go on the raid with them against my will."

"Who are these hunters? Where is their camp?"

Diamond saw Kibble's incredulous stare. "If I knew where the camp is, I would surely tell you. My friends are still captive there."

101

"That is quite a story. Uh, huh."

Silence broken only by an occasional "Hmmm" followed. Outside, the muffled sounds of people yelling, dogs barking, and children playing were the only distractions.

"So where did you come from when you got lost in the woods with your friends?" The investigator squinted one eye and focused the other squarely on Diamond's face.

"That is harder to explain, sir. You see I was helping my friends who were running from some people who wanted to do them harm. We are from a town quite far from here. I'm sure you have never heard of it."

More silence ensued. "My boy, that is just too hard to believe. Why do you not know the way to the thieves den when you had just come from there? Were you asleep on the trail?"

"Their camp is very well hidden. They did not even allow me to know how to go or come from there. I wore the cloak they gave me which hid my surroundings from my eyes. The cloaks hide the men from being seen by others, as well. My cloak was snatched from me suddenly, and there you were to find me. The others ran away, but you would not have been able to see them anyway. They are very clever at avoiding detection. I am not lying. I am telling you the truth. I swear." Diamond knew it sounded very farfetched. Who was going to believe such a story?

"You say they wear cloaks. At least we know now how they come and go without being seen. But how do they know where to look for our cattle and grain? No, there has to be more to this."

Just then Rickter came through the door looking meaner than ever. "You worm the truth out of him yet, Kibble?"

"Well, Rickter, he's got a story that is hard to get hold of, that is for sure. But he just does not look like the type of man to be out robbing folks in the middle of the night."

"He's a smart one. Don't believe them lyin' ways of his. Sneaky, that's what he is," Rickter said, determined to get to the bottom of things.

"Ask him yourself if you don't believe him."

Both sat in disbelief shaking their heads. Rickter fumed and looked at Diamond with such hatred and threat that Diamond drew back physically.

"I hope you hang for your crimes. You can't get away with lies like this. What proof do you have of any of your story?"

"I can only tell you that I am not from that place. I was only there for a few weeks. They speak a different language that I do not understand or speak. Their leader knows our language. He says he is from our part of the world, not theirs."

"Well, that is interesting. Who are these people that they live so close, and yet do not know the language that is commonly spoken from far and wide? What else?" Rickter asked still unbelieving.

"If I can think of anything that will help you I will tell you. One request only and that is, if you find this group of people, please do not hurt my friends who are being held captive by them." Diamond tried to think of any other information that would help.

"A well-told tale, if you ask me," said Rickter. "What proof does he have? None. Nothing on him except this lump of glass in his pocket. Who carries a lump of glass in their pocket? Lock him up!"

*

Diamond felt himself being hauled limply across the room, through a barred passageway, and into a tiny compartment. Dumped on a low bed, he was grateful that the interrogation was over for the time being. The bed, though hard, was a great improvement to the stone floor. A cup of water and a dry crust of bread passed through the bars at the hand of the one to whom he had told his tale. Diamond again tried to think of a strategy, but none came to him.

*

"Have you heard the news?" Kibble asked the guard on duty who entered the building. The curiosity of all within earshot was instantly aroused, including Diamond who strained his neck to hear.

"Lord Crumblestone himself is going to hold an official investigation. Since he is the closest thing we have right now to a constable, he ought to be able to get down to the truth of this matter."

"What is Crumblestone doing in these parts?" asked the guard.

"He said he was passing through on his way to wherever it is he lives. He is some kind of officer of something. I don't care who he is as long as he makes sure this prisoner gets what's coming to him."

Hearing the name Crumblestone, Diamond noted the similarity to Chiselstone. *Perhaps he is from Bellicosa*, he thought. *What if he recognizes me? But then again, I have never heard of him. Lord Prince, please help me in my hour of judgment. Vindicate me and deliver me and my friends!*

*

Morning dawned. After a poor night's sleep, Diamond ate his crusts of bread and drank the foul tasting water that had been resentfully shoved into his cell.

The noise in the street seemed to signal that the mysterious Lord Crumblestone had arrived. Through the wooden walls of the jail cell, sounds of horses and carriage reached his ears. Crowds of towns people milled about laughing, murmuring threats, and recounting to each other the losses they had suffered.

It wasn't long before Kibble opened the cell door and led Diamond out into the main room. A stool in the center of the crowd seemed to be the designated place of shame for the prisoner. He sat down. Through the crowd, two men brought in a larger chair and placed it in front of the stool, in anticipation of the seating of the Lord and judge of the day.

A sudden hush signaled the entrance of the distinguished courtier. Looking at his fine suit of clothes, it was easy for everyone to tell he was a wealthy, and most likely, powerful man. Diamond squirmed with awkwardness, but determined to hold his own.

"High and grand Lord Crumblestone, we welcome you to our humble town of Wanderdown," began a portly gentleman who looked to be the mayor. He rambled for several minutes of eloquent greetings before Lord Crumblestone interrupted. "Let's get on with this. I must leave in the morning and I have a long journey. Is this the criminal you told me about?"

The mayor bowed and presented Peace Keeper Kibble. "Yes, of course. We are grateful for your assistance with this most important development in the case of the mysterious gang of thieves. All listened as Kibble recited the long history of thefts and raids, then recalled the significant capture of this lone thief. He went on to describe the story Diamond had given about his position in the robbers camp.

"You have been most thorough, good citizens. Thank you for that account. I must say, this is a very interesting story." Lord Crumblestone turned to Diamond and asked, "Is it true, young man?" he paused to reposition his spectacles. "Mondo, is your name? I hear that you claim to have been captured by these people and they forced you to participate in their raiding party?

"Yes, your Lordship."

"May I ask then where you are from in the kingdom? Does the town have a name?" The Wanderdownians nodded to each other acknowledging the cleverness of the question. "Now he's got him on the run," they declared to each other.

Diamond felt a moment of panic but opted for the truth. *As long as they do not ask me for a family name, I am safe*, he thought. *Mondo certainly is a name no one would recognize.* "Your Lordship, I am from Bellicosa, by the sea."

"Ahhh," said the Lord in a stuffy, arrogant tone. "That is a boon. I am from there as well. So if you are truly from Bellicosa, you will be able to answer my questions." Those observing the skill of the Lord beamed with satisfaction. Surely, the imposter was trapped now by his false confession.

"Where was your home? And who are your people?" demanded Crumblestone.

Diamond thought before responding. He did not want to lie, but the truth could mean his life was in danger as well. "I was raised in the home of Lord Chiselstone, up upon the mountainside, not far from the castle of the king. My people were humble slaves of his Lordship, of no account."

"I've been to that estate. Yes, Chiselstone, a real brute. I lost many a game to him. Do you know of his business?" asked the Lord.

"I do, your Lordship. He produced the best knives and swords in the kingdom. His name is well-known for those weapons." Diamond saw a look of mild surprise cross the Lord's face.

"And do you know what has happened to the Lord most recently?"

"The last I heard, he had remarried and was not doing well with his life." Sadness crept into his voice, so he ended his answer there without elaborating any further.

"You sound like an educated fellow. If you were a slave, then how did you serve in that household?" asked the Lord.

"I aided in buying and selling, your Lordship. I am an expert in the study of weapons and the art of carrying out business."

"Hmmm. I suppose you have a reason for no longer being in that household? Do you bear a slaves armband? Did you run away?"

Diamond felt himself getting in deeper than he had anticipated. How long could he go on making up lies? "I did run away, your Lordship. The master of the house was no longer in control of affairs. The new arrangement left me without the labor for which I was trained."

Lord Crumblestone looked very happy with himself to have found an additional charge to lay against the prisoner. "That makes you a runaway slave. I shall have to charge you with that crime. Do you prefer that to what these townspeople believe you are guilty of?"

Diamond's heart sank as he realized he was convincing people of his innocence for one crime, but being found guilty of another. There was no getting out of his predicament. "I am guilty, your Lordship, of running away. But I am not guilty of being a thief. I have told the truth about that."

"If you are educated—and I can't imagine Chiselstone allowing that—then add these figures and give me a correct sum of them." Crumblstone held out his hand and snapped his fingers for Kibble to hand him the instruments for writing. He then wrote hurriedly a list of numbers and placed them before Diamond. The task was simple, for numbers had always been one of the young man's strong skills. In the end, it took longer for Crumblestone to check the sum than it did for Diamond to produce it.

"I believe you. I think I see the truth of it now." Lord Crumblestone turned to the silent crowd and pronounced, "This man was captured in the hope that he would be an asset to the band of thieves. He himself declared that he did not want to help them. No doubt, they intentionally abandoned him rather than kill him."

"But, your Lordship," Kibble interrupted. "What makes you think this is so?" Diamond braced for his answer.

"The thieves came in the night like usual, right?" Everyone nodded their heads. "They did not steal anything that night, correct?" More nodding. "They drew the attention of guards in the town, something they never had done before, also correct? Then, lo and behold, one of their own is left behind. Has that ever happened before? Of course not. They simply betrayed him into your hands."

At this revelation, Diamond was dumfounded. Had Gem known that they planned to send him into a trap? He remembered the look on Gem's face as they retreated from him that night. Diamond had to believe the worst. How could he do it?

"But, your Lordship, wouldn't they be concerned that he would tell us information about the band? What if he told us too much and they were compromised?" asked Rickter.

The Lord shook his head back and forth and explained, "He hasn't been able to give you any information that is helpful. What? That they speak a foreign language, that they live in the trees? What good does that do? What do you want to do with this man?" asked the Lord.

The men gathered and conferred. No one could come to a decision. He was guilty by association. He had been willing to participate in a crime. He should be punished.

"This is my decision. I will take him off your hands."

"What? Why would you do that? If he is a runaway slave, we can hang him here."

"Why should you bother. Perhaps I can glean more information from him. I will personally make sure he receives the punishment he deserves. He is guilty of a crime against the Kingdom and should answer for that. I will take him with me. Is it settled?" The crowd reluctantly agreed, having no better plan for the prisoner.

Diamond hung his head in despair. Once back in Bellicosa, he would be discovered to be Damon, the son of Lord Chiselstone. Going back to his former life would be worse than punishment as a runaway slave. What would happen to Jewel and the others? How had their lives become so complicated and distant from the future he had imagined?

Soon all the disappointed spectators had gone, leaving Kibble alone to hand over his prisoner.

"First thing in the morning, I will be here to retrieve the scoundrel. You should be very thankful that I was in the area today. Justice has been done."

"Yes, your Lordship," replied Kibble with a hint of confused doubt in his voice. "Will he stand trial as a runaway slave?"

"Indeed, yes. I will see that he is punished for all his crimes."

*

At first light, Lord Crumblestone welcomed Diamond into his carriage seating him on the opposite side, and then signaling to the driver to begin the journey.

"Well, Mondo. What do you think of this turn of events? I will wager that you thought you had fooled me into thinking you are a runaway slave, right?" said the Lord with a cunning sneer. Diamond steadied himself in the jolting vehicle and wondered what this man might discover.

"I don't know who you are, but I will find out. You have never had a slave's armband on your arm before. But if you choose to be a slave, I will surely make you one. Now you are my slave, and I have big plans for you."

"Are we headed back to Bellicosa," asked Diamond meekly.

"Oh, no. My plans are bigger than that."

The carriage bounced over rutted roadways that wound through the deserted main street of the town. Small, bent and wrapped around in a ragged blanket, one lone figure stood close to the path of the oncoming vehicle. Diamond thought that one of the town's peace keepers had risen early to make sure the trouble maker was finally on his way, hopefully never to return. Glancing down from his window seat he looked into the unmistakable face of Furcula.

CHAPTER 14

REVENGE

High over the forest, the night sky revealed ancient trees frosted in moonlight. Soft light filtered down through the branches where Gem sat in the near-dark opening of his cave home.

"What should I have done?" he muttered half out loud, half expecting some voice to answer. He picked up a small stone and threw it violently against the cave wall. The sight of Diamond hunched down to the ground, watching as he and the hunters ran away into the woods, had been etched on his memory. The full force of guilt and shame crushed his spirit.

"I should have known."

Tears welled up in his eyes thinking about the pain felt by Jewel during days of uncertainty, and missing her husband. Abandoning her own hut, she had moved in with Ruby after the loneliness was too hard to bear. Day after day she wept, refusing to be cheered, and looking mournfully to Gem for answers of which he dare not speak.

Diamond was right, and now Gem understood all too well. Diamond had been their leader. From him came the constant reminders of their future goals and the hope in the great one they believed would deliver them from this current enemy. Diamond was the strong one who was willing to stand up for what he believed, while Gem admitted to himself his own weakness, going along out of fear for his own safety.

The chill of midnight slithered down his spine like a serpent. He shrugged and grabbed at the comfort of his rough bedding. Thoughts of what Diamond may be enduring plagued his mind. Squeezing his eyes shut, he lay upon the straw bed and sought escape in sleep. A rustling sound from a nearby clump of underbrush did not alarm Gem who had grown used to small night visitors of the rodent kind. He pulled his quilts over his head and went to sleep.

A silent figure drew nearer, watching, observing. Rista knew she was taking a risk creeping about in the middle of the night. She had done it many times before and not been caught. Mysterious sights had been her reward—sights she could not talk about to any of her clan, especially her grandfather. These strangers possessed something she did not understand, but it had provoked an intense curiosity and attraction she could not resist. Creeping nearer the cave, she wondered if Gem was still awake.

Without warning a silent burst of lightning flashed before her eyes. Shocked and surprised, Rista could barely suppress a muffled scream of terror as she fell back to the ground. She turned and ran back into the forest, but not before catching a glimpse of an enormous, ghostly animal rising high overhead threatening to drop down and trample her beneath its powerful legs. Gem awoke for a brief moment at the sound, but drifted to sleep when no further sounds erupted.

Nearer the stairway into the lofts above, Rista turned to look back. A faint glimmer of flashing light remained in the distance. Once inside her own shelter, she could not sleep. What had just happened?

*

"What has gotten into Rista?" asked Ruby as she and Jewel served the newly baked loaves of bread to the waiting men. "She looks like she has not slept." Both women stared as Rista dragged herself to the meal line. Agafa approached from where he had been seated, and from the distance it appeared that they were having a lively conversation. Arms began to wave and fingers point. Rista turned away, but Agafa grabbed her arm to prevent her walking away. Ruby watched as Rista wrenched her arm from his grasp.

"What is wrong with those two?" asked Gem, who arrived just in time to see the argument. "I hope I didn't do anything this time. Agafa already has decided I am his enemy. I surely do not need any more trouble from him."

The three tried to focus attention elsewhere. An unmistakable tension hung in the air and everyone in the camp felt it.

"Rista," came a crusty voice from the shadows. Furcula summoned his granddaughter with a stream of Gazrak words they understood to mean he wished to know more about the disagreement. Obediently, Rista came to him and proceeded to explain. Gem held his breath and did not move as Furcula shot fleeting glances in his direction.

"This cannot be good," he said in a low voice. "Somehow I think this is my fault. What have I done now?" He tried not to look in her direction.

The conversation did not last long. Holding her hands over her eyes, Rista quietly sobbed. The sound of the grandfather's speech did not reach far enough to be heard by anyone else, but it was evident from his stern face that his words did not please her. She gathered up her skirt and ran away from the camp into the depths of the woods.

*

The moon rose high overhead, its light making little difference to the tree dwellers. When the sun was gone and the camp fires had gone out, there was only sleep, the distant cry of an infant, or perhaps some late night conversations in the dark. Nestled into the heavy branches, the leafy niches formed a honeycomb of resting places. Heavy quilts provided cushioning over the floor made of slender sticks and warmth on the cold nights.

Ruby and Jewel, after a day of working alongside the other women in the camp, whispered softly before settling down for the night. Soon only the sounds of nocturnal creatures were likely to mar a good night's rest. The feint crackling of a twig signaled that someone had not found their bed as yet.

"Jewel," came a whisper, and then, "Jewel."

"Rista, is that you?" replied Jewel trying to be as quiet as possible.

"It is. May I come inside?" said Rista. Jewel was amazed at the young woman's ability to have mastered even the polite forms of her new language.

"Come." said Jewel and Ruby simultaneously. With the grace and ease of an expert, Rista crawled through the low framed opening and crouched in the corner. Jewel reached out to touch the frightened girl as she shivered in the darkness.

"What is it, Rista? Why are you shivering? Why have you come to us this way when it is so late? You should be in your own bed by now." Jewel pulled a quilt around Rista's shoulders.

"I afraid. I see very big..." Rista sought for words to describe what she had seen.

"What did you see, when?" asked Jewel. The two could hear Rista moving about in the dark trying to demonstrate with waving arms what she could not find words for.

"We can't see anything in the dark, Jewel. We will have to have some light in order to see what she is trying to tell us.

"That might prove awkward. How do we explain the light?"

"I have a feeling it is all going to come out soon anyway, don't you?" Accepting Ruby's point, Jewel reached beneath her bedding and brought out her prized necklace. She rubbed its large green stone lightly and a dull green luminescence lit up the small cubicle where they huddled. They watched as Rista's eyes grew large with amazement and momentary relief from her distress.

"Shhhh," warned Ruby. "Now tell us what you saw."

The awestruck Rista sat motionless gazing between the necklace and her two friends. Finally she spoke.

"At cave. I wait in dark. Gem no see me. I see very big *hopu. Hopu* and man on top. Like fire."

"Was it some kind of animal?" asked Ruby. "Like this." She mimicked the motion of a rearing horse.

"Ei!" replied Rista in her native language.

"Was there a man sitting on the creature's back?" asked Jewel.

"Ei! A man, very big man."

Jewel and Ruby looked at one another in silence. "This is going to be difficult," said Ruby. "How in the world do we begin to tell her about the Prince when she can barely understand us, or us her?"

"What you say is true, but think of what she is telling us, Ruby. If she saw the Prince, that means he really is here with us. He knows where we are. He is taking care of us."

"This is so strange. I do not understand why the Prince seems to have left us here, but somehow he is here in the midst of our predicament. How can that possibly be true?" Ruby shook her head in disbelief and the pale green light faded to a soft glow.

"Prince? You say Prince?" asked Rista. "I afraid of Prince."

"No, no. Don't be afraid of the Prince. He is good. I will tell you about him." Jewel cleared a space on the floor and began what she knew would be an arduous task. She took a tiny leaf and placed it at one end of the space, and then placed her glowing necklace far to the other side.

"This little leaf is Gazrak. Very small. This necklace is the City of Light. Very big. Very bright. Very good place." Several small items were added close to the Gazrak leaf to stand for others villages and towns. Painstakingly, Jewel attempted to describe the world as she understood it to one who knew only the confines of the Gazrak camp.

"You come to Gazrak from City of Light?" asked Rista.

"No. I go to City of Light. My home is here." Jewel pointed to a small marker representing Bellacosa.

"You go? Why? Grandfather say you no go, stay here."

"Grandfather is a bad man. He says we stay, but the Prince says we go." Jewel could see that she was getting in deeper than was wise.

114

"How are you going to explain that one?" Ruby chided. "She doesn't know her grandfather is bad." Rista looked confused and alarmed.

"I will try a different approach." Jewel found some tiny stones and put them close to the leaves representing other villages close to Gazrak. "This is food. Meat, grain." Jewel then used a small twig to represent Garzack hunters. Pushing the stones away from the small leaves toward the Gazrak leaf, she explained, "Gazrak men take food from other villages. Villages have no food now. They are hungry. Gazrak is bad. Grandfather is bad."

Rista looked horrified. Ruby bit her lip and said under her breath, "Now you have done it. If she tells the old man, we are in more trouble than I can imagine."

"How else can I tell her what she needs to know?"

"Why tell her anything? She will not be able to leave any more than we are able to leave. There is no way out of here."

Rista reached out for Jewel's hands. "You tell me. I see Prince. He is good. I am afraid but I want."

"It is very late and we are all tired. You go now. Tomorrow we will talk again. Go and sleep," Jewel insisted.

*

"Tomorrow there will be another hunt. I must go, though I fear it is getting more and more dangerous," Gem reported. "We have plundered so many villages, the day will come when they trap us and this will be all over. I do not see how they can continue to succeed."

"If you say no you will wind up like Diamond, and who knows what that is? Each time you leave I worry that I will never see you again." Ruby's motherly warning made Gem wince.

"We don't belong no matter how much we try to fit in. I heard the women talking today about who I will marry now that Diamond is gone. I can't bear it." Jewel wept.

Ruby and Gem did not know what to say. Jewel was right. Gem knew that she loved Diamond. Even with him gone, she mourned his loss and refused to accept it as final.

"You know, Jewel. Diamond, wherever he is, will have a good future. He told me about a dream he had that he would become a leader, that he would lead all of us to a great victory over the enemy. I didn't believe him at the time. I was even angry with him for suggesting that he would rule over us, as if we were slaves again." Gem tried to comfort Jewel, but he could see his words only deepened her grief.

"Were you angry enough to leave him behind on the hunt that night?" asked Ruby in an accusing tone.

Not thinking about the consequences of his confession Gem said, "I heard the men say they planned to harm Diamond. I didn't know what they would do. I could not stop them."

"You heard that and you did not warn Diamond? Could you at least have told him to watch out for a betrayal?" Ruby continued.

"It wasn't like that. If I had tried to stop them, they would have left us both behind."

"So rather than help your own brother, you ran away," cried Jewel. Gem could not retreat from the murky truth. There was no going back, no excuse that sufficed. Gem had indeed betrayed his brother, leaving him behind to who knows what kind of fate at the hands of the town people.

Jewel pulled out her beloved book and began to read. The words reminded her of their mission, which it now appeared, was lost to them as well. She read aloud:

"The Prince has promised me that he will deliver me from this place. My life is in danger, but he is faithful. He knows the enemy. He is stronger than my enemy. He has a plan for me that is sure and good. No enemy can take that away from me."

Jewel stopped and cried out to the Prince, the son of the High King, "Please hear me. Deliver us from this horrid place. Let us go to your place, the City of Light. Let me be with Diamond again."

116

*

Jewel slept fitfully, tossing and turning in the small space that the tree dwelling afforded.

"Jewel, wake up. You are having a bad dream."

"Huh? What? A dream, yes, a dream." Jewel shook her head and passed her hands over her face which was wet with tears.

"That poke with your elbow was the last straw. What were you dreaming anyway, that you were putting out a fire?"

"I am sorry. No. It was not a bad dream, but it was stranger than that. I dreamed that I was standing at the top of a long flight of stairs. A woman came through a door and beckoned me to come to her. She smiled so warmly and held her arms out to me. I descended the steps and when I got to her she embraced me with such love that I started to cry."

"What did she look like? Emerald, or Lady Chiselstone?"

"She looked very strange. Her hair was done up with very fine ribbons. Her clothes were brightly colored, with a necklace of ornate beads, and…."

"Yes, what else?"

"Her skin was dark, like mine."

"That doesn't sound like a bad dream. It probably means nothing. Go back to sleep. And keep your elbows to yourself."

*

Gem pulled the forest cloak over his head with a jerk. He kicked the dust under his feet and snapped at Agafa, "I am ready. Of course, I am ready. I am always ready." He was angry at himself, angry with Agafa, angry at life.

Rista ran to Gem and offered him a last drink from her cup. He took it, offered a word of thanks, and set off with the men. Rista spied Furcula watching from the shadows with an angry look. His eyes met Agfa's. She saw both men nod imperceptibly and a stabbing pain of fear pierced her heart.

*

It was two days before the hunters returned. Everyone noticed

117

the small amount of supplies they brought. After an interview with the men, Furcula proclaimed, first in Gazagan and then in the language of the strangers, "We will celebrate nonetheless. I have decided that Agafa and Rista are to be tied together in marriage."

Agafa's face brightened with a rare smile that showed the gap in his yellowed teeth. He had expected to be censured, but instead would be rewarded with what he sought most—the hand of Rista as his wife.

Rista did not smile. She stiffened with alarm, her eyes wide open in shock. "Come, my dear," said Furcula. He beckoned her to stand close to Agafa and be congratulated by the villagers. No one moved as all sensed the tension produced by the announcement. "What? Are you all not happy to hear that the long-awaited event will happen at last?" He turned his gaze to Gem.

"King Furcula, you know that your granddaughter does not regard Agafa well. Though she once made a promise to him, she will not be happy to be his wife," said Gem in his bravest voice.

"Is that right? And has she told you this? Has someone else stolen her affections and interfered with my plan?" asked Furcula. The old man's face flushed with anger. Jewel moved closer to Rista who then held tightly to her friend's arm. "She will do as she is told. The ceremony will be tomorrow. Tonight we begin the preparations."

The hunters gathered around Agafa, patted him on the back and mumbled their support. Rista and Jewel turned and walked away slowly, not knowing what to do. Furcula spoke in Gazrakian and pointed to the trees above. Bursting into tears, she ran to the stair tree and disappeared.

*

All that day and the next the women prepared food, however little there was of it.

"There will not be much left after this feast," observed Ruby. "Ouch! The dull knife! Oh, I miss Diamond and his sharpening skills!" She looked toward the fire pit area where men prepared for the dancing and singing that was part of every Gazrakian celebration. The celebration was now hours away.

"I wonder how Rista is feeling," said Jewel. "This is a sad day. She wants to be married to Gem. Why can't Furcula see that and allow her to have her heart's desire?"

"Perhaps this is part of a grander plan. How could Gem ever leave here if he was married to Rista? She is a good girl. I like her and would want her for my son, but how would it ever work?"

"I suspect that after this we may not see Rista so much. She will not be allowed to spend her spare time talking to us. Do you suppose she needs us to help her get ready for the ceremony."

"We barely know what a Gazrak wedding is like. Was your wedding a typical celebration? I wonder if Furcula will do a trick with his magic bones and declare the bride and groom made for each other," said Ruby with a sneer.

*

It was time to begin. Furcula wore his best waistcoat over baggy, ill-fitting pants. Agafa had washed his hair and it hung in soggy ringlets he kept nervously pushing behind his large ears.

The central fire had been kindled and was crackling from the damp wood. The women had spread flower petals around the logs where everyone would be seated. People gathered. Clapping in time to the log drum, the villagers drifted in while flutes picked up a lively tune. Someone produced a stringed instrument and attempted to pluck the tune. It soon became obvious to the three that it had probably been stolen, as the new owner had no idea how to render music from it.

Urged forward by the two women, Gem presented a sullen countenance. "I do not want to witness this. It isn't right. She will be so unhappy. I cannot bear it," he said in a low voice.

"We have to be here, Gem. We cannot make trouble for Rista. She has to obey her grandfather." The strangers took their places as far from the proceedings as they could manage and still be present.

Furcula gave a command for the bride to be fetched and two young women scurried away behind the trees to lead her out into the open area. A hush fell over the crowd as they waited. After a short while, the two burst from the trees and shouted, "Rista is gone!"

"What? That is impossible," shouted the king. "She does not know her way in the forest. She is here somewhere. Everyone spread out and find her. Rista! My dear one. Come back!"

It was no use. Though they all searched high and low, Rista was nowhere to be found.

"I saw her go up into the trees," said the young woman who had been put in charge of her. "She went to her room. I am sure of it," said another. Agafa was dumfounded. Nothing like this had ever happened in Gazrak. Everyone knew that to wander in the forest meant certain death. Finding a way out meant capture. How could she have been so silly? they all asked each other.

"She will return when the sense comes back into her head. And when she does, we will make sure she does not leave again." Furcula's ominous words were noted by the three. "In the meantime, Agafa, organized a search party. Gem, you will go with them since this is all your fault."

Ruby held onto Gem's arm, every muscle in her body tight with apprehension. "Why do they want you to go? You would not be any help since you do not know the woods well." She turned to see Agafa bending down to listen to Furcula's instructions. What was he telling him? she wondered.

The day was far spent by the time the party was ready to head out. Gem joined the group secretly arming himself with a knife against he knew not what threat he may face.

"What will they accomplish if it is dark?" asked Jewel.

"I hope by now Gem can handle himself in the forest. This will be another test for him."

*

Dusk overtook the men more quickly in the depths of the woods. This was the first time Gem had a good look at the surroundings since they were not going on a hunt this time. They spread out looking behind every tree and rock, under every bush and fallen log, moving steadily in one direction. Gem wondered when they would begin the march back since it was almost completely dark. Still, they moved on until it was impossible to see any more.

"Hello. I cannot see where I am going. Can someone tell me where you are?" No one answered his call. He stopped and listened. Silence. *So was this the plan, to leave me in the middle of nowhere?*

A sudden blow to the back of his neck brought Gem to the ground. The pain was severe and he could not recover enough to get his senses. Shoved, smothered, and tightly bound, he was thrown over someone's shoulder. He could hear the muffled laugh as he was carried along.

"What are you doing?" he yelled to no avail. "Let me out! It was not my fault! I did not make Rista run away!" It was no use. They were not listening. Was he to be thrown to the towns people, who would capture him as they had Diamond?

With a thud Gem landed on a hard surface, the cape he was wrapped in barely providing any padding against the stony ground. He felt himself being rolled over several times and worried that a cliff may be at the end of his journey. Repeated sounds in multiples reached his ears and gradually grew fainter until they stopped. It was deadly quiet. No forest animals or crickets. No birds of the night. *Where am I*, he wondered.

Gem remembered his knife hidden in his boot. If only he could reach it. After working at loosening the wrap, he finally found the top of the weapon and worked it up and out so that he was able to cut his way out of the bindings. Complete darkness met his eyes. "Hello," he yelled only to hear a hollow echo in return. He felt around with his hands and found the sides of his prison to be hard, cold stone. Feeling farther, he found large stones rolled into the entrance of the cave with more and more smaller rocks blocking any way to dislodge them.

So this is my punishment. They have left me to die in this cave.

CHAPTER 15

IN THE PRISON

After the guards shackled his ankles, Topaz was left to sit or stand in his assigned place with other newly inducted prisoners. Two men stared at him with grim, threatening expressions, while others gazed at the floor in silence and utter hopelessness.

Topaz gathered his courage and whispered, "What is your name?" He waited and got no response. "Anybody here feel like talking?" Still there was silence, as if they were all deaf. Topaz waited for some time before trying again.

"I was arrested for crushing an image of the dragon, how about you?"

"Hah!" cried a prisoner. "Hail to the man who dared crush the image!"

"I hope you gave it a kick while you were at it!" cried another in anguished voice.

"Maybe you should have burned it!" mumbled another.

"It was an accident. I did not mean to…Oh, well." Silence returned.

Just then, a guard sauntered into the dank prison entrance. "Thieves over here," he yelled, ordering those men to a dark hallway on the right.

"Let's see, any murderers? Not today. Just one assault. You, over there." The guard shoved one burly prisoner toward the exit. "You can't push me around," he shouted. "I'll show you. I'll get you for this!"

"Save it, rat face. No one moves from this place unless I say so."

A second guard came for Topaz. "Well, what do we have here? A blasphemer! I don't get one of those every day," he announced through a huge grin.

The guard reached out to grab Topaz's chain, yanking hard toward the passageway that led away from the left side of the room. He followed obediently wanting to avoid further offense. Heavy darkness made further observation of the interior of the prison difficult. Why no one escaped from the Tenebrose prison became more and more clear as each twist and turn of the building defied any organized pattern.

*

To Topaz's amazement, the cell to which he was assigned was not as bad as he had anticipated. It was dark, but there was a tiny beam of light that found its way in through a small window high on the wall. The walls and floor were constructed of hewn stones of varying sizes, not so skillfully laid one upon another. Filling one corner of the cell was a raised platform strewn with straw, serving as a bed. A short stool provided the only seating.

Lying on the straw was anything but luxurious. The smells of the prison cell evoked scenes of putrid vegetation, though there was no growing plant life in sight. After a short while, Topaz's nose adjusted. Then, all there was to do was wait for something to happen.

Late in the day new sounds reached Topaz's ears. Voices, movement on the stone pavement, and the clanging of metal grew louder. Someone was making the rounds, perhaps delivering water or food. That was most welcome after a very long day. Rising from his pallet, he stood at the barred doorway and tried to see who it was.

"Tojaz. Jopaz."

"It is Topaz, Master," came another low voice.

"New prisoner. Right. He needs a drink. No, wait. I need a drink. I will be right back." The sounds of retreating footfalls echoed down the passageway.

"Here is your water for the day," said the young man who appeared hauling a low cart loaded with pails of water and bread. Without looking up, the prison servant stood checking a chart he held in one hand. When he did look at Topaz, surprise overtook his expression. The servant stared at him for several seconds before speaking.

"Is something wrong?" asked Topaz, noting the strange look on the servant's face. Handing over a metal cup of water, he replied, "I'm sorry. You remind me of someone."

Topaz hardly knew how to reply. The young man was tall with fair hair and skin, very much unlike his own dark skin and short-cropped, black hair. He was neatly dressed in clothing befitting a servant, but his appearance showed a degree of dignity Topaz had not seen in men of his class. He realized that he himself did not look like a man of his class either. Gone were his plush robes and embroidered tunics. All the traces of his heritage were left behind for the sake of the mission.

"Do you know someone who looks like me?"

"Not exactly. But I do know someone you resemble in many ways." Mondo changed the subject. "It says here that you insulted the Dragon. Whew! That's creates a dilemma. Tell me, was it done on purpose? Somehow you don't look like the average dragon crusher."

"No, it was an accident. I was distracted by the sight of a beautiful woman." Both men laughed.

"Here is your allotment of bread. I added a bit of cheese. I won't be around again until tomorrow morning."

"Tell me, what is to happen to me now? Do I just sit and wait out my time?"

"As you have seen, the Prison Master is not always at his best. I will try to find out for you. For now, I have to move on. Many men are waiting for their portions." The cart squeaked out of sight, the sounds growing ever fainter until silence once again prevailed.

Discouragement began to set in. *Does Ameth know I am here? Is there any way for them to work for my release? Is there any way to succeed with the plan? Everyone was counting on me, and now look at where I ended up!*

Days passed. No word came as to how long the sentence was to be. Nothing happened. The young servant came and went doing his duties all the while remaining kind and considerate. This was certainly contrary to what Topaz expected. He found himself longing to talk to someone, anyone.

It was time once again for the morning allotment of food. Perhaps this day, a conversation could be struck.

"Topaz, here you are. Bread, water, a little soup today."

"I need to talk to you or someone. Did you find out what my sentence is? How long must I be in here?"

"The Master will come around soon. He will determine the finality of your sentence, so speak humbly." said the servant.

"He does not seem to have his mind on his work. Can I really count on his judgment?"

"I will speak to him and make sure he makes the right decision. Do not worry."

"I have friends in Tenebrose who may have come asking questions about me. Is there a way to find out if they have come?" Topaz debated with himself about how much to reveal. "You see, I was trying to find a job as a wood carver when I stepped on the dragon. I just want to work in that trade to be of help to the kingdom."

"I am not sure about helping the kingdom. I do not think I want to spend the rest of my life that way. I would be careful if I were you. The kingdom is a dangerous place," said the servant. "You and I are both prisoners here. You are in a cell. I am a slave with little freedom to do what I wish to do.

"How did you end up here?"

"It is a long story and there is no time to talk, though I do enjoy your company more than most of the prisoners here. There are many very unhappy people in this part of the prison. I would like to know how you got here, as well. You are not like the others and you are so young. I hope you can find a way to be released."

The servant's words gave hope as he waited.

*

"Next prisoner." A voice in the passageway roused Topaz from his daydream. He rose from his stool as the cell door opened. Before him stood the pompous Prison Master who looked over the top of wire spectacles with a furrowed brow. He no longer wore the green mushroom hat and the bulky robe. He looked the prisoner up and down, then turned to his servant who prepared to write down the sentence for his master.

"What is it I want to know?" the official stammered slurring his words.

"Name. What is his name. It is Topaz," replied the servant.

"Oh, yes, yes. No family name?"

"None given, sir."

The Prison Master turned to Topaz, "Citizen of Tenebrose, I assume?"

"No, your honor. I have been living in a distant part of the kingdom."

"Not familiar with the laws and customs in Tenebrose? You look like…never mind. Not from around here. Write that down. "

"Yes. I mean no, I am not."

You are accused of blasphemy, is that correct?"

"Yes, your honor."

"Crushed a dragon image and cursed it, the report says."

"It was an accident, your honor. I meant no harm. I merely wanted to find work as a wood carver. I did not watch where I was stepping and the dragons were before me on the ground," pleaded Topaz.

"Very careless. Your failure constitutes a crime in this part of the kingdom. Write that down. Very careless. I said that, didn't I?"

"I am very sorry indeed for my crime. I did not know what I was doing."

"Nonetheless, you have committed a crime which normally brings a punishment of hard labor." The Prison Master muttered something to the servant in a low voice which Topaz could not hear. Writing quickly, the servant finished his report and bowed as the Master turned to leave. The servant reached out and gently redirected the Prison Master in the opposite direction.

"I apologize for my master. He is incapacitated by overindulgence; you know what I mean?"

"How long must I be here? What hard labor will I have to do?"

"I think your friends have tried to negotiate with the Master. We will see if they are successful. In the meantime you must wait to see the outcome. I will come later and we will talk."

At the mention of a possible conversation, Topaz grew excited. It had been very lonely in his cell and he longed for someone to talk to, especially someone like his servant friend.

*

"Psst," came the loud hiss through his cell door. "Are you awake?"

"Yes. Can you come in or must you stay out there?"

The cell door opened in a slow motion to avoid any noise. It was late at night and all was dark.

"I do not know why I am doing this. I will be punished if I am found visiting with a prisoner. I have earned some special favor from the Master of late, so I feel I can risk it."

"Thank you for taking the chance. It is so good just to talk to someone," Topaz confessed. "What is your name? Am I allowed to know and call you by name?"

"My name here is Mondo. That will do for now."

"About that long story, do you have time to tell it? How did you come to be servant in the prison?"

"I cannot tell you all, but I will say that I was brought here by the power and might of one who knows all our stories." At these words from Mondo, Topaz felt a tingling sensation in his chest. Of whom did he speak?

"I was a free man, but then I was taken as a slave by Lord Crumblstone, and brought to Tenebrose to serve him. He put me to work with his business affairs, which were in great disarray. I was doing well until the Lord was away for several days. During that time, his wife kept badgering me to change some figures in his accounts. I refused. In her anger, she lied and told the Master that I had robbed his accounts of money. I do not think he believed her, but his wife insisted I be sent to serve with his cousin, who is master here in the prison. The truth is, he is in danger of disaster with the way he has managed. I have saved him great embarrassment by correcting his mistakes and making sure this part of the prison is run well."

"So you are not really a slave? I am not really a wood carver," said Topaz. "I came from an island far away from here, but I think my roots are here in Tenebrose. I should not talk about it. Somehow I can trust you. I come from a family of wealth and privilege far removed from slavery and prison."

"How did you come to pass yourself off as a wood carver? What did you hope to gain by that?" asked Mondo.

Topaz ground his teeth and frowned. How badly he wanted to share everything about Ameth and the plan to infiltrate the palace. "I cannot tell you much. I will say that I, as well, am here because of the power and might of one who is greater and who has a plan for my life. Though I confess, I did not expect this part of the plan."

Silence ensued for a moment as each man pondered what to say next. "Do you mean the Prince?" whispered Mondo.

"Yes," replied Topaz with great excitement.

"Do you mean the son of the High King?"

"Yes."

"I thought as much. With a name like Topaz, you must be one of the King's men. We are here together, neither of us in the place we expected to be. Our paths have been very different, but we have been brought here for a purpose. We will find out soon what that plan is to be, I am confident of it. Until then, do not mention to anyone about the Prince."

"I will heed your warning. One thing I would ask. Are you aware of the other followers of the High King? Have you heard anything of their activities?"

"Do you mean outside of the prison? I have not. There are those who are imprisoned here for following the Prince. Keep all this to yourself for now. I must go. Until tomorrow." Mondo quietly crept out and closed the door.

Topaz could not sleep after the encounter with Mondo. His heart raced with the thrill of finding, in that brief time, a bond of kinship.

*

Days went by very slowly. He had nothing to do but sit and think. Scanning the walls over and over again did not get any more entertaining with time. Mondo's visits were always brief, as his work required haste and efficiency. Late night proved to be the only time they could take more time to talk.

"Tell me more about your family, Topaz. Did you have no other siblings or cousins?"

"None that I know of. My mother would not speak about the past. I only know from others that my father disappeared under circumstances that must have been tragic. It left my mother with a great sadness and fear. She was extremely protective of me, despite the fact that there were no real dangers where we lived. It all seemed so foolish to me, that is until I met Master Ameth."

"Who is Master Ameth?" asked Mondo.

"He is an amazing man, very old, but very wise. He has studied the history of the kingdom and seems to understand the times and events of our day to such an extent that others look to him for guidance. I knew him only as Ameth, or Amethyst, as he is really named. But his followers call him Master Ameth."

"Amethyst, as in the precious stone? Is he named by the Prince?"

"Yes. He truly is the Prince's man. He saved my life from hoodlums who stole my money and possessions. I got everything back except the gold. That adventure is a long story. But in the whole affair, I did meet the Prince. He called me Topaz."

"You must tell me more. I long for news of the Prince. I must hear more about this man, Master Ameth, as well" said Mondo.

"You may in time for he is in Tenebrose. It was he who brought me here." Topaz paused and lowered his voice. "I believe I can trust you, Mondo. Master Ameth brought me here for a reason. He and others like him believe I can help their cause. They wanted me to hire on as a wood carver so that I could work inside the palace grounds. Some important event will soon take place and they want ears inside to know what to expect from, you know, the Ultimate Ruler."

"How do you know about the Ultimate Ruler?"

"We know all about him. Master Ameth has taught me about the history of this city. The man who calls himself the Ultimate Ruler was once the head servant of the High King in the City of Light. He stole a precious possession of the king's, the Promise, as it was called, and now he uses it to turn himself into the fierce dragon. It is by this that he brings fear so that all will obey his command. If he did not have the Promise, he would have no power over the people."

Mondo let the information settle in his mind as Topaz continued.

"Did you know that my people originated from this place? You see the color of my skin, my hair. We are people who populated the city called Abundant before the king was overthrown and Malpha came to power. You are inside this prison so you may not have seen the city as I have seen it. It is a miserable place."

"Judging by the misery in here, that is no surprise. There are people in this prison, Topaz, who have your characteristic coloring. I believe some of them have been here for a long time. I wonder if anyone of them may have information about your family. What was your father's name?"

"There is the problem. No one would ever tell me my father's given or family name. Perhaps my given name may mean something if anyone remembers my family." The prisoner lowered his voice. "My former name is Tofar."

"Tofar. I will remember the name. I will try to find out for you. When I come again, I want you to tell me the history of Tenebrose, and more about this Ultimate Ruler."

*

Mondo sat with quill in hand writing painstakingly the daily statistics of the prison. His neck ached with the tedious bending over the soiled entry page. It was almost time to fetch the late afternoon rations and begin the same laborious task assigned to him every day, week after week, month after month. Managing the prison had become very monotonous. The occasional improvement in the system added some flavor to the tasteless occupation.

His mind drifted into lonely sadness missing the love of his life, his precious Jewel. No longer was he Diamond: husband, friend, brother; now he was Mondo, slave, serving in an even lowlier place than Gazrak.

Then there were the dreams. Why still the dream of fighting an enemy alongside Gem and prevailing as leader, warrior, and hero? Now he was having dreams about a tiny white flower. It fell from his hand into the soil and grew instantly into a towering tree that bore bright yellow fruit.

Leaving his post, Mondo headed to the kitchen where the prisoners rations were prepared. It was a primitive room with nothing more than a large brick oven at one end and an enormous mixing bowl stand at the other. The cook wore a filthy apron over worn tunic and breeches. To say there was a lack of precision in his work was putting it mildly. He cared not what went into the bread and he cared not what came out of the ovens. The goal was to have something ready for the daily allotment for each prisoner.

"I hate this place. I hate this work. I hate those men. I hate it all," Diamond overheard a guard say to the cook. He entered quietly to collect the loaves that were stacked on the floor, load them on his cart and leave.

"You there," the guard called out. "You are the servant of Crumblestone, aren't you?"

131

"Yes," said Mondo, the humble servant.

"Tell that wretched man we demand more food, more sleep, less work. This is the rottenest job in the whole kingdom. Nothing but abuse and filth from morning to night."

"I will tell the Master what you have said," replied Mondo.

"No, forget it. I will tell him myself, that is if he will even listen. He is not known for listening. But I will make him listen. You hear me? I will make him listen, and things will change around here."

"Easy there, Ranker. You may end up on the other side of these barred doors if you aren't careful," said the cook.

"He wouldn't dare. He is a sniveling coward. He does not have the courage to stand up to a mouse. We will see that he listens."

Mondo made a mental note to speak to the Master about the guards. Debating what kind of recommendation to make on their behalf, he continued with his chore. Sounds of the disgruntled guard shouting threats as the cook tried to bring calm followed Mondo but a short distance before the thick prison walls shut them out.

*

Down the stone passageway clanked the old wooden cart, giving fair warning to the prisoners that their daily meal approached. Topaz's stomach growled. He was anxious to see Mondo again for other reasons.

"Topaz, here is your bread and water," said Mondo in a loud voice. "Here is some cheese I saved for you," he said softly poking his head inside the door of the cell.

"Thank you, Mondo." Topaz received the food and began to eat. "Have you heard any news? Has anyone come asking about me? What about the hard labor sentence?"

"No news, but I have determined to use my influence to get your sentence reduced. I believe I can do it."

"Have you been able to speak to any other prisoners who might remember my family?"

"Not yet. I do not go into that part of the prison often. Those prisoners are not here because of a crime they committed, but are guilty of being a "threat to the order of society", or so I am told. Tell me, is there anything else your family might be identified by?"

"There is one thing, but I don't think it will help. When I toured the city with Master Ameth, I saw a mural on the outer wall of the palace. In it a man of my lineage was painted being trod upon by the dragon creature. The man had a tattoo on his arm of a small flower. That same pattern of flower is on an amulet I was given. I think that flower design is important, though it may be merely a symbol of our ancient society as a whole. It may not have significance for any individual family in the former kingdom."

"A small flower? Was it a white flower?" asked Mondo.

"I believe it is. Is the color important?"

"Perhaps. It may be a coincidence."

"What do you mean? Do you know this flower?" asked Topaz.

"I keep dreaming about a small, white flower. And fruit trees. There is not likely to be any connection between your symbol and my dreams. I will keep what you have said in mind," said Mondo as he left the cell.

*

Mondo reflected on all that had happened since leaving the Gazrak. Having time to think eventually led back to those he left behind. What was happening to them? Would he see them again? He was lost in thought when voices echoed through the hall. Shouts became louder. Not the usual shouts of angry prisoners. One of the guards dashed toward Mondo and yelled, "Where is Master Crumblestone? We have trouble in the deep cell block."

"He was here not long ago." Mondo hurried through the immediate area looking for the Prison Master. In a side room, a sleeping form lay on his back with several empty bottles beside him on the floor. "Here he is! Wake up, Master. There is trouble in the deep cells."

"What? Where? Trouble?" slurred Crumblestone trying to sit up but finding himself unable to do so. The guard and Mondo both tugged until the green-robed Master stood upright. "Mondo, you know what to do. Go fix it." he said before collapsing again into a heap.

"Master, I cannot fix the problem. You must go. Come. We will help you."

The two men walked Master Crumblestone around the room several times to stabilize him. "Good. Good. I will go. Here I go." Mondo and the guard followed close behind to make sure he did not fall over. Through the labyrinth of passageways, they descended toward the deep cells.

"What is it? What is the problem?" the Master probed down into the dark below him.

"It's Ranker, sir. He and the other guards have rebelled. They have taken the ruler's number-one prisoner. He is not in his cell. We don't know where they are. He left a message saying they will kill Falgar if we don't listen to their demands," came the reply.

"Oh bother. What is this about? Demands? What demands? Why would he want to harm a prisoner, and why should I care?"

"Pardon me, Master, but the prisoner is Falgar. You know, the man the Ultimate Ruler has a particular interest in keeping alive," said the other guard.

Crumblestone finally understood the situation and became alarmed. "Master, if something happens to Falgar, we will all be headed for the gallows. Ranker and the others know this," reported the guard who stood nearby.

Mondo listened carefully trying to discover the significance of the name Falgar.

"I...I have a headache. Tell Ranker he will be horse-whipped and sent to do hard labor for this outrage. I will not have it in my prison. Mondo, go down there and tell him now!"

"Master, he is not there. Only the letter he left behind is there. We do not know where Ranker and the others have taken the prisoner."

"They must be in the prison somewhere. Search until you find them."

Mondo glanced around the room at the other guards who stood

nearby. As he looked into each face, it was obvious that the men did not intend to comply. "Yes, Master," he replied. "Leave the matter to us. You may go back to your affairs and we will see that it is done."

When Crumblestone had left, Mondo addressed the guards. "Do as the Master has commanded and report back to me as soon as you have finished searching." The men grumbled among themselves. "When you have found that your search was in vain, I will take that news to the Master."

The men saw that Mondo understood their intentions. Turning to the lowly prison slave as they departed, one guard said, "We want Crumblestone's downfall. We will take our demands higher if necessary, until things get better in this prison."

"If that is your desire, then send one of your men with a message to Lord Crumblestone, the Master's cousin. He will listen to me. I am sure of it." Mondo quickly wrote a letter, signed and sealed it with the Prison Master's seal. "Go now. The sooner we end this standoff the better, before news of the rebellion brings more trouble."

As the guards made an appearance of searching the prison, Mondo decided to investigate the disappearance himself. Descending the steps down into the deep cells, he was intrigued by the mystery of a prisoner like Falgar being valuable to the Ultimate Ruler. After many months of serving in this dark building, he had not heard even a rumor of the existence of the deep cells. Why was it kept a secret? Who was Falgar?

There was no one to stop him. The guards did not care now who went where. They were occupied with their plan to hide Falgar from the Master. At the bottom of the stone stairs, a circular room came into view. It formed a hub from which five individual barred cells extended. Mondo walked slowly from cell to cell peering inside to see who might be imprisoned there. Three cells were empty. Only one person remained in each of the two occupied cells.

"You there, what is your name?"

A shadowy figure moved closer to the bars and revealed a thin, frail man clothed only in rags. His hair was matted and pulled back into

135

a braid tied with a strip of ancient cloth. His skin was shrunken and gray and he looked half dead.

"Who are you? What is happening? Where have they taken Falgar?" asked the prisoner.

"I am a servant here in the prison. I am looking into the disappearance of your cell mate. Falgar has been taken by the prison guards and being held somewhere in the prison. I do not know where he is. Who is Falgar? Why is he in prison? Why are you here?"

"Are you a spy for the ruler? Is this another one of his tricks to obtain the secret of Komatal? You will not hear anything from me, torture me as you will," replied the prisoner.

"I assure you, I am not here to torture anyone. I am a lowly slave owned by the Master's cousin, Lord Crumblestone. I would be punished severely if I were discovered wandering down into these deep cells. Since the Master and the guards are not really in control of things at the moment, I thought this was my chance to explore."

"Do you know of the history of Tenebrose? This is the place where those who have resisted Malpha are kept. One by one, he has worn us down until each king revealed the secrets of his kingdom's wealth. Falgar and I alone are left."

"What is the secret of Komatal?" asked Mondo.

The effort to speak with such passion had left the prisoner exhausted. He sank down to sit on a low three-legged stool. "Go away," he said breathlessly. "I will not tell. I cannot tell."

Mondo was speechless. The injustice these political prisoners suffered weighed heavily. "If I could help you, I would." As he turned to leave, he passed the final cell where Falgar had been kept. He gazed inside at the harsh conditions the men had lived with for so many years. Then something caught his eye and his attention was immediately fixed. Upon the back wall of the cell a simple drawing had been etched, no doubt with a stone for a tool. It was a small flower with multiple petals, a stem and two leaves.

CHAPTER 16

FALGAR

"Cousin! I am here to call you to account for yourself. What is this you have allowed?" A booming voice echoed in the Prison Master's ears as he tried to rouse himself to attention.

"I have fixed the problem," Crumblestone said in a groggy blur of speech. "Tell them, Mondo. You fixed it, right?"

"The guards have done a thorough search and have found nothing, Master. Falgar has not been found," replied Mondo.

"This is outrageous! You know, of course, that Falgar is the former king of what was once called Abundant. But how would someone like you know of such things? If the Ultimate Ruler hears that his prisoner has escaped, or been taken by someone, he will be furious. His wrath will fall upon us all. What do you have to say for yourself?"

"Your Lordship, I believe this can be remedied quite easily. If you give me a chance, I think I can put things to right."

"You, Mondo, will have your chance. I believe you can do it. Cousin, you are relieved of your duties. Out! Out with you! Mondo, you are in charge. You are now appointed to be the head of this prison.

You have shown yourself to be trustworthy and capable. But don't forget, you are still under my command. Remember also, this is a prison. Now find Falgar and restore order here immediately."

The disgraced Prison Master slunk away to his quarters to gather his possessions and leave, throwing a resentful look back to his successor. Lord Crumblestone retreated leaving Mondo standing in a daze, astonished at the turn of events. Facing the guards, he said, "Tell Ranker he has his demands. I will personally see that the men are treated fairly. Now go! Have Falgar back in his cell by the end of the day. Report back to me when all is accomplished."

The guards quickly disappeared as Mondo pondered what his new responsibilities would entail. Who would now feed the prisoners? Who would do the record keeping and other duties that he had done for months? An idea bounced around in his thoughts. He raced away to find the answer.

"Topaz!" yelled Mondo, as he inserted the key in the prison door lock. "You won't believe what just happened."

"Something pretty important I would guess. Aren't you afraid of yelling like that? The Master will hear of it and we will both be in trouble."

"I AM the Master, Topaz. I was just made the Master of the Prison. And I need someone to take my place feeding the prisoners. I choose you! Come. Start your new duties. This is your 'hard labor' sentence." The elated new Master leaped into the cell and began to push his confused protégé out into the passageway.

"How can you be serious? What happened? Aren't you a slave?" asked Topaz.

"Yes! I think Lord Crumblestone trusts me, and he does not trust most other men."

"Are you going to wear the green robe and hat like the previous master?" Topaz laughed at the thought.

"I thought you would look good in that outfit. That hat would go nicely with your fuzzy hair sticking out the side. Seriously, you have a lot to learn, so pay attention."

*

It wasn't long before the report of Falgar's return reached Mondo. Ranker and the other guards obeyed their new master, despite his age and lack of experience, realizing he was the key to their ability to survive in the prison. Any other man would have had them whipped and imprisoned for their rebellion. Improvements were soon put in place which were gratefully received.

When all seemed to be taken care of, Mondo decided it was time to meet the infamous King Falgar. Making his way to the deep cells once again, he found his way to the lower chamber. But this time would be different. Mondo had given orders for the two prisoners to be given extra rations. With a hearty salute, the prison guards on duty acknowledge his approach.

"I have come to see Falgar," he announced. Peering into the cell in the dim light, the prisoner could barely be seen sitting in the shadows. He stepped forward upon hearing his name. "I have nothing to say. I will never have anything to say. You are wasting your time," said the thin, bent man.

Mondo observed his dark grey skin now wrinkled prematurely with age and poor living conditions. The look on his face was one of determination and fierce dignity. He held a secret and no amount of deprivation or torture would make him reveal what he knew.

"I did not come to bring you more sorrow. My name is Mondo. I am the new Prison Master, incredible as that may sound. I do not know much about why you are here, but I am sure I will be hearing about it. They say you were once the King of Abundant. I know very little of what you have been through, but I mean to treat you well."

Falgar did not speak. He looked away, the muscles in his jaw hardening in resolve. Mondo noted his stature, tall and muscular despite the opportunity for a normal life of activity. His hairline receded slightly emphasizing a graying mass pulled back tightly and bound into a braid with bits of string that had once been colorful. His ragged shirt revealed ornate tattoos in black ink across his chest and arms.

"There is someone I wish you to meet. His name is Tofar. Does that name mean anything to you? He is a stranger here in Tenebrose, but he is much like you. I think he may formerly have been from this kingdom." Mondo watched Falgar's face as he said the name Tofar. He did not flinch or show any signs of recognition.

"I know no one by that name."

"Well, I had to ask. This young man is searching for someone who can help him find any family members who may still live here. I have one more question. Does that flower design on the wall behind you mean anything special? I have had a strange dream about just such a flower."

"It means nothing," came the terse reply.

"I must go now. I want to help you if I can. I am not a very good Prison Master, I guess. I do not wish to see people suffer. They will probably throw me out soon, as I would be too soft on criminals. You can keep that between the two of us."

As the new master ascended the steps, he barked a command to the standing guard. "Double the rations for these men and see that they have clean clothes."

*

Topaz pushed the unwieldy cart across the stubborn surface of the hewn stone floor. Growing more accustomed to his new responsibilities brought new light to his eyes. Still, the knowledge that the Prince's men and women outside the prison walls would be worried for him was a weight upon his soul. The role of prison servant was a step in the right direction, but a long way from where he was supposed to be—the palace of the Ultimate Ruler. His only hope seemed to be Mondo's friendship.

"I have a task for you today that I think will help your cause," said Mondo after thinking long and hard about it. "I will have a guard show you to the deep cells. There you will bring food to the prisoner, Falgar."

"You told me he does not know the name Tofar. What do you think he will tell me? What should I ask him?"

140

"He trusts no one after so many years in captivity, and after being treated so poorly. His secrets are bound inside and no man can make him reveal them. Meet him. Tell him about your family if you dare. There may be some link you can discover," said Mondo.

Gathering several loaves and lumps of cheese, Topaz followed the guard down into a part of the prison that brought shivers throughout his body. Not only was it cold and dark, but the atmosphere reeked of some evil presence. The question gnawed at his mind, *Why do these men have to suffer? What have they done?* Surely the Ultimate Ruler was an evil man.

As they neared the cells, Topaz felt his courage rise. How he longed to see someone of his own lineage. Wondering how to address the prisoner, he suddenly felt awkward. Perhaps Falgar had been an important man in his day and warranted respect. For this reason Topaz used a formal term of address.

"Master Falgar, I have brought you bread and cheese. The guard comes with water."

Falgar rose from his bed and slowly walked toward the unfamiliar voice. "Who are you?" he asked with a tinge of suspicion for the unexpected visit.

"My name is, or was, Tofar. Master Mondo told you about me. How I came to be here is a long story, but I am told we have some things in common. I wished to meet you, so here I am bringing your rations. Falgar was silent for a long time as Topaz stood uncomfortably next to the bars.

"What do we have in common? Who are you?" asked Falgar.

Looking carefully into the dark cell, the young servant observed the prisoner. "For one, it was not that long ago that I had long braided hair bound with colorful strings similar to yours. It pained me sorely to have it cut off. Now you see it grows again. A most unruly mop. If I had means, I would chop it once more."

Falgar stepped closer and stared into the face of his visitor. "Where is your home?"

"I have lived most of my life on a distant island; a very long way from here. But I believe that perhaps my family came from Tenebrose, or I should say," Topaz whispered, "Abundant."

Falgar received the loaves and began to tear off pieces to eat. "Tell me about your family," he asked.

"When I left home, I was carefully instructed not to talk about them to anyone. There is much secrecy surrounding my family. They won't tell me why, but they say there is great danger associated with our name. I was hoping you could tell me something. That is asking too much, I am sure. What would you know, being so long in this prison cell?"

"I can tell you this. If the ruler's men have sent you to break down my resistance, then they have failed. This is a clever twist on their plot to wrest secrets from me, but it is to no avail. Tell them that." Falgar turned and spat on the floor to show his disgust, then retreated to the rear of the cell. Topaz's heart sank.

"I am sorry. This is not a plot or any clever scheme. That drawing on your wall matches an amulet I have in my possession. Well, I do not have it at the moment, but I know there is a connection. I will find out what it is. There is a purpose even for a diversion here in this prison. I will know my name someday."

Without another word, Topaz turned and found his way up the steps and away from the deep cells. Falgar faced the wall and stared at the flower design, a tear running down his cheek. He closed his eyes and shook his head.

*

"I had hoped for more," said Topaz looking dejected. "He thought I was some kind of spy for the Ultimate Ruler. Should I try again or should I give up?"

Mondo stood behind the ancient podium at the entrance of the prison directing guards and new prisoners to various locations. Dressed in the requisite green robe and a more modest version of the mushroom hat, the Master listened with partial attention. A large ledger book was propped open before him, and a stack of new documents crowded the remaining space.

"That is but one closed door. Others will open. Perhaps it is time to turn your attention back to your original plan. I may have the power to see you transferred to the palace. Laborers are always needed and the prison is a source often used to provide recruits. Because of your work of service here, I believe I can change your official status from blasphemer and spy to something more acceptable to those who receive workers there. Maybe even 'wood carver'." Mondo smiled and waited to see Topaz's reaction.

"Then my mission can go forward. Ameth and the others will be pleased. Do you really think you can do it?"

"There is also a problem of overcrowding." Mondo stared at the ledger again with dismay. "It looks like I will need your cell soon. Now go about your work." The young servant prisoner wasted no time in complying with the order.

Finding a pen and paper, Mondo began to craft a letter to Lord Crumblestone outlining the difficulties a sudden influx of criminals had caused. *Here is my chance!* he thought. "I will need to identify several prisoners for a work force to send to the palace," he said out loud to himself as he wrote. He continued, "In particular, I have a skilled wood carver who would be a good candidate." He finished writing and held the letter up for a final inspection. *I think this will do it.*

CHAPTER 17

ONE STEP CLOSER

Sounds of horses' hooves and wheels grinding on the crushed rock driveway reached Mondo just inside the doors of the prison. This was not the normal mode of arrival for new convicts, which piqued his curiosity. Stepping aside from his official post, he saw his master Lord Crumblestone emerge from a large, ornate carriage. The Prison Master bowed before his superior.

"Lord Crumblestone, to what do I owe the honor of this visit to your humble servant?" Mondo had come a long way from the days when he treated his own father—a Lord himself—with disdain and disrespect. In fact, he had learned all the right things that a slave must say to a Lord. Even as he bowed, he reflected on his change of status and way of life.

"Well done, Mondo," said Crumblestone observing the improvement to the wardrobe. "You even look the part." The Lord entered the building and searched for a place to talk in private. "Over here, I have news." Another man had arrived in the carriage as well, and stood at a distance.

"How do you like that new carriage? A real jewel, don't you think?"

"It is very fine, indeed," said Mondo wondering where this was leading.

"I thought you would agree. It is one of the benefits of my new placement. I have been promoted to assist the Ultimate Ruler in his latest venture—a top secret project."

"That is good news. You are an important man in the kingdom."

"Ah, what you do not understand is that I will need you by my side. You have the skills I need to properly carry out the Ruler's wishes. I will come for you tomorrow. Be ready to move to the palace for our new assignment."

"But, Master, what about the prison? Who will be Master here?"

"Do not worry about that. I have appointed another to take your place. Be ready tomorrow morning," said Lord Crumblestone as he motioned to the man who had accompanied him into position at the prison entrance.

Mondo's stunned expression was soon followed by a look of authority; he now saw the need to instruct the new Master on the workings of the prison. His mind raced with details.

"Lord Crumblestone, if you received my letter, do you approve of the transfer of skilled prisoners to the palace work force?"

"You do not need to worry about that any longer. The new Master will deal with it. But, yes, of course. Transfer them. Finish whatever you began."

Whatever I began, thought Mondo. *There is one thing I must do before I leave.* Descending into the deep cells, it seemed only right to warn Falgar that a new master would be in charge. He reached the lowest point and called out to the lonely prisoner. "Falgar! I have news for you."

"What news?"

"I am leaving tomorrow. A new master will arrive here at the prison. I do not know what kind of man he is. Things may go well or not go well with him. I am sorry to leave."

"You have been good to me, and to Wingar. We will survive. Thank you. Tell me, is the young man Tofar still about? I have not seen him again."

"The young man you accused of being a spy? No. You discouraged him so much, he did not have the heart to return. He is a good lad. He means only to find his family. You might have helped him," said Mondo with a sympathetic tone. "He has been transferred to the palace work force. I am going to the palace as well. Do you have anything you wish me to convey to Tofar?"

When Falgar replied his voice was heavy with emotion. "Be careful. Do not trust anyone." He paused before saying softly, "Remember me."

*

Daylight faded. The last hour of Mondo's responsibility as Prison Master had come. He tidied the ledger and documents, again making sure all was in order. Early that afternoon, Topaz had bathed and been outfitted with clean clothes. Mondo himself had overseen the trimming of his unruly hair, all in preparation for his new role as palace artisan.

The heavy doors of the prison entrance screeched at the daily ritual of opening locks and bars. The guards had almost completed their routine when a tapping sound could be heard. *Who would be coming to the prison now?* they wondered, looking at each other in surprise. Mondo signaled to the men to leave the door open a crack while he investigated.

"Who is there? What is your business? We are closing the doors now so come back tomorrow." he yelled at the stranger. A piece of parchment, folded and sealed, appeared through the narrow opening, and an indecipherable voice said something. Mondo examined the envelope before carefully opening it. Inside a note was addressed to the Prison Master.

May I please make an inquiry about a prisoner in your care?

I am willing to pay a fine or ransom for his release if necessary.

Please reply.

With gratitude for your mercy,

♍

"Who are you? Which prisoner are you inquiring about?" Mondo asked loudly. One of the guards put his ear to the crack and relayed the answers, "It is a messenger for another. He is asking about the young man who serves the food, Topaz."

"Open the door. I will receive him," commanded Mondo. Standing in the last light of day was a poor beggar in rags. He stepped forward bowing low in fear of being unable to escape when his task was completed.

"Who is it that is asking about Topaz?"

"I do not know his name, sir. I only bring this letter to you. He asks for a reply."

"Tell him that it is too late. The man he asks for has been transferred to the palace work force as a wood carver. Tell him that all is well," said Mondo with emphasis on the last phrase in the hope that the message would be delivered with the assurance of that for which they had planned. He thought for a minute before concluding the reply. "Tell him that further communication will come to him through Mondo. Do not forget that name!" The beggar backed away through the doorway and into the street before running as fast as he could away from the dark prison.

The door closed for a last time. Walking back to his quarters, Mondo gazed in disbelief at the signature. Who was it asking after Topaz? Was it the man Ameth, about whom his prisoner friend had told him? Was it a coincidence that he signed his name with that particular symbol? Could it possibly be the same person whose warning was the beginning of their journey to the City of Light?

*

Morning dawned and, true to his word, Lord Crumblestone appeared in his new carriage. Mondo had few possessions to call his own. He stepped up into the luxurious cab feeling at once rich and free, and poor and shabby. "You will need new clothes, my man. I will see to that. Our lives are about to change once again."

CHAPTER 18

NO TURNING BACK

Never-ending darkness filled Gem's senses. Utter blackness—cold and penetrating—brought him to the realization that the end of his life stared him in the face. There was no way out. He tried to move the stones, but they were wedged in tight, layer upon layer. The men had done their work and made sure he would not be heard from ever again. Gem contemplated how many hours he had to endure before he would starve and lose consciousness.

Thirst took hold of his mind. He could think of nothing else but a cool drink of water. *How long have I been here?* he wondered after what seemed like days. Sleep relieved some of his misery, but not for long. He woke again to find nothing changed.

"Why?" he cried aloud though there was no one to hear. Gem knew he could answer his own question. Why was he even asking? He had betrayed his brother. Diamond was right. He should have listened. But if he had listened, how would things have gone any differently? Misery engulfed him. There was no comfort in rehearsing the past or what might have been.

Gem grew weaker. His parched lips burned. His stomach ached with hunger.

"I'm sorry. I was wrong." What else was there to say? Surely,

149

some supernatural power would rescue him. The Prince? What were the chances that he would be given yet another chance to get his life right? Was the Prince able to get him out of this hole? He remembered his key and brought it out of its pouch. There was no lock to put it in this time.

"Help! Please help me? I don't want to die. I will do whatever you want me to do," mumbled Gem. Tears fell from his face and wet his scraped fingers that held the blue stone. A glow began to rise and fill the dark space. Seeing the light brought more tears. He stared at the key for a long time wondering how it could help move the great pile of stones from the cave entrance and concluded that it was useless. He replaced it in its leather pouch.

The lonely hours continued. How long had it been? The sound of moving rock woke Gem from his trance. *You are loved! You are forgiven!* The words flashed in his mind. Was he dreaming? He lay still and listened. Someone was moving stones outside the cave. After an hour, small beams of light appeared aimed like arrows striking his chest. He sat up and tried to see who was bringing the world back to him. Some of the stones were no longer tightly wedged so he started to remove them from the inside. Finally the breach grew large enough to allow Gem to see his rescuer. Rista's tear stained face stared back at him. She continued her work feverishly, pitching rocks in all directions. He saw that her hands were bleeding.

Gem crawled out and held Rista close. She was crying hysterically. "I am sorry," she wailed.

"How did you know where I was," asked Gem.

"I ran away. I follow you, Agafa and others. Dark night, hide cave. I cannot see. I....I ask Prince to help. Where is Gem, I ask. This good, yes?"

"Yes! This is good! You saved my life. Thank you." Gem breathed heavily.

"Here is food. Eat," said Rista as she handed Gem a handful of winter berries and a small loaf of bread.

"Where did you get the bread?" he asked.

"I run away, take bread." Rista retrieved a bundle she had brought from Gazrak.

"Is there water? I am very thirsty."

"Come, I show you." Rista took Gem's hand and led him to a stream not far from the cave. He knelt down and drank deeply of the cool water. Soon he was refreshed enough to lay down on the mossy bank to let it restore his strength. Rista washed her blood-smeared hands and face then sat down beside him.

"We cannot go back to Gazrak. What will happen to Jewel and my mother? Furcula will blame them for your leaving."

"He no hurt Jewel and Ruby. They work hard. I go back to help them."

"You cannot go back. They will make you marry Agafa. That would be bad. What are we to do?"

"Ask Prince," said Rista. Gem smiled and turned to face her.

"How did you get so smart? You are a mere girl from the depths of the forest. I know very little, but you! Who are you?"

"I am Rista," she replied and as she spoke her face glowed with a warmth and strength that he had not until now seen.

"I see who you are. I see Prince, he helps you. He will help us. You ask him."

Gem realized that Rista was right. He had not thought of the words of the Prince for some time. He removed the golden key once again and held it out for Rista to see. She touched it lightly and admired its jewel that sparkled in the sunlight. The blue stone began to pulsate as if to urge them to connect to a greater power.

"The Prince gave me this key. I will tell you all about it when you can understand more. You have never even seen a lock, or even a door or a prison. I have used it to get out of some bad places."

Gem held one half of the key and Rista placed her fingers around the jewel end. With his other hand Gem reached out and grasped Rista's free hand.

"Oh, great Prince, help us now. You have always helped me in the past. We do not know where to go. What do we do next?" asked Gem.

"Oh, great Prince, help us now," repeated Rista.

A peaceful quiet settled on the forest and floated down to rest upon the two. Neither one spoke for several minutes, then all at once, Rista arose and said, "We must go now. Agafa and hunters soon come to find me."

"So you have decided not to go back to Gazrak? That is good. You and I, we will go together away from this place."

"The Prince will rescue Jewel and Ruby," Rista said with a strange confidence that amazed Gem. She looked up and studied the wind in the trees, the sun above them, and pointed away from the stream. "Here is the way. We must go now."

CHAPTER 19

THE PALACE

Mondo observed the drab, ominous grounds that surrounded the palace. Approaching a king's palace would normally create a reaction of awe at the sights and sounds of great wealth. Instead, there was only a collection of tasteless attempts at decoration. Effigies of the dragon sculpted in various media—green shrubs, wood and stone littered the visible portions of the grounds. The high entrance stood at the top of a flight of steps and bore a dragon head with a beady, red eye carved into each of the two doors.

Lord Crumblestone was greeted by servants as he descended from the carriage. As a slave, Mondo expected to help with the baggage and to see that his Lordship was in need of nothing. To his surprise, the servants did not have the same assumptions. Wondering why this was so, he remembered that his position with the Lord had risen in recent days since leaving the management of the prison.

The interior of the palace was dark, having few windows that allowed light to penetrate through stained-glass portraits of angry beasts.

"This way, your Lordship," said the servant as he led the group up a flight of stairs and down a long hallway. A large apartment in one wing of the palace awaited them, with a connecting room designated for Mondo alone. It was well furnished and there was a line of long narrow windows with a view of the opposite side of the palace from the entrance. Mondo could see vegetable gardens and patches of forest. A walled section of the grounds that had no gate appeared to have an orchard inside.

"You are looking a bit disreputable, my boy. Change your clothes before being seen by anyone important. You will find some things in the chest that I had delivered to your room."

"Thank you, my Lord. Is that what I should call you?" asked Mondo.

"That will do. Tonight we will dine with the Ultimate Ruler, so try to behave yourself. He is not a man to be trifled with. Let me do the talking about your background. We do not need to tell anyone I took you out of the hands of a lynch mob, do we now?"

Mondo opened the chest in his room to find several sets of very fine, though excessively colorful, clothing. He chose the least extravagant and ostentatious, but still felt foolishly overdressed. Amazed at his apparent rise in status, he was not sure how to respond. Was his master such a high official that this luxury was warranted for a slave? And now to dine with the highest ruler in the land—even if he was the evil ruler that the diary and Topaz had reported him to be— would be a benefit never expected in his lifetime.

The servant again directed them down the hallway and stairs to a long, narrow dining room lit by enormous hanging chandeliers with hundreds of candles. The walls were painted with dark murals from floor to ceiling. Even the ceiling was covered in images. Mondo couldn't help but look up and fix his eyes on an unending series of battle fields littered with armies in full fighting gear, swords, cannons, catapults, and battering rams. He longed to look at every detail, but was alerted by Lord Crumblestone to attend to the business at hand, which was finding a seat fitting for his Master's station in life.

Alarmed at being shown a seat beside the Lord, Mondo spoke quietly to a servant, "Has there been some mistake? I am the Lord's servant. Should I be seated here?"

"You are Mondo, are you not?" returned the servant.

Mondo nodded, not knowing what to say. "Your Lordship, is it proper for me to be seated next to you at such an occasion?"

"I do not make the decisions here, so do as you are instructed. We will see in time what the Ruler has in mind. I am as puzzled as you are."

When the company of officials had assembled and were seated, a clinking sound signaled the group to rise for the entrance of Malpha, the Ultimate Ruler. Mondo did not dare raise his gaze and look at the ruler, lest he be pointed out as a servant who had been accidentally placed with the important people of the kingdom. Finally, when the others sat down again, he sat as well.

"Greetings, Lords," said a gravelly voice from the far end of the long table. Mondo strained his eyes to see the fierce Ultimate Ruler Malpha that he had heard about only in hushed tones. What he saw was an old, shriveled man propped up by ornate robes, and balding under a crown of golden leaves. Looking around the room, it seemed that the others saw something far different. Perhaps it was the ruler's reputation for turning into a dragon that made everyone else tremble in his presence.

"I have called you here this evening to welcome Lord Crumblestone from his recent post overseeing the enforcement of kingdom-wide compliance to my order of submission. I am overjoyed to report that obedience to my command is almost complete. Only small pockets of resistance remain. There is no other ruler than myself. No one resists the Dragon King, Malpha."

Everyone donned their most pleased, though obviously resentful, expression and nodded toward Lord Crumblestone. Mondo smiled a half smile and tried to look enthusiastic, hoping that his eventual work for his Master would be inconspicuous. The idea of bowing to the odious pretender grieved and disheartened him.

The ruler went on for several more minutes praising himself and his leadership before he got down to the business of the evening.

"It has been brought to my attention that recently one of my most prestigious prisoners was taken for ransom in my very prison," Malpha said with a very severe frown. "I was spared the details, and it was a good thing, as I would have blasted the whole place into ashes, had I known." The audience feigned looks of fear and respect for their leader. "One thing that was made known to me was the presence of a courageous and cunning young man who was able to find my prisoner, punish the offenders, and restore order. He is also praised by others as being able to defeat chaos and corruption at any level and thereby advance the cause of the kingdom." At the mention of the word 'corruption' Malpha glared intensely at the faces of the present company.

Mondo had a horrible sinking feeling in his stomach, anticipating what might be the consequence of his apparent accomplishments.

"Let us raise our hands to Mondo, servant of Lord Crumblestone." Everyone raised a fist above their heads and said in unison, "Honor to Mondo, servant of Lord Crumblestone!"

"Stand and be honored, Mondo!" Malpha commanded.

Rising from his seat at the table to be honored created a mix of emotions for Mondo. On the one hand, he was grateful, but on the other hand he knew there was more to the story which, if discovered, would not please the ruler. On his right, Lord Crumblestone was looking annoyed, and it occurred to Mondo that perhaps he had hoped to be credited with the improvement and success at the prison. In a flash, an idea occurred to the young hero and he acted upon it.

"I could not have brought about this success without the help and guidance of my Master, the Lord Crumblestone. Let us honor him as well." It was shocking for a humble servant to speak up in such a crowd of dignitaries, but as the event had been brought up by the ruler himself, all seemed pleased.

Mondo was anxious to sit down and become invisible. At the sound of a large metal gong, servants appeared with tray after tray of food. The guests ate until they were almost unconscious. Groans and burping sounds dominated the atmosphere and the conversations died down. Once again Malpha stood to speak.

"We have waited long for the kingdom to be united under my rule. I am the most powerful and only ruler of the land, and now everyone else knows it. They will respect my authority or else be punished. No one dare defy me and my power." Here the ruler let out a loud laugh for emphasis.

At this point, the attendees were barely aware of what their ruler was saying. Being clearly unimpressed with their reaction to his declaration, he turned aside and appeared to take a drink from a flask. When he returned to face the crowd, he placed his hand on an object just under the table before giving out a mighty roar. Green flashes of light filled the room and stirred the sleepy lords to attention. A ghostly green haze of smoke rose up before them, and the giant serpent of the Ultimate Ruler's reputation materialized to bring fright and awe. Mondo was at once fascinated and horrified by the ferocious apparition. Was it a real dragon or just an impressive shadow of something real? His mind flashed back to the all-but-forgotten moment when he was knocked overboard while at sea many months before. The same terrible vision of threatening fangs and red glowing eyes returned.

As quickly as it had appeared, the dragon shriveled down into a tiny wisp and seemed to fizzle into the opening of the flask. Malpha stood with an evil grin searching the faces of his audience for anyone who did not look terrified. His eyes fell upon Mondo who still gazed curiously into the space the fierce dragon had occupied only moments earlier. "Young man! Mondo!" yelled Malpha. "Do you not fear the dragon?"

"Oh, yes, of course," said Mondo apologetically. "It was very frightening." He tried to sound convincing, but unfortunately, he had felt not a shred of fear of the beast.

Malpha visibly shuddered and staggered back as he heard the reply, a response that only Mondo noticed. *You have with you the power to overcome evil,* he heard in his mind almost like a clear voice. Where had it come from? The thought kept repeating itself over and over. *Do not be afraid. You will overcome him.* Mondo felt himself stand tall and straight with a strange confidence. Everyone else in the room seemed bent and small.

No more was said. The group was dismissed. Malpha sat looking completely exhausted by the demonstration. He held out his flask to a servant who refilled it from a silver pitcher.

*

Crumblestone led the way back to the rooms in the upper chamber of the palace.

"Who are you? I have made you a slave, but you simply refuse to remain a slave. You must think you are a high-born lord," said Crumblestone with an annoyed and threatening tone.

*

Late the next day, a formal invitation arrived requesting Crumblestone to enter the throne room and come before the Ultimate Ruler, his majesty Malpha.

"This had better be the appointment I have been waiting for," said Crumblestone to his servant. "I know that an important event looms in the future of the kingdom, and I will be at the center of it. I have worked my whole life for this opportunity." He looked himself over in the looking glass, straightened his waistcoat, and nodded in approval. "You should change your clothes."

Mondo was confused. "I thought you wanted me to wear these fancy clothes before the ruler."

"I have changed my mind. Wear the prison clothes and look the part of a slave. I will not have you out-shining me in lordly dress."

After he had changed back into his rough, worn clothing, Mondo followed Crumblestone, obediently walking a few paces behind, down the grand staircase, and on toward the throne room. Clearly, the lord was angered by the memory of Mondo being honored during the last evening.

The party walked through a maze of halls before arriving at a large, ornately decorated room. At the far end sat the ruler, his face tense and eyes all-seeing. An evil energy emanated from him that dominated the room. Dressed in robes made of a bulky, green fabric, his body looked larger than his face. In one gnarled hand he held a glowing ball, and in the other, a silver goblet from which he kept taking sips.

Others stood beside him looking anxious and jumpy, ready for the least command from their master. Immediately to his right stood a proud official in a long, black robe. On his head, a tall, black hat that covered his forehead arched upward and pointed directly to the ceiling like a menacing thorn.

Everyone in the room knelt down except Mondo. Suddenly an arm was thrust toward him and he found himself pulled down into a kneeling position by a man next to him.

"Excellent! Excellent! Lord Crumblestone, you are welcome. Come forward and bring your protégé," said the man in black. Mondo gulped and moved forward as Crumblestone whispered in his ear, "Lord Chancellor to you."

"Your Ultimate Rulership, Lord Chancellor, we are honored by your invitation. How may we serve you? As you know….."

"Never mind all that," blustered Malpha. "Oh, my head. Very bad night's sleep." At this, a servant delivered a small cup of liquid. Malpha closed his eyes and drank as if he hadn't had water in days. "Where was I?" asked the ruler.

"Pardon me. I was only saying…" Lord Crumblestone tried again to make his speech.

"Silence! The Ultimate Ruler speaks," said the Chancellor.

"Here is what I need, Crumblestone. I cannot find anyone who knows how to get things done around here! What is the matter with all you numbskulls? I ask for some small thing and what do I get, a bunch of idiots."

"Yes, your Rulership. I understand. I do know how to get things done. I promise…" said Crumblestone before being again interrupted.

"Not you. I want that servant of yours, Mondo. Now, Mondo, can you get things going around here or not? Speak up, boy." commanded Malpha.

Mondo's mouth hung open in amazement as he searched for words. Lord Crumblestone saw Mondo's hesitation and jumped into the conversation once more. "Yes, indeed your Ultimate Rulership. He will begin immediately. What is it that you want him to do?"

Malpha looked annoyed with the self-important Lord. "Can he speak for himself? Look, I have not had a night's sleep in weeks. I keep having a dream that my whole celebration is coming crashing down around my feet. What is so difficult about celebrating my ascendency to rule the entire empire? A rather important occasion, wouldn't you say?"

Crumblestone made a last attempt to insinuate himself into the ruler's good graces. "I will see that this humble servant of mine does all that you require."

"Mondo, I am putting you in charge. The whole thing. Get it done. Fail, and off with your head! Or something even worse! And by the way, why are you dressed like a peasant? Whose idea was that?" Malpha shot Crumblestone a disparaging look.

"I will do as you ask," declared Mondo. Everyone in the room gasped. Not only had he not addressed the Ruler by his supreme title, but he had usurped his master.

Crumblestone sought to control his surprise, anger, and embarrassment. What was the audacious idea of appointing a servant to be in charge of the entire celebration event? How could his plan have gone so wrong? He turned to Mondo while asking his final question to the ruler. "How may I serve your majesty at this time?"

"Mondo, let Lord Crumblestone know as soon as you decide what task he should have. Now, everyone away. Go about your work and leave me to my rest." Malpha looked decidedly weaker as he rose and left the hall.

The Chancellor stepped forward and addressed Mondo. "Please stay here and I will instruct you regarding your task. Do you understand that you have been elevated higher than anyone in the kingdom?" he asked with stern authority. "That is, with the exception of myself."

"I am most humbly honored. I have the greatest desire to make the Ultimate Ruler's dreams come to pass." The meaning of Mondo's statement did not seem to register any alarm.

"Very good. You will now have a title. You are to be Chief Samaran of the Order of the Great Dragon."

Mondo stood flabbergasted and speechless before the Chancellor who walked slowly around looking the young upstart up and down. "You certainly do not look very impressive. His Ultimate Rulership must know what he is about. Hmmm." He paused before giving his final command.

"Lord Crumblestone, you may leave us."

CHAPTER 20

THE WAY OUT

The day was far spent. Hours had passed with no word from the hunters who had gone to search for the missing Rista. A strange wind blew through the trees high above the camp creating an ominous moaning sound.

"I fear the weather is changing. They may be caught in a storm," said Jewel. "Rista may not have taken her cloak."

"Rista is the least of our worries," replied Ruby. "She is a smart girl. It is Gem I am worried about. The villagers are blaming him for her rebellion against Furcula's wishes. He has tried to fit in and avoid offending, but I fear Rista has charmed him indeed. He feels deeply for her despite the knowledge that this would upset the way of things here."

"She has never wanted to marry Agafa. That was her grandfather's plan. How else could she have escaped from that unpleasant prospect? If she does make it to the outside world, how will she survive there?" Jewel could not stop thinking about the scenarios that played out in her mind. All of them seemed to end in unhappy possibilities. The future looked grim and without promise. "I do wish Gem would return soon with the men."

Jewel and Ruby had retired to their tree top bedroom when the hunters finally lumbered into the camp. In the dark, the two women prayed for a safe resolution to the day's events.

*

The morning light brought with it a sense of dread. Everyone was down early to find out what had happened. Had Rista been found? Had Gem suffered any consequences for his perceived guilt?

Ruby listened intently to hear conversations as the women whispered among themselves. "What are they saying?" she asked Jewel, who had a better grasp of the language.

"I sounds like Rista was not found. Come, Gem will tell us what is happening." Jewel hurried away toward the cave, and Ruby scurrying close behind.

"No one is here," they said at the same time. They looked at one another in dismay. "What do you think this means?" asked Ruby. Jewel began to cry.

"This is enough. Where is Furcula?" Ruby stormed away to find the king. "Furcula? *Momo betere*? Where?" she yelled as she went through the camp. The Gazrakians looked at her in shock and thought she had gone mad.

"Are you looking for me?" said Furcula stepping out of the crowd. He scowled and squared his shoulders as he prepared to do verbal battle with Ruby.

"Where is Gem? Why is he not here? Have the men abandoned him to the outsiders like they did to Diamond?"

"You are making many assumptions. Do you not believe that Diamond was captured due to his own foolishness? Is it not hard to believe that Gem, as well, may be lost because of his desire to escape from this place? I believe he has gone just as Rista is gone. Undoubtedly, they planned this untimely departure. In fact, I charge him with this crime. My granddaughter would never leave of her own accord. She would not defy my wishes for her marriage. It was Gem who poisoned her mind."

Ruby's anger boiled over. "You are insane! Gem did not do this. If anything, it was Rista who planned this "departure" as you call it. Gem has worked hard. He has cooperated in every way with your evil schemes, even to the point of betraying his own brother. He did this for you and these men. How have you repaid him for all his efforts?"

"Come, Ruby," urged Jewel. "It is no use. Maybe Agafa will tell us something." Ruby hurried past Furcula, disgusted and unconcerned for what might result from her outburst.

*

For the first time, Gem saw the enormous trees and dense underbrush of the forest. Other forays had given no opportunity for observing the surroundings. Always he had worn a camouflage covering and followed only the feet of others in front of him. How would he and Rista ever find a way out, and where would they go? How would they survive in an unknown country? His thoughts drifted back to Gazrak, his mother and Jewel. What was to become of them now? Was there a way to rescue them?

Rista did not seem to be bothered by such questions. Gem was surprised by her determination and confidence as she pushed onward. "This way," she said again and again, looking into the trees, then down at the ground, then side to side. Gem wondered what she saw that made her choose one direction over another.

At one point she stopped to listen to the sounds of birds and insects. Gem could hear no other clues. He listened as well, but could not make out what she heard that spurred her to the left or right. "Did you hear that?" she asked after another hour of walking.

"Hear what?" Gem listened again. In the distance he thought he heard barking. "I think it is a dog."

"What is dog?"

"A dog is an animal. Sometimes dogs are good and sometimes dogs mean trouble," said Gem before he realized that dog also meant they were nearing some kind of human outpost. "Wait, what will we tell people? How will we explain where we have come from?"

Rista did not understand his concern. "Come. We find dog. We can eat."

"No. No. We cannot eat someone's dog. Oh, Rista, you have so much to learn. What have we gotten ourselves into?"

The trees were thinning so that the sky was visible for the first time. Rista stared up at the clouds before looking curiously at was the beginning of farm land. "What is this place?" she asked.

"This is where people grow their food from the ground. This is where Agafa and the men take the food of others and bring it to Gazrak. They steal. Then the people here have no more food. You see? What they do is wrong." Gem wondered again if she understood. "The people here will not like us if they think we are from Gazrak. We must not tell them."

"Jewel tell me that Agafa steal. I hear this word. It is bad to steal?" she asked.

"Yes. It is bad."

"You go with Agafa. You steal? You are bad?"

"Yes. You are right. I was bad, but I want to do the right thing now. I want to be like Diamond. He is the good brother."

Thoughts of his brother infused Gem with a sense of purpose.

"We find Diamond now?" asked Rista

"Yes. We will find him."

CHAPTER 21

THE PLAN

The grand hallway was alive with bustling slaves and servants. A lone dignitary walked with purpose, measuring each step as he approached large, double doors. Bowing before him, the lowly palace staff buzzed with the news that a new official was present. Malpha had wasted no time in announcing to all the appointment of Chief Samaran Mondo. Whatever he wished was to be their command.

A uniformed guard opened the doors allowing the entrance to the apartment where Lord Crumblestone waited. Mondo braced himself for the lord's reaction.

"Am I to be bowing to you now? Chief Samaran is it?" Lord Crumblestone shook his head in disbelief.

Mondo broke into a smile and relaxed his studied high and mighty stance. "I am very sorry about this. You know I had nothing to do with it. I still cannot believe that Malpha would even notice me, let alone put me in charge of his celebration. I do suspect that part of it may be that, if I fail, he can easily dispose of me. What do you think?"

"I think that Malpha is smarter than he appears at times. You are right that you are disposable. One mistake, and your life will be forfeit. Perhaps I should be glad that it is you and not me with this insane appointment."

"I will do what I have to do," said Mondo with a degree of resignation that Crumblestone did not quite understand.

"By the way, I still hold your future in my hand."

"Would you threaten me, Lord Crumblestone? Will you reveal to the Ultimate ruler that his new Samaran is but a criminal from a foreign land?"

A sly smile appeared on the lord's face. "I have not told you this until now but, I have searched out your real identity. You are Damon Chislestone, son of Harraster Chislestone. I know your father. In fact, we are distantly related. So that makes me some sort of cousin, and equal. That takes some of the bite out of having to bow to you as Chief Samaran."

"How did you discover this?"

"To start with, you simply do not behave like one who has ever been under someone else's authority!"

"I am sorry. I have tried," lamented Mondo.

"Then I traveled to Bellicosa, and it did not take long before I heard the story of a young master who disappeared the same night that three criminals escaped into the wilds. No one was certain, but it seemed that there was some kind of magic involved. They even claimed you had believed that ridiculous story about a prince. That is the way of rumors and fairytales, right?" Crumblestone found the whole of it hilarious.

"And then, there you were in Wanderdown claiming to have been captured with your three friends—your friends the wanted criminals."

"I told the truth about all of it, except about my name. The men of Wanderdown came up with Mondo. Do not ask me how that happened, as I am not sure. I only know it was fortuitous. I have been keeping my real name secret so that I do not endanger my friends. Their involvement in crime was unintentional, and had much to do with my mother's errant ways. I could not let them suffer for her wrongs. Perhaps you heard that it was her servants who were blamed for her crime. So cousin, I am surprised that you did not improve my circumstances knowing that I was a blood relative, and your equal. Should I be angry with you for that?" asked Mondo.

"I think I did right by you. Look where you are now. And, it seems that you may do with me as you wish. My silence has brought your promotion. I assume you wish me to remain silent."

"Please do not reveal my identity. No one here knows the matters of Bellicosa, or even cares. I feel that my adventure as a young slave named Mondo has profited me. I sense a great purpose in it."

"I will do as you ask. Be aware, however, that you owe me some future favor. I have lost the position to which I most aspired. Surely, my cousin, you will see to it that I have a favorable assignment as compensation." Crumblestone's expression was sly and conniving, though Mondo sensed that a loyalty to family seemed to be playing a part in his willingness to grant secrecy.

"I do have something I wish for you to do. I think you will enjoy it."

"I am intrigued. Go on."

*

Stepping out of the shadows, a short, robed figure approached the Bellicosan lord as he passed the lower chambers on his way out of the palace. "Lord Crumblestone, may I have a word with you?" The lord recognized the rasping, female voice of Mucosa Drain.

"Mistress Drain, you are looking well," he said with difficulty. "How is Master Drain? I thought he was threatening

168

people somewhere in the south. Did I get that right?"

She attempted a smile that failed to turn the sides of her mouth upwards, achieving more of a grimace. Her boney nose curved down like the beak of a carnivorous bird.

"Hmmm. You are always so charming. But Malpha caught you this time, did he not? So the new Chief Samaran is your former slave? Did I get that right?"

"We had arranged for it to look that way. Our plan is working out beautifully. You will be surprised how well we are doing," said Crumblestone, knowing her curiosity would now be piqued beyond endurance.

"I will be keeping my eyes on him. There is something about him I do not trust, and you as well, for that matter." She turned and appeared to float ghost-like down the passage into oblivion.

Crumblestone laughed out loud. He turned and hurried out of the palace to order his carriage to be readied at once.

*

In his chamber above, Mondo meditated, waiting for some inspiration. He reached into a pocket and brought out his beloved stone. Rubbing it once again with his shirt sleeve, he brought it to a gleaming shine. It was clear and bright, telling Mondo that he was really Diamond, and he was exactly where he was supposed to be. He thought back to his dream of leading his brother and others in a battle against evil, and asked himself if this was just a dream or something that would come to pass.

"Lord Prince, what is it you want me to do here? How can I play the part in your great plan?"

Pacing back and forth in the room, Mondo thought over a hundred possible scenarios. *How do I plan for an event that everyone thinks is amazing, yet will end in disaster?* Ideas started to come. *This is so outlandish and unconventional. Can I get away with it? There is only one way to find out…*

Mondo's hand reached out, hesitated, then pulled the

169

tasseled cord that hung next to an ornate desk in the main room of the living quarters. A servant entered quietly, bowed, and asked, "What is it you wish, Master Samaran?"

"I wish for you to send a message to the Ultimate Ruler's chief officers. Tell them to meet in my chamber here in one hour. I have a plan."

CHAPTER 22

TOPAZ IN THE PALACE

Blurred vision and unsteady hands caused by a poor night's sleep rendered the Palace Workforce Commander into a foul mood.

"Who is this arriving at this hour? I have not opened the gate yet," he barked to the prison guard who stood waiting at the main gate.

"New workers for the palace detail, Commander."

"Did we order more workers? I do not remember sending in such an order."

"Yes, Commander. Three men, to be exact. Two to dig and plant, and one to carve wood."

"Wood. Did I ask for a wood worker?" He scratched his bald head before putting on his official hat to complete his almost-fully-dressed appearance.

"A wood carver, Commander," said the guard emphasizing the word 'carver'.

The Commander opened the gate and marched the men

171

to a small building behind the main palace. "In here until I get this worked out."

Once inside the main building, the commander sought the head of the household staff. "What's happening? I have three workers that I didn't ask for. Is someone in here changing the orders?"

"A big change is coming. There are rumors that Malpha is about to start preparations for his celebration. There may be more workers ordered before you know it."

"One of these new workers is a wood carver? Why would I order a wood carver?" The commander continued with a foul stream of language, turning the heads of all present.

Topaz tried to look inconspicuous, waiting for instructions on where he was to go next. Looking at his order sheet, the commander searched for more information about his new recruits.

"Come from the prison, have you? What was your crime? Says here that you accidentally broke a carving at the woodcarver's shop? That is a crime?"

"Yes, sir. I tripped over it, and it was crushed."

The commander shook his head in disbelief.

Just then, a servant came before the commander with a written note. The Commander opened it, read the contents, and continued to shake his head.

"It says here that I am to make sure that a woodcarver is recruited immediately. When said person arrives, he is to be sent before the Chief Samaran for orders, for an important job."

Nose to nose, the commander stared at Topaz saying, "This is my lucky day. How did the Chief Samaran know that today I mistakenly ordered a woodcarver, and here he is? What a coincidence," he yelled angrily. "And you coming with no tools? How is that going to work? You, servant. Take this woodcarver to the Chief Samaran."

*

Following the appointed servant, Topaz tried to imagine what awaited him in the presence of the Chief Samaran, whatever a samaran might be. He wanted to observe the layout of the palace, but the servant sped down hallways so quickly, there was no time.

The servant knocked lightly on the large doors to Mondo's chamber. Another servant opened one side of the doors.

"The Chief Samaran's request for a woodcarver has been fulfilled." Bowing, the servant turned and left Topaz standing outside the entrance. From within, he could hear a man's voice.

"Who is it, Gerwin?"

Topaz was shocked to recognize the voice. He entered and saw Mondo standing in the middle of the room. A look of surprise and joy overtook his face.

Giving a sideways glance at his servant, Mondo tried to look stern. "Come in. You must be the new woodcarver I asked for. What is your name young man?"

Topaz reacted, quickly catching on, but amazed at the confusing scene before him.

"Yes, master Chief...Samaran. I am Topaz."

"Gerwin, you may go. Topaz and I have work to do to plan for the carvings I need for the celebration."

Once they were alone, Topaz immediately asked, "How did this happen? What is a Chief Samaran, anyway?" Dazed and astonished, the younger man looked at his new superior in disbelief.

"It is a long story, but essentially, the Ultimate Ruler heard about the incident in the prison with Falgar. He was so impressed that the matter was peaceably resolved, that he wanted to appoint me to be head over his whole celebration for the rulership of the empire. I do not understand it myself," said Mondo, lowering his voice almost to a whisper. "I believe it has to be part of what the Prince has for me to do."

"What about Lord Crumblestone? Is he still your slave master?" asked Topaz.

"That is also a long story, and I shall tell it in time. Right now, I have sent Crumblestone on an errand. You may say that we have an understanding."

"Is there a way for me to contact Ameth and let him know I am here?"

"I have some ideas. When you do make contact, somehow I must meet him. There are burning questions I have that long to be answered. What do you know about Ameth's story? Where is he from?"

"He did not tell me much about his story. I only know that he has traveled all over the kingdom and learned much along the way. He taught me about all that has transpired in the past."

"Did he tell you that your family came from this place, formerly called Abundant?"

"He did. I saw the painting on the outside wall of the palace."

"Did he explain that former Abundanites are held in suspicion and not frequently promoted to positions of high rank?"

"Yes, I did receive that warning. I know I must be careful. What do you want me to do? What carvings shall I make?"

"I do not know yet, but you will need to obtain tools and supplies. That will mean you will be able to move about and contact your people."

"How can this be? This is so much better than we planned. Now I hope I can remember the skill of my youth and manage to be a woodcarver!"

"Go now. I will give the command that you are to be allowed to come and go freely," said Mondo. He walked Topaz out the door and put him in the charge of a servant to see him out of the palace.

Turning back to his chambers, he saw from a sideward

glance the shadowy figure of an old woman whose long nose drew attention to her pinched, frowning face. She watched as Topaz passed down the hallway, then she slipped away in the opposite direction.

CHAPTER 23

THE TRAP

"Rista, my dear. Can you come help me with this meat? You are so skilled at cutting and chopping. My hands get so tired these days."

"Yes. Mistress. I come." Rista dropped the bundle of hay into the barn and headed for the cottage door.

"Can you finish?" she yelled to Gem across the farm yard.

"Do not worry. I will feed the rest of the cows. You go ahead." Gem jumped down from the tall stack of hay and headed for the barn. He could not help but think back on the last weeks since Mistress Melly Potter had taken Rista and him into her home.

They had been wandering about the country looking for food and shelter. Looking across a field of hay, they saw the old woman hacking at the hay, trying to harvest it by herself. The couple hurried in her direction to see the sweat pouring from her brow and the look of pain on her face as she stopped to brace her back with one hand.

"Let me help you! I have a strong back, and you look tired," said Gem. Not waiting for a reply, he grabbed the scythe out of her hand and began to swing it back and forth. In no time, a pile of hay was laid down before them. Gem paused to wipe the sweat from is face with his rough shirt sleeve.

"Thank you, son. You look pretty tired yourself. You had better come to my house and eat something." The look of relief on both grubby faces told the old woman her intuition was right. They were hungry and tired.

"The name is Melly Potter. Who are you and where have you come from?"

"My name is Gem and this is Rista." At that point, he did not know what to add about where they had been.

"We live in forest. We leave that place and look for new place," interjected Rista.

"You must be a foreigner. What forest did you live in?"

"Long way away," Rista added.

"We are looking for a new place to live. It is true. We know nothing of this area."

"Well I could surely use some help from two strong young people like yourselves. You see, my husband died some time back, and I have been trying to run this farm by myself. It is 'near impossible. And on top of that, there is a band of thieves who have been stealing my poor cows. If you can help me keep them from stealing, I will be eternally grateful to you."

"I am sure I can help with that, Mistress Potter. That is one chore I would love to do for you." Gem felt confident he could outsmart the Gazrak, since he had become an expert at thievery.

"You know, they caught one of those thieves some time back. He got what was coming to him, though."

Gem gulped and wondered if he had the nerve to ask what happened to the thief. Mistress Potter saved him the trouble.

"They sent him off to prison, they did. Hard labor, I heard tell. He had some strange story about being captured by a tribe of wild savages. Heh, no one believed him, of course."

"What is savage?" whispered Rista to Gem, who did not want to answer the question.

"Oh, sweetheart, a savage is someone with no manners. They are uncivilized, cruel, and heartless."

Rista realized that the mistress was talking about her own people and turned to Gem with a lost look. He quickly changed the subject.

"Where shall we sleep? Do you have room in your tiny cottage?"

"I have only one small bedroom besides mine, with only the one small bed."

"I will sleep in the barn, if you do not mind. Keeping an eye out for those bandits will have me up at night anyway."

"I will get you the spare quilts."

Lacking the courage to tell her they were not married, Gem and Rista accepted the arrangements gratefully.

*

Working long hours each day, Gem and Rista helped Mistress Potter catch up with the work that had been waiting to be done. Gem thought about how he could prevent the Gazrakians from raiding the farm. Each night he herded the cows into a corral surrounded by a rim of thorny branches.

"How will this keep the cows safe, Gem?" asked the old woman.

"I am hoping that the thorns will penetrate through the bottom of the thieves footwear and discourage them from coming closer."

"Won't they be wearing boots?"

Gem had to think fast because he knew that the hunters did not wear boots. "I do not believe they will. I have heard that their footprints are hard to discern because no clear boot print can be seen. So they must be wearing something soft and thin on their feet."

"Gem, that is a very clever deduction. I hope you are right." Mistress Potter wondered who could have told Gem this vital bit of information.

"I will stay up for a while, waiting in the dark to hear if anyone comes."

*

After many nights of dozing off in the dark barn, Gem heard the cows becoming restless. Shaking himself awake, he waited for any unusual sound. He crept closer to the corral.

"Ugh," came a whispered groan, then another. It was a moonless night, the most popular time for the hunters to strike. Faint whispers reached his ears, some rustling of capes, then nothing. His plan had worked. Back in the barn, he slept the rest of the night on the hay stacks. In the morning, he inspected the thorn branches and found one pile disturbed. A small red spot remained on one of the sharp points. Gem smiled and headed for breakfast.

*

"I think we foiled the thieves last night," reported Gem.

"Did your plan work? Did they step on the thorns?" asked the amazed hostess.

"I heard noises in the night, and I found signs of disturbance on the branches. I think they changed their minds and left."

"Oh, Gem. That is wonderful. You are a genius. Extra cream for you this morning!"

Gem thought for a moment before continuing. "Mistress Melly, you have been so good to us. It is we who are deeply in your debt."

"Nonsense. You have saved my farm from ruin."

"We have loved to be here with you. The truth is, we will eventually have to move on and find a more permanent place. We have a destination in mind. It is called the City of Light. Have you heard of it?"

Rista added, "We go to see Prince."

"I have heard rumors of such a place. I thought it was a myth. Are you sure it is for real? I have heard that the Prince does not exist. Someone made up stories about him."

"We are sure he is real. We will stay a bit longer, but it will soon be time to go. We will miss you."

"Oh, I do not want to talk of such things. Let us celebrate our small victory over the thieves and be happy."

*

A new morning dawned bright and warm. The animals grazed contentedly and the chores were almost finished.

"Gem, I want you to go to town for me. I need some supplies and I am just too old to carry all that back here. Take the cart and make a day of it for you and Rista."

The young couple looked at each other with glee. They had a plan.

*

Rista did her best to bind her orange locks into a mass and pin them in place. Wrapping a bright scarf around her head and straightening her best dress, she was ready for the journey to town. Gem had tried to explain about towns, about matters of dress and manners. This was a new adventure. She wondered if she could remember all the important things he had told her about how to behave.

"Be sure to get the dark molasses. Take this lump of fresh butter to barter with the storekeeper. Hurry along before it melts. It will be hot today."

With her two hands holding on to Gem's arm, they set off in the donkey cart. Rista giggled at the sensation of riding over the rough road. When they hit a bump, she whooped and held on tighter.

*

The road into Wanderdown was dusty and dry. Spying a drinking trough, Gem steered the donkey in that direction.

"Now we just have to remember what Mistress Melly told us about where to go. We must see to the supplies first before the butter turns into a puddle."

"Then we go find other place, right?" Rista held on to Gem's arm and jumped up and down with excitement.

"Right. Be patient."

The two made the exchange and found that the supplies were easy to purchase. The storekeeper was delighted to see the butter and quickly removed it to a cooler place.

"Now? Now?" cried Rista.

"Now!" responded Gem.

*

Parking the donkey cart in a shady spot, the two walked on down the street arm in arm.

"Pardon me," he asked a stranger on the street. "Can you tell me where the law office is?"

"Keep going along here and turn right at the next lane," came the reply.

After the turn, they looked down the street and saw a crowd gathered outside one of the buildings. "Looks like we may have to wait in line. That is the building we are looking for." They drew closer and listened to people in the crowd talking.

"It is Lord Crumblestone, and he is going to give a speech," said one.

"Why has he come back to Wanderdown? Is there some pressing legal matter again for him to decide?" asked another.

"Listen, he is about to begin."

Gem and Rista tried to get closer to see Lord Crumblestone. A stout, dignified man emerged from the interior of the building. He was dressed in such finery that Rista could not help but murmur in a low voice, "Ooohh."

"Quiet. Listen," whispered Gem.

"Citizens of Wanderdown, it is my pleasure to be once again in your fair town. You will recall that last time I was here, I performed an important duty of criminal justice. The lone thief caught in the forest was deemed to not only be part of the notorious gang, but a runaway slave as well. His punishment at the time was to be sentenced to prison. I did convey him all the way to Tenebrose where he spent many months in prison."

At these words, Gem felt a return of grief, but resolved to put the feelings out of his mind.

"Now I come to you with new information. I have cracked the case. After an extensive investigation, by myself, I have determined the identity of the head of the gang of thieves. Additionally, I have determined where the gang's hideout is."

Rista grabbed onto Gem's arm again and held it tight. "Do they talk about my people? Who does he mean, 'the head of the gang?'"

Gem put his arm around Rista's shoulders and whispered in her ear, "They mean your grandfather."

"What will happen to him? What will happen to the Gazraks if they find the village?"

"I do not know, but perhaps the time has come for them to pay for their crimes."

Tears began to form in Rista's eyes. The speaker continued.

"I have found out that the thieves have a spy here in Wanderdown. That is how they always know where to go to steal and plunder. That spy may be listening to my voice right now."

At this, the townspeople cried out, "Who is it?" They began to look around for a possible suspect. A woman turned to Gem and cried out, "Here he is. This is the man. I have never seen him before. He must to the one!" Gem stepped back in self-defense and said, "No, it is not me."

"No, madam. That is not the man we are looking for. The man you want is someone you see everywhere and never notice. I alone know who he is. I am not going to point him out to you because I have a message for him. And here it is. 'You are holding three people hostage in your camp. They must be released immediately. If they do not appear in this town in three-day's time, your camp will be raided, everyone arrested, and you will be hanged. If the hostages are released, you may be given some leniency in your sentence. But know this: your reign of terror is over!'

The people were stunned by the speech. After a short pause, as the meaning of the message sunk in, they all shouted 'Lord Crumblestone, our hero!'

Slowly the noisy crowd dispersed leaving Rista and Gem standing in the street holding each other. "We knew this was going to happen, Rista. The good news is that Jewel and Ruby will be released."

"Three hostages. He said three. Who is number three?"

"Me! I am number three. Do we dare tell them our story? Maybe

I will be sent to prison as well."

"Will we still be able to marry?" asked Rista dejectedly.

"That is what we must now go to find out. Come on. We have to talk to Lord Crumblestone."

CHAPTER 24

REVELATION

"We would like to speak to Lord Crumblestone, if you please." Gem asked the most authoritative-looking person in the room. Rista cowered by his side, fearful of the new and unpredictable circumstances.

"I am the Keeper of the Peace—KoP to you. Who are you and why do you wish to speak to him?" returned the officer.

"We have information about the gang of thieves he spoke about just now."

Every head in the room turned at once towards the strangers. Surrounding them on all sides, the staring eyes bore down on them like a great weight before one asked, "Who did you say you are?"

"I will tell Lord Crumblestone my story. Please. May I speak to him?"

Hearing the commotion, Lord Crumblestone was drawn into the main room of the Peace Keeping office. "You wish to speak to me? But, of course...."

"He says he has information about the thieves' gang."

"My name is Gem and this is Rista."

The lord immediately recognized the name Gem. "I know who you are. Come. We will talk in private." Leading them to a back room, he looked them over carefully. The awareness that Gem was, by blood, a relative—Crumblestone being a cousin of Lord Chiselstone's—was not forgotten by him.

"I take it that you were able to escape from the Gazrak's camp."

"How did you know that?"

"I have come here with the task of rescuing you, dear boy. I have gotten acquainted with your half-brother. I have not heard all the details, but apparently you betrayed him so that he was captured by the men of the town. Do you want to hear what has become of your brother?"

Gem was overcome with remorse. "I know what I did. I am very sorry. I almost paid with my life. Rista saved me from a sure death at the hands of the Gazrak."

"No doubt you have a story to tell. Your brother has spent many months in prison. From what I hear, you know what prison is like. Am I right?"

"Yes. Will you now send me back?"

"No. But I am going to take you to Tenebrose. There the Chief Samaran will decide what to do with you."

"Where is Tenebrose? Who is the Chief Samaran?"

"He is one of the most powerful men in the kingdom, second only to the Ultimate Ruler," Crumblestone said sternly. "Well, there is the Lord Chancellor, but he is less trustworthy, if you ask me."

"Why is he interested in us? How does he know who we are? Has the small matter of my criminal past gone all the way to a city I have never heard of?"

"Let us not worry about that now. All will be clear in time. Tell me about this woman you have with you, Rista."

Gem was thoroughly confused, making it hard to concentrate on what Lord Crumblestone was asking. After a moment, and unable to

185

find any possible answers, he replied.

"We escaped together. We wish to be married. That is why we came here today, to find an officer who can officiate a wedding."

"We can see to that matter." Crumblestone waved his hand to dismiss what he considered a triviality.

"Once that is accomplished, return here in three days. If the other two hostages have not been returned to us, we will raid the Gazrak village. If they do arrive, we will take them with us to Tenebrose and leave the Gazrak problem to the men of Wanderdown."

*

Gem and Rista rushed out of the Peace Keepers office and down the lane to find their donkey cart, their heads full of questions with no clear answers. It had been so much longer than they thought to reach their goal. Now, all haste had to be made to return to Mistress Potter's farm by dark. As they turned the corner, Gem saw a shadowy figure lurking between buildings. He stopped suddenly, causing Rista to look. She gasped.

"Grandfather, is that you?"

"It is you, is it not? You are the spy they are after!" exclaimed Gem.

"Well, what do you know? I should have known that she would rescue you. Rista, I order you to come back with me. You cannot leave us and go with this outsider."

"Did you hear what Lord Crumblestone said? They are going to raid the village. You must bring Jewel and Ruby to Wanderdown, or you will hang! He knows who you are."

"Diamond did this. He told them. I should have had him killed instead of merely left to the townspeople. But then, I thought I had killed you. But look, here you are. Whatever happened to good old-fashioned assassination?"

"Grandfather, you did this to Diamond, and to Gem?" Rista cried.

"I did it for you, my dear," was Furcula's sarcastic reply.

186

"No! I go now. Goodbye," yelled Rista running away down the street.

*

Darkness crept over the landscape. The road ahead grew fainter and fainter. Fortunately, the donkey was better at navigating than the humans, for he knew his way home and was hungry. A large, silvery-white moon began to rise, casting its light over the terrain. In the distance, an outline of the farmhouse emerged with dots of yellow light shining from the windows.

*

"Goodness, where have you been? I was worried sick that you were headed to the City of Light and taken my only donkey with you." declared Mistress Potter.

"We are very sorry. There is a good reason for our late arrival, and we will tell you. But first, may we eat? It has been a very long day."

*

Savoring every bite of the steamed potatoes, Gem closed his eyes to let the relief of a full stomach settle upon him. Rista ate in moderation, poking here and there at the familiar vegetables.

"Where is your appetite, my dear? Is something troubling you?"

Attempting a smile, the young woman clung to Gem for support. "The day was very good. But sad, too. Gem can tell you?" She turned her gaze to him as if to say, 'it is time'.

"Where to begin…. As you heard and told us the first night we were here, the gang of thieves—who are really known among themselves as Gazrak—left one of their men behind some months ago. Only, he was not one of their own. He had been a captive who was forced to join their hunting…ah…stealing trips. You said yourself that people did not believe his wild story about being one of four who were being held against their will."

"That is right. But what does that have to do with you?"

"I was one of the men being held by the Gazrak people."

At this revelation, Mistress Potter gasped in horror. "No, Gem. Are you telling the truth?"

187

"It is true. Rista is one of the Gazraks, but don't judge her harshly. She was raised by these people, but she did not know what they were doing. She was adopted by their leader, and we do not even know who her real parents were. She saved my life and helped me escape from their treachery. We did not know where we were, but you took us in and helped us survive."

"Oh, my land, Gem! Why did you not tell me when you came?"

"We were afraid you would think we were thieves and turn us in to the KoP," confessed Gem.

"And how do you know about the KoP?"

Gem and Rista looked at each other as he continued, "We met him today, I believe. We did not tell you before, but we were not married when we came. We wanted to get married. Rista is my true love." Rista's face radiated joy and love as she stared at Gem, and they held each other's hands.

"Get on with it. What then?" begged Mistress Potter.

"Oh, yes. We went to find someone to marry us. What we found was a crowd gathered to hear a speech by a Lord Crumblestone. They said he visits Wanderdown once a year to look after his estate. He gave a speech and revealed that he knows who the head of the Gazrak gang is. Acting as a spy, the person actually comes to Wanderdown to learn about where to steal next!"

"Was he there? Did you see him?" asked the old woman, who had not heard such good gossip in years.

At this, Rista's face turned to a frown, pain and sorrow now seeping through what had been joy. Tears welled up again as she said softly, "It is my grandfather."

Mistress Potter's eyes widened with surprised concern. Had she been housing the very family of the enemy gang?

"My dears, this is awful. What did you do?"

"Lord Crumblestone threatened the spy, thinking perhaps he may have been in their midst at the moment—and I think he was within earshot.

"Threatened? This is getting better all the time. Go on!"

"The thieves must bring the three hostages to Wanderdown in three-day's time or their leader risks being hanged! He said they know where the gang's village is and will raid it and arrest everyone. I have to tell you, that is hard to believe; the village is very hard to find."

"If you escaped, then there are only two hostages to set free."

"That is how it is. I had to speak to the lord to tell him about Rista and me. He says that if the two are freed, he will take all four of us to a city called Tenebrose."

"Why would he take you away from here? Can you not stay and live here?"

"There is one more fact that I have not shared with you. The man who was caught months ago and sent to prison, is my brother. And it was my fault that he was abandoned in the forest and found by the Wanderdown men. I did not even tell the lord about that. I must go and try to free him from prison. It is so wrong for him to be punished for something he did not do."

Mistrss Potter sat stunned by all the new information. She shook her head and chuckled. "Wait until I tell Minerva about this. In my very own house all this time." After some reflection on the plan for spreading the news, the mistress added, "Well, did you get married?"

Gem and Rista smiled once again. "Yes!"

"Well then, let us celebrate!"

CHAPTER 25

RESCUE

Fading light signaled the close of another day. One more day of backbreaking work and little cause for cheer would be followed by one more day of the same. Jewel sat on a bumpy log staring into the central fire pit, elbows on her knees and head cradled in her hands. Thoughts of lost hope and an empty future pricked at her mind.

"Come," beckoned Ruby. "It is time to go up. Mosquitoes will soon be tormenting you if you stay there."

"I cannot go on like this. How are we supposed to keep trusting and hoping when we hear nothing but grumbling Gazrakians. Why is there no relief and deliverance? Are we to give up and just become like these people, lost to the outside world and resigned to a life of chopping up food for gobbling Gazrakians?

"You are sounding almost poetic this evening. I especially like that phrase 'gobbling Gazrakians', very picturesque. How about 'greedy, gastronomically gluttonous,…" Ruby stopped mid-sentence to let the humor hang in the air.

Jewel could not help but laugh. "I should have the skills of a diarist and write my poetic thoughts on this journey that is taking us nowhere."

"Ah, more poetic thoughts. You should consider more seriously learning how to write. At least your reading has improved. Speaking of which, let us retire to the trees and read from the one book that we do have. Maybe we can find something to cheer us up."

The two women moved toward the hidden stairway to the lofts above. "It has been weeks and we have heard no word about Gem or Rista. Do you think they found their way out of the forest?" asked Jewel.

"There is no use trying to guess. We will have to content ourselves with 'no news is good news'. Did not some wise philosopher say that once?"

"I have never heard that said before, but it seems the best advice."

Muffled mumbling could be heard in the high, tree-top dwellings. People were settling down for the night in the blackness of night. Jewel and Ruby crawled into their small space and pulled rough quilts over themselves to ward off the chill of a light breeze.

"Some days I long for a normal bed and a lamp," said Ruby.

"We could go on for some time naming all the things we have a longing for. I have a longing to know if Diamond, Gem and Rista are safe. I long to see them all again, to see the Prince, and arrive at the place we hoped for—the City of Light. Oh, well. Go ahead and read something to me."

"The man in the diary did not end his book on a final note. We do not know if he made it safely to that city? I wonder if he is still alive. Maybe he lived so long ago that he has died by now.

I wonder if we will ever know. Let me see. Shine your green light over this way so I can see the page. Here is a good paragraph."

*

The next morning found the women as usual, lighting fires and preparing to bake their crude loaves of bread. Water boiled in a caldron for making a tasteless, grainy porridge that was becoming very tiresome for Jewel and Ruby.

Furcula squatted close to the fire silently watching the preparations. He poked at the coals with a stick before standing. He had his bag of bones at his side and the two women wondered if he was about to make some proclamation in the name of his gods.

"What can it be about today?" whispered Ruby. "Are the hunters going to take us into the woods and lose us like they did with Gem and Diamond?" She was joking, but the thought never left their minds that it was a possibility.

Raising his arms in the air, Furcula shouted, "Listen, my people. The gods are angry. I will discern for you what they are saying to us."

"Here we go again." Ruby turned her back on the crowd and continued with her breakfast.

"Someone in our midst has brought trouble for us. We are in danger." Sounds of panic rippled through the group. Agfa stepped forward and shouted in the Gazrak language, "Who is it who has brought this trouble? We will find them and banish them from our midst."

"Not me. I did not do it," quietly teased Ruby.

"Shush," warned Jewel. "He is serious."

"I will ask the bones to name the troublemaker." He proceeded to shake the bag and toss the contents into the air. All were looking closely when they fell to the ground and formed a neat arrow pointing in a direction that even Furcula was shocked to see.

All eyes followed the arrow point to the person standing closest.

Furcula could hardly believe his luck. Ruby and Jewel stood directly in the path of the point. His job of convincing everyone of their need to be banished was now so much simpler.

"Ah hah! It is the two foreigners. They have brought the trouble. They must be banished," shouted Furcula.

Stunned shock showed on the faces of Ruby and Jewel. Speechless and helpless, they did not know how to react. Both stared at the ground and the obvious arrow pointing in their direction. How did this happen? Was Furcula capable of real magic?

Silence hovered over the small crowd as the news took hold. Women began to whisper to each other and speculate on how the two could have brought trouble to the village.

"You will leave us now. Get whatever possessions you have and be prepared to leave immediately," commanded Furcula.

Jewel and Ruby did not wait for any additional instructions. Running, then climbing into their small nest in the trees, Jewel quickly retrieved her green dress, the diary, and her precious necklace. Ruby grabbed a spare shawl but had nothing else of importance worth taking. They climbed down and presented themselves for the departure, still in shock from the sudden change of direction in their lives and the uncertainty of what was ahead.

*

Morning fog lay like a blanket over the flat farmland beyond the forest. Jewel and Ruby dropped in an exhausted heap on an outcropping of large boulders. After walking all night through brambles and bushes, tripping over fallen trees and sharp rocks, and being continually prodded along by hostile Gazrakian hunters, the sight of treeless terrain was a relief.

"I cannot go another step. If they keep pushing us, I will die. I am sure of it," lamented Ruby.

Jewel raised her gaze to look behind them and was surprised to see that their captors had disappeared.

"They are gone!"

"What? They were just there a minute ago. What happened? Why have we been left here?"

Jewel's mind tried to fathom the possibilities. She was too tired to come up with any answers. Hungry, disheveled, and overcome with fatigue, they both collapsed on the ground and went to sleep.

Blazing sun and heat woke the sleepers. Bees buzzed, insects chirped, and a crow cawed from a distant tree. Otherwise, all was silent. Stiff and sore from the long night of hiking, they stretched and looked around for some clue as to what they should do next.

"I am so hungry. The hunters could have at least left us a hunk of bread," complained Ruby.

"I guess we do what we did the last time; we walk."

*

Gem rose very early from his night of restlessness in the tiny room in Mistress Potter's home. He looked at Rista sleeping peacefully and did not want to wake her, just in case his mission brought disappointment. It had been two days since they had returned with the news of Lord Crumblestone's demands of the Gazraks. One day remained before the deadline to return the hostages to Wanderdown. *They will not bring the women into the town,* he reasoned. *The hunters will leave them before being seen. How will they know which way to go?*

He unlatched the door and crept out into the foggy morning. After walking for the better part of an hour, he was within sight of the forest. Scanning the trees produced no sign of any living being. From the far right edge, a small wagon drawn by a horse approached driven by a single figure.

"Ho! Gem," shouted KoP Kibble. "I see we are on the same quest. Do you think it is possible that they will appear today?"

"I do not believe their leader, Furcula, will wait for the whole three days. But we will see."

The sun increased in strength. Gem and Kibble looked at each other and shook their heads.

"Not today, I'm thinking." Kibble climbed into the wagon and turned the horse towards Wanderdown. "Wear a hat next time. You will burn up in this sun."

Two grubby faces poked out of the long grass at the side of the road. Ruby waved the driver down and shouted, "Help!"

Gem ran from behind the wagon and grabbed Ruby and Jewel as they emerged from an overgrown ravine.

"Gem, where did you come from? How are you here? Where are we?" Ruby stumbled over her words trying to understand and ask the myriad questions jammed up in her thoughts.

Tears flowed as the three savored the moment of relief and joy. Jewel had to ask, "Have you heard anything about Diamond?"

"He is alive. It is a long story and I will tell you all. Right now, we must get you to Wanderdown and Lord Crumble-stone."

*

The wagon rolled into the outskirts of the town. Almost immediately crowds began to gather on either side of the road. People waved and cheered. Pointing to the women, some shook their heads in sympathy. Ruby could almost understand their words to each other by looking at their facial expressions and the movement of their lips. She did not know whether to happily soak up the attention or be angry at the pity they expressed for her own sorry-looking state.

Entering the center of town, the wagon stopped in front

of the Peace Keeping office. Lord Crumblestone greeted them with all the pomp he could muster. He addressed the crowd, "Citizens, this is the first step towards a solution for the Gazrak gang. These poor captives were rescued this morning by your honorable Keeper of the Peace, Horatio Kibble. As you can see, my plan has worked. Now, all that must be done is to locate the gang's hideout, and the rest will follow."

Gem listened carefully, noting that the rest of the plan would not be easily accomplished. Crumblestone finished his speech and ushered the three into the office.

"Lord Crumblestone, begging your pardon, but we are starving. There wouldn't be some bread or water close by, would there?" Ruby looked a most pathetic sight. All present echoed her request, and soon, it was being carried beyond the building. People scurried here and there, and before long, a flood of food arrived at the door. They ate voraciously, but it was not long before the Lord began his interrogation of them.

"What do you remember about the trail leading from the camp?"

"Long."

"Twists."

"Turns."

"Trees."

"Hmmm. These answers will not help us. Do not any of you know how you got in or out of that place?" Kibble asked in exasperation.

The questions went on for some time before Jewel looked faint and Ruby kept falling asleep. Finally, Kibble and the others left the room to form a plan. Gem could not resist asking the obvious question of Lord Crumblestone, "How will the men of Wanderdown find the Gazrak village to arrest everyone?"

"That is not my problem," Crumblestone said in a low voice. "You have been my problem. And now, I have solved the problem. Let Wanderdown solve its own." Raising his voice again, he hailed Kibble, "Take these former captives to Mistress Potter's home to prepare for our journey."

"Your Lordship, will we be able to find my brother in Tenebrose?" Gem asked as they climbed back into the wagon. The courtier laughed.

"The Chief Samaran will see to that when he hears your case, though I would not get your hopes too high. He does not look favorably on people who abandon their own in a time of trouble."

CHAPTER 26

COMMISSION

Fed and scrubbed, Mistress Potter sent the four on their way on a bright, sunlit morning. The son of Peace Keeper Kibble—a strapping young man—needed work and agreed to help the widow with the farm chores once Gem and Rista were gone.

Gem had enough time to gather some of the farmers together and give them instructions on how to prevent any more loss of cattle or food, just in case the gang should try to strike again. Strangely, the men of Wanderdown never did find the Gazrak camp. However, the thefts mysteriously ceased. It was assumed that the group had moved to another location. Later, some suspected that they had never really existed.

The morning of the departure, Jewel donned her green dress in an effort to be acceptable in a city. Ruby wore some castoff clothing from Mistress Potter. Gem and Rista had put a few belongings together from their stay at the farm, but none of them looked very civilized. They met the carriage they were to travel in outside the KoP office, said their goodbyes to all, and waited for Lord Crumblestone to appear.

"The Lord left this morning in another carriage," remarked Kibble as if it was common knowledge that they would not be traveling with a lord. "He said to tell you he has business along the way and did not wish to keep you from a direct route to Tenebrose. He sends his regards. His servant and driver will make sure you are taken care of on the journey."

Gem was the most surprised by this revelation as he thought they were meant to travel together. As it was, the carriage only seated four comfortably and their party numbered an unexpected fourth person. He held onto Rista's arm which was looped through his own and mentally gave thanks for her. She was a gift that he did not deserve.

"We are not yet headed to the City of Light. In fact, Tenebrose may be a very long way from that city. But I am thankful that we will be a long way away from the Gazrak," said Jewel. Rista bit her lip and held on tight to her husband.

*

One surprise after another followed as the journey unfolded. Crumblestone had left instructions with his driver to make sure they only stayed in the finest of accommodations along the way. It was particularly obvious that Jewel was to be favored above the rest. The lord had brought a great trunk with him which was now in their possession. All four marveled at the finery contained within.

"Why has Lord Crumblestone done this? These clothes are better than any I ever saw in Bellicosa," Jewel observed as she handed Rista some of the many items meant for the shorter woman.

"He must have taken a liking to you, Jewel," said Ruby. "Look at the luxury he has bestowed on you! I am not complaining, mind you. But I am as mystified as you are."

"Look at this! I can hardly believe my eyes. Here is a genuine Chistelstone sword and sheath. I think this is supposed to be for me, but why?"

"Now I am worried," Ruby added. "Perhaps this Chief Samaran has us mixed up with someone else. This is probably not even intended for us, but for some dignitaries he is expecting. We will have to explain to him who we really are, just slaves from a tiny kingdom by the sea!"

"I would not go that far, mother," said Gem, still admiring the sleek weapon in his hands. "I wonder as well. Who is this man? Why is he favoring us this way?"

*

Climbing the stairs to the upper chamber challenged Ameth's tired limbs. Determination and a sense of purpose drove him upward to the goal. He knocked. Jasper opened the heavy door.

"Come in, dear Master. You have been so patiently waiting for some development in our cause. I am sorry that this affair has kept you here way beyond your expectations."

"No, my friend. I believe that patience will be rewarded. However, I must confess, events have not gone as planned or hoped. Something good will come of this yet." Ameth sat down on a cushioned chair and rested. "I am getting old. Perhaps the word is *very* old. The Prince told me that I shall see the day of deliverance for the kingdom in my lifetime. I still believe that. Besides, I have used the time to continue my research into the history of the kingdom. I started that many years ago, and now that I am here in Tenebrose, I have more questions about its history."

"You are faithful, Master. And, I imagine you are curious about Topaz and his quest to find his family. There are many former Abundantites here from whom to gain information."

"Yes, and I must be careful that no danger comes to him because of my looking into the matter. We have already suspected important connections seen in his possession of the amulet. I did not tell Topaz this, but some years ago, I heard of such a prize. The tales were so fantastic as to be unbelievable."

"I do have news of Topaz that may cheer you," reported Jasper. "My messenger has returned from the prison. He reports that he

200

arrived at the prison just as the doors were closing for any business. He managed to deliver your letter to the head of the prison. The response was only a verbal message, but a significant one, indeed. You will be glad to hear that, strange as it may be, our young man, Topaz has been transferred to the palace to work as a woodcarver."

Ameth perked up, sat up straight, and seemed revived after his exertion of the stairs. "This is remarkable. How did it come to pass? Is there anything else to report?"

"Yes, the prison master said that if any messages are to be sent to Topaz, they should be addressed to Mondo. I think that was the name he gave. I have no idea who Mondo is, but it must be someone in the palace. We can make inquiries and try to find out who he is. Maybe he will know how this transfer came to be." Jasper was happy to see that his report was bringing renewed hope to his old friend.

"You have done well, Jasper. Remind me what instructions we gave Topaz about contacting us once he was inside the palace."

"Since we do not know how to get messages to Mondo, it is difficult to plan to communicate through him. We told Topaz to watch for our young spy outside the palace gate in the hope that he would find a way to convey information deemed important. Now that we know he is there, we must engage the young fellow again and tell him to keep a watchful eye for our woodcarver."

"This is good news, Jasper. Such good news. It is a beginning. Now we must wait for the next step, whatever that may be. And I will continue my research in the meantime."

*

Topaz loathed the thought of having to carve dragon images for the celebration. He hoped that Mondo would think of decorations that would provide an alternative. In the meantime, Topaz planned an outing outside the palace to obtain the best wood for the projects.

"Commander, I have been ordered to purchase wood and tools for the carvings the Chief Samaran wishes to commission. You are ordered to allow me to pass through the gate and return

201

when I have completed my task." Topaz tried his best to sound mature and authoritative.

"I do not take orders from the likes of you, Abundanite. Prisoner. Bring it in writing signed by the Chief." The Commander of the Gate spat out the words in contempt. "Highly unusual, I say."

Topaz returned a short time later and handed a written document to the commander.

> *To the Commander of the Palace Gate: my servant*
> *woodcarver has been ordered to purchase supplies*
> *from the city of Tenebrose. Please see that the gate*
> *is opened for him to leave and return this day.*
> *The Chief Samaran*

Reluctantly the commander handed back the note and opened the gate. Topaz took a deep breath of air and walked through, a free man, at least free for several hours while he tried to navigate the town. No sooner had he walked outside the gate when he spotted the familiar, young spy sent to watch for him. Topaz walked confidently along the lane until the entrance to the palace could no longer be seen. Turning to the lad, he spoke as one would to a stranger.

"Tell me if you can, young man. Where can I go to buy tools and wood? Is there such a place in this city? If you don't know, can you lead me to someone who does know?

"Yes, sir. I know someone who knows quite well where you should go. Follow me." It was a good thing that Jasper had hired an intelligent boy. Not far from the palace was a market where everything imaginable was bought and sold. The spy led him there, lest someone find it suspicious that he disappear into a private dwelling.

"Off you go. Bring someone back that I can deal with. I will wait here." Topaz did not know if anyone had followed him or if palace guards would be keeping an eye on him.

Topaz waited for some time before an unfamiliar man approached and spoke to him.

"I have been told that you are in need of assistance." A quick wink told Topaz that his advisor was someone he could trust to communicate with Ameth and the others.

"Hello. The name is Topaz, and I am new at the palace. I have been commissioned to create carvings for the celebration that will soon take place. Unfortunately, I have no tools or wood. The Chief Samaran has promised to provide whatever is needed to purchase the items needed. Can you help me?"

"A few questions first, if I may. Oh, my name is Carnelian."

"I will help you in any way that I can. What do you need to know?" asked Topaz.

"I need to know what tools you want and what you are going to carve. And who is the Chief Samaran? I have never heard of that name before."

"Ah, I need an array of different gouges and a mallet." In a much lower voice, "he is on our side. His story is complicated, but he can be trusted. He is also known as Mondo. He is the one who got me reassigned from prison to the palace."

A uniformed guard walked by close enough to overhear the conversation and Topaz quickly changed the subject.

"And you can deliver those tools to the palace tomorrow. I will give the order to have them received by the gate commander."

Carnelian responded in kind, "And the wood, how big must the pieces be?"

"Hmmm," Topaz considered the question and made a quick decision. "I think perhaps I should go with you to the wood yard and pick out the best pieces. I will meet you here tomorrow and we will go together."

"Done. I will meet you tomorrow. If you are unable to come for some reason, send the boy to tell me. He will be waiting at the gate."

There was so much to tell Carnelian, but it would have to wait until they could talk in private. For now, Topaz was thrilled that he had made contact.

CHAPTER 27

THE ARCHIVES

"Wood carver Topaz wishes an audience with the Chief Samaran."

"Bring him in, Gerwin."

Mondo sat at his large, wooden desk that had been richly carved with trees and animals. While the servant was still in the room, he sought to sound official and busy with important tasks.

"Ah, Topaz. Just the man I wish to see. Come and hear my plans." Gerwin exited the room and quietly closed the doors. "Did you make contact?" asked Mondo in a low voice.

"Yes. I met a man named Carnelian. He is the King's man, and will make sure I get the supplies I need to begin my carving, that is, once you decide what it should be."

"I must meet the man, Ameth. Can Carnelian arrange a meeting with him? There are so many questions I have; I believe he may have the answers."

"I will try. He is very old and it would be best if he did not go far from Jasper's home in order to meet you."

"I have so much on my mind. I think I have a plan for the

celebration, but I need to talk to someone who knows the Ultimate Ruler's main weakness," he said barely whispering. "You told me once that his power comes through the object called the Promise that he stole from the High King. If we can take it away from him somehow, perhaps we will be able to destroy his ability to crush the people of the kingdom."

"Until then, what shall I carve?"

"I think it will be a large standing statue of the Ultimate Ruler himself. When I report to him, I will make sure that this is what will make him happy. See if you can get a very tall, broad tree trunk. You will need some larger tools to rough out the shape. Ask Carnelian to help you bring the tree. Put it in a place where you can keep it secret for as long as possible. This will also keep you out of sight in case your presence has drawn undo attention."

"This will be quite a project. I hope I am up to the task."

*

"Magnificent Ultimate Ruler, your Chief Samaran, Mondo wishes a word with you about your celebration." The servant announced the presence of the newest and highest in the regiment of appointed officials.

"Enter! I am anxious to hear how the plans are proceeding." Mondo strode into the rooms with purpose and confidence—traits that always made an impression on the Ruler. "What do you have to show me?"

"Your Rulership," began Mondo, never quite sure how he should address the self-styled leader. "I will lay out before you what I have so far. One concern is for the invitations. It will take time to send out word of a date, have everyone prepare, and then travel to Tenebrose. We need to put the date far enough in advance to be assured that the greatest number of important people will be able to attend."

"Agreed," said the Ruler with furrowed brow and squinting eyes.

"A great amount of food must be grown for the celebration meal. I must assign a large number of people to grow the food, which will also take some months."

"Agreed," he said again with thoughtful nodding of his head. "Though I do not know why you cannot go out and take the food from those who have it."

"Well, I am not sure the citizens of Tenebrose have that much to take. Moving on. A program must be devised. I must know what you want to take place at the ceremony so we can prepare and plan for it." Mondo had a long list of items yet that needed the Ruler's approval. They went through each one until it was finished.

"One more thing," added Malpha. "I want Falgar brought to the palace and placed in the dungeon. I do not want to risk his escaping again. He will be part of the ceremony as I parade his defeated ilk in front of my guests. Once he called himself king of Abundant. Now he is a vanquished shell, no longer able to threaten anyone. They will all see who is above all, victor over all kingdoms." He laughed an evil laugh as he contemplated how it was going to feel to be superior to all known rulers.

"I will see to it right away, your Rulership," said Mondo trying not to show a reaction to the request.

"There are rumors that Falgar has a son. My soldiers have not been able to locate him, but I hear they are close. That would be even better—to have Falgar and his son on display. I will find him yet."

Diamond pretended to ignore Malpha's threat. The mention of a son of Falgar disturbed him. It was a new detail that could disrupt the plans.

"I have one more request as well. Are there records of all the towns and villages in the kingdom so that I may be sure that all the appropriate people are invited from each place?"

"Good question. Ask the Chancellor. This place is too big for me to keep track of all that." He laughed again and added under his breath, "You could probably ask Falgar. He knows his way around here." He waved Mondo away and turned to his drink which was always by his side.

Thoughts were jumping around inside Mondo's head. The stories about Falgar were true. He had been the King of Abundant before he was imprisoned. Imagining the poor man paraded through the ceremony set his mind to work on finding a way to prevent it. It was too degrading. *I must find that room with the archives and records?*

*

Using the archives as an excuse, Mondo found his way from the top floors of the palace all the way to every room on the main floor and below. After a thorough search and not finding anything, he relented and sought the Chancellor's advice.

Ever a suspicious man, the Chancellor was reluctant to hand over the keys. "Can you not just send riders out to tell people to come to the celebration? Why do you have to know of every town and village.?"

"I believe this will be more effective. The Ultimate Ruler wants as many people to attend as possible. We do not want some distant king or mayor to be put off by not officially receiving an invitation, do we?

*

Dust and cobwebs obscured the ledgers stacked one upon the other in the closet-sized room. No one had consulted the archives in years, nor had the room's door even been opened. Mondo brushed aside the offending webs and wondered if the names of places and people may be outdated. Perhaps his efforts were in vain. Choosing a volume, he blew away dust and opened it to the center. Handwritten entries about taxes paid filled each page. He chose another and repeated the process. Slowly a list of towns had been carefully copied into his notes.

Finding a large book from the old kingdom of Abundant piqued Mondo's interest. He carefully examined each page for information about past kings. The handwriting was difficult to read; the pages were worn and faded. Finally, a name riveted his attention. It was a page of birth records. Perhaps some clue could be gained into the identity of the rumored son of Falgar. Whatever he found, Mondo determined to keep the knowledge to himself. He did not fancy anyone else suffering, as the former king would suffer, if Malpha got his way.

Falgar was listed as the son of Misgar, who was the son of Balshar of the House of Andar. On the next page there it was: Tobar, the son of King Falgar, House of Andar. Mondo felt his heart pound as a suspicion began to grow. The name was so similar. Could it be a variation of the name Tofar? The mother was listed as Queen Jebel. Looking around, Mondo found a scrap of parchment and placed it in the record book. A new and frightening dimension to the plan arose.

After hours of searching through the archives, a weary Mondo headed back to his chamber. He had to put Topaz and Malpha out of his mind and get back to the business at hand—invitations.

*

"Scribes over here!" Mondo yelled above the din of dull conversation. "The rest of you will seal, sort, and write addresses." The job of directing everyone who had been recruited to help with the invitations was daunting. He went through the room, "As neatly as you can, scribes. No sloppy work accepted. Do I have to call in a dragon to get this done right?" At least when this part of the job was finished, they could all relax for a while.

Mondo glanced down to the invitations lying on the stack of outgoing mail. He saw the names Lord and Lady Chiselstone and company. Tempted as he was to grab it and tear it up, he resisted. There would be such a large crowd, it might not be difficult to avoid them all. The last thing he needed was to have his parents on hand to identify him as a Bellicosan runaway. Since Violencia was now his step-mother, he wondered if his mother would be allowed to join the group. A wave of sadness swept over him thinking about her and their final parting.

*

A knock at his door, Mondo motioned to Gerwin to answer. "Message for the Chief Samaran from the wood carver." Mondo took the note and opened it quickly. At last, a meeting with Ameth had been arranged.

"I am going to inspect the wood carving being done in the city." Giving last minute instructions to Gerwin, Mondo walked down to the front entrance and summoned his private carriage. Shortly thereafter, he was on his way. Upon arriving, he stepped down in front of an enormous trunk of tree that was partially covered with a blanket. Topaz stood in front to greet him and discuss the project. Mondo was ushered into a shaded area where an old man stepped out of the shadows.

"Master Ameth, this is my friend Mondo, who is now the Chief Samaran at the palace of Malpha."

"I am pleased to meet you at last," said Mondo. "You do not know me, but I think I know you."

"It is a pleasure to meet you as well, Mondo. Or should I call you Chief Samaran?"

"You should call me Diamond."

"I am pleased also to hear that name, for you are a follower of the Prince, as I am."

"I am a follower of the Prince because of you, dear Master Ameth. Did you know that?" said Diamond.

"Ah, tell me the story, for I perceive it is a good one." Surprise registered on the faces of both Topaz and Ameth.

"My former name is Damen Chiselstone of Bellicosa. My home

is the estate of Arcana which I suspect you know about already. Am I correct in that?" asked Diamond.

"You are correct. And how is it you know who I am, since I left that place so many years ago, long before you lived there?"

"I would never have known, if it were not for a humble servant who discovered your secret study room in the back of a closet. She found your diary and kept it. Through reading that, we both came to understand about the Prince. We have wondered through all these months whatever happened to you. How did you escape? Were you still alive? I can hardly believe that I am seeing you at this moment."

"I think we both have stories to tell. Yes, I am alive. But where, may I ask, is the servant you mentioned who found the diary?"

Diamond hesitated before answering. He had not told even Topaz about this relationship. "Her name is Jewel. She was my mother's servant. Through a series of unusual circumstances, we became acquainted. She could not read the book and asked me to help her. To shorten the story somewhat, she will be in Tenebrose soon, I hope. I sent Lord Crumblestone to bring her and two others here."

"Do I understand correctly that she is no longer a servant?"

"You do understand. She is actually my wife. We became separated when I was mistaken for a criminal and sent to Tenebrose to serve as a slave in the prison."

"You have risen significantly in stature since then, I see. You must be a very talented young man. With such an important position, I believe the Prince has placed you in a key location. You are planning Malpha's celebration. What do you think will happen? Do you have a plan?"

"I do. Nothing is certain yet, but I believe it will be a time when we can take back the Promise and deprive Malpha of his power over the people. I will need your help. I want you to alert every follower of the Prince you can find and urge them all to come to the celebration."

"We will do as you say and spread the word."

"Topaz, we must conclude our business here before I go back to the palace. I must tell you that when you meet Jewel you will be surprised." Diamond slapped Topaz on the back and laughed.

CHAPTER 28

REUNION

"Who goes there?" yelled the Gate Commander.

"It is the carriage of Lord Crumblestone, returning at the command of the Chief Samaran."

The heavy gate swung open and the horses lunged forward, knowing that they were almost home. Down the long driveway and around to the front of the palace, they had brought the journey to its end. Four faces peered out the windows with wide, alert eyes and gaping mouths.

"Where are we?" asked Gem. "This is very strange. Why are we here?

"This whole trip has been a delicious nightmare," said Ruby. "I keep wondering if I will wake up back in Gazrak."

"I just hope that someone here will explain, and then tell me where Diamond is being held. I so long to see him, to know if he is safe," added Jewel.

Rista said nothing. She was in awe of the new surroundings and feeling very timid and fearful. She held on to Gem and would not let go.

They all stepped down from the carriage with their new belongings placed on the steps. Servants came out, picked up the trunks, and hurried inside. The four felt constrained to stay with the baggage so they followed the servants through the high doorway. Inside the front hall, darkness overtook them.

"Please come this way." They could not see the man's face well for his dark complexion blended with the shadows. Dumbly, they followed up a broad stairway and down another hallway. Finally, they stood before a set of doors and the servant knocked. Another servant inside the doors opened and brought the guests into the room.

"Where are we?" asked Gem of the servant.

"This is the chamber of the Chief Samaran, Sir. He will be with you in just a moment. Please wait here."

Gem whispered to the others, "He called me Sir. It must be the new clothes." They all agreed.

The servant turned to face Jewel. "The Chief Samaran will see you one at a time. First will be the Lady Jewel. Right this way."

"What?" stammered Gem. "Lady Jewel? He must have us confused with someone else. I knew it. Jewel is no lady! Are you going to go in by yourself?" Jewel frowned and whispered, "I am a goddess, remember?"

"Silence. The Chief Samaran has commanded it. You will wait here while he interviews the lady." The servant led Jewel into an adjoining room and closed the door.

"Oh, what now? Have we jumped out of the cooking pot and landed in the fire?" Ruby was more distressed than Gem. "What will he say to her? Will he make her a slave again? What is going on?"

*

Jewel stepped into the room and saw the Chief Samaran's back turned to her. He was dressed in a long flowing robe of fine silken material. On his head was a hat, the style of which Jewel had never seen. It was very royal.

"You wish to see me, Master Chief Samaran?"

Diamond turned around to face her with a huge grin on his face. He raised his hand to silence her surprise as she stood in complete shock. He rushed to her side and they embraced. "Is it really you? How? Why? I do not understand? Lord Crumblestone said you were in prison."

"I was a servant in the prison for many weeks. Due to some strange circumstances, I was promoted to Prison Master. Then I came here with Lord Crumblestone, and before I knew it, I was promoted to Chief Samaran. I do not understand it myself. I sent Crumblestone to free you from the Gazraks and bring you to Tenebrose."

"Why did you keep us in suspense all this time? I was very worried."

"No one here knows who I really am. That is, except Crumblestone. He is from Bellacosa, so it did not take long for him to do some digging and find out my identity. He has agreed to keep it a secret. As for you, you are now Lady Jewel, and no one can say anything different. The Chief Samaran has proclaimed it."

"You must tell the others. We have all been worried, thinking of you in a dark prison, suffering. It was most distressing."

"I am sorry but I had no way to communicate with you. I still have some things to settle with Gem. I assume he awaits on the other side of the door."

"One new development has occurred. He is now married to Rista, and she is here as well."

"How did that happen? Did Furcula allow that?"

213

"Gem can tell you that story. You must believe me that he has suffered from the hand of Furcula, as well. Do not be too hard on him."

Diamond summoned his servant once again. "Send in Lady Ruby next," he commanded. The servant complied, calling out, "Lady Ruby, you may now enter."

Ruby slowly walked through the high doorway, hearing the door close firmly behind her. She stared into the beaming faces of Jewel and Diamond and froze. For several moments she could not speak, and then almost screamed.

"What! How? Who?"

"Well, do not look so shocked. Did I not tell you I would be great some day?" said Diamond laughing at himself and the dazed woman before him.

"No! It cannot be. Has my delicious nightmare just turned into the sweetest of daydreams?"

"I will explain all in time. Right now, I want you both to sit quietly over at the side of the room. I need to make my brother suffer just a bit for his abandoning me to the good folks at Wanderdown." Diamond whispered in the ear of his servant and sent him to fetch Gem and Rista. As they entered the room, the servant left them and closed the door. The Chief Samaran turned his back to the visitors.

Disguising his voice he growled at them saying, "Who are you and why have you come to this city?"

"My Lord, Chief Samaran, you bid us to come before you. We do not know why. I was recently rescued from a band of criminals. Lord Crumblestone told us you wished to help us. We could certainly use some help."

"Help? Like you helped your brother? Is that the help you want?"

"No, indeed, Lord Chief. I did not help my brother when he needed me. I am most woefully sorry. We heard that he is in prison here in this city. If we could please see him, help him, find a way to release him, we would be so grateful."

"So you want him set free? Will you pay for his crimes? Will you serve his term in prison so he can go free?"

Gem's face hardened. He looked at Rista who frowned mournfully. "Yes, I will even go to prison if he can be released."

"Good. You realize that you are in my power. I can do anything I please with you. I am your LEADER," said Diamond with emphasis on the last word. "It will be as you wish. Your brother is set free at this very moment." Diamond turned to face Gem and Rista with tears in his eyes. The five flew together in a great hug. Tears flowed. Sounds like wailing of relief and joy came from Gem and Diamond as they embraced.

"I did not believe you. You were right. The Prince has made you leader over the rest of us. And to such an extent that I would never have believed possible. Will you ever forgive me?" Gem cried.

"You are forgiven. We are together again. Let us celebrate.

*

That evening great platters of fruits and vegetables arrived for their meal. A large side of bobbit accompanied by the finest of wines rendered the guests fully satiated.

"You must all sleep here tonight. We must plan where each of you will best be located so as not to arouse suspicion. Only one other person here knows who I am. He is sworn to secrecy. But I remind you, Lord Crumblestone does not know of our allegiance to the High King. Our goal right now is to prepare for the celebration of his rule over the whole kingdom. Only the Prince knows what is in store for him."

Diamond set up sleeping arrangements for each guest in his vast chamber, then gathered them once more for one final talk before they all slept.

"I have good news. You know that I worked in the prison for many weeks. While I was there, I met a young man who had been imprisoned for some petty crime—only the prison master

215

seemed to think it was not so petty. He is a follower of the High King and has met the Prince!"

The four listeners smiled and shared with one another what a good sign that was. "Is he still in prison?" asked Gem.

"There is so much to tell I hardly know where to begin. No, I was able to get him sent to the palace to work in preparation for the celebration. He is working as a wood carver. I gave him a large project that will keep him busy for some time. Anyway, he introduced me to someone." Diamond's words tumbled out like a mountain stream. "It is none other than the man who wrote the diary many years ago, and whose wisdom we have been encouraged by all this time."

Three of the listeners jumped with surprise and joy.

"Who is this man?" asked Rista.

"His name is Ameth, short for Amethyst. He is very old now. He was the man who had the secret room. Jewel found his diary and we have treasured it for all these months. I hope you still have it in your possession, Jewel. I told him about us, though not all the details. He was very pleased that his book helped us. I am hoping that we may all meet soon."

"Oh, he is alive then? And he is here in Tenebrose? I have many questions for him," cried Jewel with great enthusiasm. She rummaged in her valise and brought out the tattered book. Holding it close to her heart she proclaimed, "I thought we would never know him. How thrilling it will be to meet him and hear him speak to us."

"That may happen very soon, my dear Jewel. I fear it is not safe for you here in the palace. I will send you and Ruby to stay where Ameth is living for a time. You see, this city is not friendly to former Abundanites. I believe that is who you are, Jewel. Now the city is called Tenebrose, but it was once the small kingdom of Abundant. When Malpha, the Ultimate Ruler, captured the king and all the inhabitants, he renamed the city. That very same king has been in prison all these years. I have seen him myself. Abundanites are unique in their dark complexion and hair. I have now seen many who look very much like you, and most of them have been made slaves."

"But, Diamond, I want to be near you," cried Jewel.

"You will be safe with Jasper and Ameth. There is great risk in my position. If I fail, I could end up back in prison, or worse! I do not want to risk your life as well." Jewel reached out and held Diamond tightly. "You must go at first light tomorrow. Ameth will be happy to hear your story, and you his."

"What about us?" asked Gem. Rista gripped his arm with both hands and tensed to hear Diamond's answer.

"I have work for you, Gem. I need someone among the workers around the palace who can keep me informed about what is being said by them. The more ears, the better. Rista may go with Jewel and Ruby. I fear that you do not know enough about the ways of this city to make a good servant. This is a house of darkness. I would rather not worry about your safety here."

Rista did not understand completely, but she did realize that she and Gem would be separated. Tears filled her eyes.

"Go and be safe, Rista. Everything will be fine. You will see." said Gem, trying to comfort her.

"We will talk more in the morning. Get some sleep now. We will have a busy day."

∗

Diamond lay awake trying not to disturb Jewel or the others as he stared into the dark room. A dull luminescence grew and glowed more brightly. He raised his head from the pillow to determine if he was really awake. The images became clear and distinct. He saw the Prince; bright, alive with joy, and waving. Slowly the face morphed into that of Falgar; transformed from the dark, miserable man and, instead, looking happy, victorious, and strong. What did it mean?

CHAPTER 29

JEWEL'S STORY

"Wake up," whispered Diamond to the sleeping guests. "It is time to go."

Slowly they all rose and readied themselves for the journey. All except Gem. He and Rista looked glum, but he was determined to see her off in a good mood. She wrapped a dark cloak around her shoulders and pulled the hood over her orange hair. Ruby had taught her how to fashion it into manageable twists and pin it on top of her head.

Ruby, whose girth was very much reduced after months of hard work and small rations, donned her newest gown. Wishing to be as regal as possible for her departure from the palace, she took as much care as possible with her grooming.

"Jewel!" scolded Ruby. "Your hair is a wild tangle. Do you not want to look your best to make your exit. What if someone sees you and thinks you are a forest waif? Come, let me help you."

"It has been so long that it mattered to anyone. I never have been very good at making my hair behave." She handed Ruby a recently acquired brush and the older woman went to work on the mass of dark, curly hair. It did not take long to braid and twist every stray strand into place. Jewel smiled her approval.

"Hurry now. We must leave. You both look beautiful," Diamond teased. "I will take you as far as the wood carver's shed. From there, Jasper will see that you get to his home. He should be waiting for you even now."

*

Lord Crumblestone's borrowed carriage pulled up in front of a space between two prominent buildings that stood close to a narrow street. In the yard, logs of various sizes lay stacked in orderly piles. Beyond those was a tall shape covered over with a rough blanket. Diamond, who had ridden up next to the driver, jumped down and beckoned the four to follow him.

"Topaz, are you here? Come and meet my family." Diamond realized that he had not used that word before to describe his wife, brother, sister-in-law, and brother's mother before. Jewel looked at him and smiled.

A tall, slender figure appeared in the early light. Jewel gasped to see that he was dark like she was. His features looked familiar, yet strange. Under his rimmed hat, wisps of dark curly hair poked out. Jewel had never spent much time peering in a looking glass, but she recognized the long, curved nose and brown, almond-shaped eyes.

"I thought you would be surprised. Did I not mention that my friend Topaz is from an Abundanite family, probably like you are?"

"I have never met anyone like me before," Jewel sputtered.

Topaz did a double take and proclaimed, "You were

219

right, Mondo. I am surprised. Where is your family? Who are your mother and father? Maybe we are distant relatives."

"I had a father once, long ago. I do not remember much." Jewel's face turned sad. Topaz sought to comfort her saying, "We have that much in common."

"Jasper is sending a carriage for you ladies," he continued. "He should be here any minute. Here he is now."

"Take heart, Jewel. You will meet other Abundanites, so prepare yourself to be amazed again and again." Diamond led them to the carriage and saw them safely on their way. The three men waved good-bye.

"Topaz, I think it would be wise for you to stay out of sight as best you can. Just in case." said Diamond.

"Just in case of what?" asked Topaz.

"I hear rumblings of threat from Malpha that could mean trouble for any young, formerly-Abundanite men. It is possible that you could get caught up in that, so be careful."

"It is a good thing my work is here then. I have much to do yet to finish the project."

"Good. And now, to my brother. Come. We will find work for you."

*

"Ah, it is Lady Jewel and her company," observed Jasper as he welcomed the visitors. Jewel shook her head in embarrassment and blushed.

"I am your host, Jasper." He led them along a corridor, up a flight of stairs, and into a sitting room. The chill of early morning was still in the air. Jasper went to the window and pushed aside the parchment blinds, allowing the sun to shine into the room.

"There now. That is more like it. I know you have not had time to eat yet. A meal will be brought right away. I hope it will be to your liking. We have bread—baked this morning, butter, sweet jam, and cheese."

Ruby's stomach was growling. Her mouth watered just hearing about the anticipated repast. "Yes, that sounds much to my liking!" she blurted out.

"Master Ameth will join you. You will enjoy his company, I am sure. I am told that there is a connection between Lady Jewel and Master Ameth. Is that true?" asked Jasper.

"It is the most amazing coincidence; all here have benefitted from the Master's wisdom by way of his diary. I am very anxious to meet him."

"Here he is now. Come in, Master Ameth. You are just in time for a meal with our very special guests. This is Lady Jewel, Diamond's wife. And this is Ruby and Rista—all related somehow. I look forward to hearing about how that is."

"My dears, it is a great pleasure. I have to say, I am a bit shocked at you, Lady Jewel. You are so like my friend, Topaz. I had forgotten how Abundanites have such similar features."

Tears came into Jewel's eyes again as she expressed her deep gratitude to Master Ameth. "Your diary kept us believing when we almost despaired of ever being free again." She took his hand and kissed it bowing deeply before him.

"My dear, this must be a good story. I am all ears. But first, I shall eat of this fragrant bread I have been smelling. Hmmm. Delicious!"

"And I want to hear your story as well. How did you come to write the diary? How did you escape from Bellacosa? Where have you been all these years?"

"One story at a time! I will tell one, and then you tell me one. To start, my older brother was the master of Arcana after our parents died. Neither of us married. He was a gambler and I was a scholar.

Being the oldest, my brother managed the affairs of the estate. He foolishly gambled and spent until there was nothing left. I, on the other hand, chose to isolate myself in my secret room and ignore his behavior.

Because of my love of knowledge, I decided to investigate the history of Bellacosa and surrounding kingdoms. I went here and there gathering interesting stories—I have always liked stories—until the day I heard about the High King who lives in the great City of Light, Illumah. Amazed, I learned about his son, the Prince, who had been sent to wrest away the kingdom from a usurper, Malpha. Yes, that was many years ago. Malpha and I are both very old, but I believe he is older still!

My brother, informed of my findings about the true and rightful High King, tried to kill me. Following a different king was the path he chose. He was serious; I was in danger. Escaping over the mountain, I found the rock under which one could not be seen. Later, I returned home hoping that my brother's temper had settled down. However, I kept my studies secret, partitioning off a section of my quarters to create my study.

I wrote the message on the wall to remind myself of where my help was to be found. I kept the diary and wrote all I had learned about the Prince, and how he helped me escape from my murderous brother. Unfortunately, he only tried again, and I left for a final time, never to return."

Ameth took several more bites of bread and jam, savoring each morsel. "And now it is your turn. How did you get mixed up with that fellow, Diamond? A remarkable young man, by the way."

Ruby and Rista sat on the edge of their chairs as the stories unfolded. Having never fully heard Jewel's story, they now paid close attention.

"My earliest memory is of being with my father. I do not know where that was. It was a room high up in a building. I could look out the window and see trees far below, and the sea sparkling in the distance. 'Julen,' said my father. 'You will always have me. I will keep you safe.'

"Your name was Julen?" asked Ameth.

"At that time, I was called Julen. After that, men came in the middle of the night. It was terrible. I still have nightmares about being wrapped up in a blanket and carried away. I do not know what happened to my father. I never saw him again.

The next thing I knew, I was standing in the slave market in Bellacosa with ugly faces before me, glaring at me and frightening me. Lady Chiselstone stepped forward and led me away. She looked so beautiful in that moment. Her three children were with her; one in particular I was very attracted to—his eyes were so kind and sympathetic. I never forgot."

Ruby shifted uncomfortably in her chair as she imagined the small child, frightened and alone. Why had she despised this poor girl so much all that time?

"I was made a slave in the house. Scrubbing floors was my job. I only saw that sweet face as I looked up from the wet, stone slabs. I imagined how it would feel if he would smile at me or look with sympathy once more. But he did not."

"She is talking about Damon Chiselstone, known to you as Diamond," added Ruby. "Get to the good part, girl."

"Oh, so he was the son of the Lord and you were the lowly slave. Who looked after you? Were you completely on your own as such a small child?" asked Ameth.

"I had a friend. She was also a slave, an old one, whose duties in the house were limited for some reason. She took me in and was like a grandmother to me. If it were not for her, I would not have survived in that place. Her name was Ralda, though in her final days she told me her real name was Emerald. I think perhaps she knew the Prince, though she never did mention him to me."

"Her final days?" asked Ameth sadly. "Did she die?"

"Yes. Right before we escaped from Bellacosa,"

Ameth appeared to experience some deep emotion. His voice became husky and broken. "Did she ever tell you her story?"

223

"No. Only, at the end, she said some strange things. She left me a gift, very precious. It was wrapped in a dirty cloth and encrusted with years of dust and grime. She must have been afraid someone would take it from her. After her death, I found it under her bed."

"Was it an emerald necklace?" asked Ameth.

"Yes, how did you know?"

"I do know. What a small world we live in. That you would know my lovely Emerald. I long to hear more of her life, though it pains me to hear it."

"How did you know her? Was she a slave in the house when you lived there?" asked Jewel.

"It is true. That is one part of my story I usually prefer not to tell. It is difficult at best. I loved her. She was a slave and I was a wealthy master. We could not even acknowledge that we were acquainted, let alone have any kind of future together. We wanted to run away, and we did. My brother chased us to the top of the mountain behind Bellacosa. I hid under the rock, but she was afraid, turned back, and was captured. I returned later to try again. They banished her to a locked room. I could not even see her. That is when I left for the last time. My brother was very angry and no doubt took it out on her."

"That is very sad." Jewel again reached out to touch Ameth's hand and comfort him. "How did she come to have the Emerald necklace?"

"I told her about the Prince. She believed me. I gave her a necklace with a green piece of glass. It cost me very little but it was pretty. She liked it well enough but could not wear it. What does a slave do with a pretty necklace? After she learned about the Prince, she said that the glass sparkled more brightly somehow. She seemed to think that the Prince would turn the glass into a real emerald. It was crazy, or so I thought. You say she left the necklace with you? Do you still have it?"

"I do." Jewel searched through her bag and brought out a

wrapped parcel. "I have not been able to wear it for some time." Slowly she unwound the cloth until the shining gold and emerald lay before them. Everyone stared at it, speechless.

Holding it up to the sunlight, Jewel began to rub the green surface. The rays bounced off the smooth facets and created a sprinkle of lights on the opposite wall. The words of the promise began to appear—safe, forgiven, cherished.

"Can this be the same necklace? I tell you, it did not look like this before," said Ameth with mouth open wide in awe. "How did this happen?"

"That is another story, but it all began after I found the diary!"

"Yes, how did you find my study?" asked Ameth.

"I was sent to put clothes away in the closet of the lady's apartment. Was that your living quarters when you lived there?" she asked Ameth.

"Yes, that is where I lived then."

"The closet was very full of gowns, sashes, cloaks, and such. In the light of my lamp, I found a set of hinges, and it was not long before I determined that there was a secret door behind the clothing."

"The mistress had never seen it before, and neither had I," Ruby added.

"My curiosity burned until I could resist no longer. When both the mistress and Bina were sleeping, I opened the door and found the dark stairs leading to your study room. Books had been thrown about, and the lamp had been smashed against the wall. A chair lay in pieces."

"Harold, no doubt. He had such a temper," said Ameth.

"Heavy with dust, a tapestry hung on the wall. When I lifted the edge to shake the dust, I saw the message, 'Cry out to the One'. Such a strange writing; I did not understand what it meant. As I inspected the books on the floor, I found your diary and decided to try to read it. Afraid of being found in this secret place, I took the book and retreated back to the apartment. My reading skills were very poor. I kept the book in the hope that someday I could decipher its message."

"You kept it even though you could not read it?"

"I was sure it would reveal some hidden story. Why the secret room? Why the destruction? Why the message under the tapestry? It was utterly intriguing."

"How did you finally read it then?"

"I will tell you after the story of our 'crime' and our escape," answered Jewel, wrinkling her nose in a way that assured the listeners that an exciting story remained to be heard.

When Jewel came to the part about her dream, she was careful to describe how she had fallen asleep holding the necklace, still in its dirt-encrusted state.

"I did not know I was dreaming. It was so real." She went on to tell of meeting the silent stranger in the dark. Transformed by the sparkling lightshow of promises, Jewel then described her awakening to the cold reality of the cave.

"Tears were streaming down my face. I did not want it to end. I wanted to stay in that warm, loving embrace forever."

"That is where I come in," interrupted Ruby. "I woke up and could hardly believe my eyes. She was wearing that necklace around her neck, and it shone and sparkled in glittering gold and emerald. I knew right away that something powerful had taken place."

Looking somewhat skeptical, Jewel added, "Ruby, whose name is really Rubina, did not believe me right away when I tried to tell her about the dream. She will have to tell her own story."

"Well, it is true. Desperation pushes a person to say things they do not mean at times."

"We *were* quite desperate," laughed Jewel.

Ameth reached for and held the necklace in his hand. As he caressed the precious jewel, tears welled in his eyes. Jewel reached over to touch his hand again, "I miss her too."

Between Jewel and Ruby, many happy hours of storytelling passed. Ameth listened carefully, entranced by the drama and purposefulness of every event. One final question brought Jewel back to the beginning.

"Tell me again about your father. Do you remember anything else about him?"

CHAPTER 30

FALGAR'S SECRET

Creaking wheels alerted the Commander of the Gate that a carriage approached. Unlike all others that came through the entrance to the palace, this one looked like a moving cage. Inside, sat a lone figure, head bowed, shoulders slumped.

"King Falgar, is it?" the commander asked the driver. "I heard he was being sent here. It must be for the big celebration."

The carriage continued up the driveway to the rear entrance of the palace. Armed guards unlocked the barred door, pulled the captive down to the ground, and pushed him into the dark interior of the building. A long, descending stairwell led to the dungeon. Falgar stared down into the blackness and dreaded whatever was to come next. Bypassing the dark hole, guards prodded him onward to a room on the main floor.

A voice from within the room instructed the guards, "Leave us now. I will interview the prisoner before the Ultimate

Ruler is to see him." It was Diamond, known only to Falgar as Mondo.

"Falgar," he said, speaking as quietly as he could. "Remember me? Mondo. My title now is Chief Samaran. Listen and please believe me. I am working hard to make sure no harm comes to you. Malpha will try to humiliate you and hold you up as an example of his ascendancy to power and your submission to his authority. Do not fear. We will rescue you yet."

"Why would you do this for me? Who am I to you?"

Diamond responded in a whisper, "I would do this for the High King and his son, the Prince. It is he whom we wish to see rise to power again."

"I serve only the High King and his son. I will never give that up, no matter what Malpha does to me," said Falgar fiercely.

"I rejoice to hear that."

"How do I know I can believe you? Are you not here serving that beast?"

"I am here because I brought you back after the prison guard uprising. Malpha thinks I am a genius for that. However, I am here to serve only the High King. Here, look at this." He reached into a pocket and pulled out a large diamond. "Look inside and see the power of the King."

Falgar held the rock up to his eye and peered into it. "I see that you are telling the truth. I trust you."

"I am named for this stone. Call me Diamond, for that is the name the Prince gave me."

"Diamond. A strange name for a strange young man."

"Malpha says he has news of the whereabouts of your son. I have seen the archive. I know that you did have a son named Tobar. We both know of just such a young man by the name of Tofar. We do not know who he really is, but I believe he is safe where I have located him for now. Malpha may be bluffing, or he may be about to capture your son. Be prepared."

"I sent my wife and son far away beyond the reach of Malpha. How could he now be where that monster can find him?"

"He has grown up and has a mind of his own. He wants to know who his father is, and he has no idea it could be you. He has left his mother and traveled far from his home."

"It cannot be him. It must not be."

"It is time for you to come before Malpha. I will be there as well. Be strong."

The Chief Samaran called for the guards to escort Falgar to his next interview. In rags and filth, he walked through to an anteroom where they waited for the Ultimate Ruler to make his appearance.

With an entourage of courtiers, Malpha slowly approached. Looking over the small crowd, Diamond saw Mistress Drain hovering near the ruler, smirking confidently as she directed her gaze directly at him.

Malpha seated himself on an ornate stool while a servant spread his heavy train out behind him.

"Bow down, slug," commanded the ruler. A guard shoved Falgar to the floor. "We meet again. How long has it been this time? Two years maybe? I think we will have better luck this time. Do you wonder why?"

"I serve the High King," Falgar spit out.

Malpha fell back temporarily before taking a quick drink from a small flask in his hand. He lurched forward again and yelled, "I will get what I want. You will see. I know that you have a son. I have tracked him down and he is here in Tenebrose. In fact, I am about to arrest him, and soon he will join you in the dungeon. See how you feel when you see your son suffering alongside you."

Falgar was silent.

"I will know where your treasure is before the celebration or...or dire consequences will result!"

Tension hung in the air as both men imagined the threat of 'dire consequences'. Both Malpha and Falgar knew that death was not an option, as he had not been able to kill any servant of the High King for a very long time. In frustration, Malpha rose and retreated to more stately parts of the palace. He had to come up with something dire enough to make Falgar disclose his most guarded secrets.

"Rise," commanded the guard. The Chief Samaran followed behind as Falgar was led away, down into the bleak, damp dungeon. Before disappearing behind locks and bars, Falgar looked at Diamond with an understanding look that said, *Keep him safe.*

*

Aching muscles greeted Topaz as he rose from his bed after a restless night. His temporary home—a mere shed in the back of the wood yard—was far from comfortable. Stretching his arms over his head, he loosened the sinews and joints that were stressed from the unusual work of pounding a chisel into hard wood. He set about cooking a meager meal of porridge and bread, the latter a gift from Jasper.

The statue of Malpha was coming along well, even though Topaz had no idea what the man looked like. As long as he looked regal and strong, everyone would be happy. The work was challenging, but boredom crept in, and doubt about his usefulness was a constant thought.

The normal sounds of morning accompanied Topaz as he cleaned up his cooking space and began to move in the direction of the never-ending project. Just as his calloused hands picked up the mallet, a clamor of horses and people altered the atmosphere. It drew closer until, in a cloud of dust, uniformed guards stormed the grounds and grabbed him. Dropping the mallet to struggle, he protested the attack.

"What have I done? I work for the Chief Samaran. You cannot arrest me." His pleas did nothing to stop the silent

231

guards from roughly pushing Topaz towards a horse that waited in the street. "I have done nothing wrong!"

*

"Chief, the Ultimate Ruler has ordered the detainment of Abundanite men, one of whom may be Falgar's son-in-hiding. One of them is the boy, Topaz."

Diamond heard the message from his servant who had heard it being passed around the palace. Without pausing to finish the documents he had been writing, he walked hurriedly down into the main hall. Another servant pointed in the direction of a large hall that was often used to interrogate errant citizens. Arriving at the entrance, the Chief Samaran straightened his garments and came before a lineup of young men who stood at attention, waiting for the Ultimate Ruler to come. Diamond located Topaz in the group and bristled at the notion that Malpha would use this to manipulate Falgar.

The young men had many physical similarities—dark complexion, black hair of varying lengths and degrees of curl. All were tall and slim. How would Malpha distinguish one from another to determine who might be the son of Falgar? The thought that possibly, none of them would qualify set Diamond's mind at ease.

Malpha entered wearing long, heavy robes of a rich material.

"Chief Samaran, see who I have rounded up. These are suspect, do you not agree? Each one has been observed and bears resemblance to Falgar. I am glad you are here to help me test them."

"Your Rulership, one of these is a servant of mine who has been commissioned to carve a statue in your honor. Surely, you will excuse him from this test and allow him to finish his work for the celebration," Diamond said, hoping his admonition would be sufficient to see Topaz freed.

"Never! If he passes the test, he may go immediately to

232

finish his task." The ruler rubbed his hands together with glee in the pleasure of this new game.

The first of the men stepped forward.

"What is your name and what is your mother's name?" asked the Chancellor loudly.

"My name is Bimal and my mother's name is Ransela," replied the man.

"What is your FATHER's name?" asked the Chancellor emphasizing the key word.

"Zimar of the house of Wilnel," replied the man.

For the final question, the Chancellor directed his gaze to all the candidates, "Where is your home?"

"On the hill called Vassel in Tenebrose," was the reply.

He passes the test. Let him go," commanded Malpha. "Next!"

Another stepped forward with the same resulting replies. "I am the brother of Bimal."

"Let him go. Next!"

Several more gave full and clear answers. Topaz saw his turn coming and wondered what reply he should give. The voices of his mother and her counselor came back to him, *Tell no one who you are or risk certain harm!* The names he could fake, but what would he say as to the location of his home? If he said the same as the others, they would know it was a lie. No one there knew him and could vouch for him being a citizen of Tenebrose. There was Jasper's house. What was the name of the location? Panic seized him.

Nervously he stepped forward when the others had finished.

"What is your name and your mother's name?" The Chancellor and the others in the room grew bored with the rote responses, suspecting that this was but another of the Ruler's games. The Ruler leaned forward in anticipation of the final answers.

233

"My name is Topaz and my mother's name is Magtel—he made up the name and hoped it was good enough to fool them. The others in line flinched and looked at him askance.

"What is your father's name and where is your home?"

Topaz knew he could not fool them with a phony name so he blurted out the truth, "I do not know my father's name for he died when I was very young."

The audience suddenly woke up and paid closer attention.

"Where is your home?"

"I am from a city far from here. I doubt if you have heard of it." The looks on everyone's faces revealed to Topaz that his answer may not have served him well.

"And what is the name of that city, young Topaz?" screamed Malpha.

Topaz's hesitation spoke the sad truth before he could utter a word. "Clovis…ville."

"You lie!" the ruler screamed again. "Take him away. Regardless of whether or not you are the son of Falgar, I declare you to be that very man. You do not know your father. He is here in this prison and you shall be there with him."

Diamond was horrified. They had not prepared for this turn of events. Was Topaz the son of Falgar? How would they ever know for sure? And what would happen to him now?

"Congratulations," said Diamond in a flat voice. "You have found your man, regardless of who he really is."

"Precisely the point. You may go now and take your wood carver man with you. I am looking forward to seeing that statue you promised."

Diamond turned to leave and hurriedly ushered out all the young men before the ruler could observe that no wood-carving servant was among them.

*

The word spread rapidly that the wood carver had been taken by guards and did not return. Jasper's spy soon heard and

234

took the news to Ameth and the others.

"What do you think has happened to him," asked Jewel.

"I fear that his true identity has been found out, my child."

"What do you mean? What is his true identity? Is he not just Topaz from a distant island in the kingdom?" Ruby further inquired.

"I suspected since the first day he came to my home, that he is the true, lost son of Falgar, King of the former kingdom of Abundance." Ameth brought out the amulet and held it before the group.

"What is it?" they all wanted to know.

"This, my children, is the Komatal. I had only heard of its existence before Topaz arrived in Betwixt. I realized when I saw it that the innkeeper who stole it knew what it is. And indeed, it is the glorious and powerful amulet of the King. This was the preeminent symbol of the kingdom. When the King was wearing this amulet, it was said to have great power. That part, I do not know for sure. It was only what people said. The fact that Topaz did not know what it is speaks only to his family's ignorance of its importance."

"If you knew this, why did you let him take on this dangerous assignment?" Jasper asked.

"It had to be," Ameth replied. "This was the only way he would find his father, even if it was dangerous. The Prince took away his fear so that he would be brave and face even the evil ruler of the kingdom."

"Will they put Topaz back in prison?"

"Malpha must have some evil purpose in taking him captive. However, I perceive that the Prince also has a purpose, as we shall see."

*

Diamond paced back and forth in his chamber. Driven by a fear for Topaz on one hand, he was also driven by the need to know for sure his young friend's true identity on the other.

Was he the son of Falgar, or were all these facts about him just coincidences?

Perhaps there were clues in the archives. Diamond left his chamber and walked casually through the palace as if he was in no hurry. Inside, he was bursting with curiosity. Having been in the archive closet before, it was not difficult to unlock the door once again. It did not take him long to find the ancient volume in which the birth accounts had been recorded. The bookmark facilitated an easy opening to the right page. Diamond read again the lineage of Falgar and the birth of Tobar. He turned the page to see if any additional information could be found. On the next page there was a record of another birth, a son; then a record of a death, the same son. So Falgar had not lied. He did have a son that had died in infancy. There were no more records after that, only blank pages.

About to give up, Diamond began to close the book when he thought to look on the pages before. In very small, and seemingly insignificant print at the bottom of the previous page, was a brief sentence. He read it carefully, taking in every word. At the thought of the implications of that sentence, his knees buckled beneath him. In that moment he felt like he had been run over by wild horses. Falgar did indeed have a secret he had never told anyone. More than hidden treasure, more than a lost son.

CHAPTER 31

THE KOMATAL

Darkness and gloom engulfed Topaz as he stepped down into the dungeon of the palace. Being imprisoned had a familiar feel, but this time the stakes were higher. His journey had brought him to this end; the search for his father may be over. What were the chances that Falgar and he were related? Topaz intended to find out.

A tiny crack of light beamed down from a small opening to the outside world high in the wall of the stone room. Once his eyes became accustomed to the dim light, he observed that Falgar sat in the shadows not far from him, waiting and silent.

"Is that you? Well, here we are together at last," Topaz offered trying to keep the mood light.

"I would have preferred that it never come to this." replied the dull voice of Falgar.

"I suppose you know why I am here. They think I am your son. How they determined that was a bit arbitrary. I come from an island far away and I do not know the name of my father. That makes me your long-lost son? I am sorry if this farce is an offense. It is possible that we are related, but a son?"

"What is your mother's name?" asked Falgar.

"I called her mother, of course. Her Chief Counsellor and our household servants called her Mistress. But I believe her name is Jebel. Does that sound familiar?"

Falgar was silent again for a moment before he asked, "Why did you come? Why could you not stay in your island home and never know what had become of your inheritance in the kingdom of Abundant? Is this what you wanted?"

"My mother and her counsellors filled my heart with fear the whole of my life. We had a peaceful existence there, to be sure. But that was not enough. I do not need only peace and ease in my life. I need to know who I am and why I am alive. I need to serve some purpose that is higher than myself. If that means danger, then so be it. I was plagued with the voices of warning and dread. But that has changed. That life-suffocating fear is no more, and I am here because I am no longer afraid."

"Do you still have the amulet?"

"Yes. You remembered that I told you about it. I do not have it with me. I was warned not to carry it, so I have entrusted it to a friend. Is that important? Do you know something about it?"

"Yes, it is important. Do you trust your friend?"

"With my life!"

"That is good. The amulet is called the Komatal. It is very valuable. It is to be worn only by the rightful King and sovereign of Abundant. If you wore it, it was for only one reason. You, my son, are the heir to the throne."

Topaz choked and coughed, holding his hand to his throat. His heart pounded in his chest and his stomach felt like it was full of squirming squirrels.

"What?"

Silence fell between them as both men realized the truth.

"I said, you are my son." Falgar's voice cracked with emotion. Tears formed in his eyes. "I am, or was, the King." he said.

Topaz could not speak. He was not sure if he should hug his father, or bow down to the King of Abundant.

"You are, or were, Prince Tobar. For your safety, your mother must have changed your name. And now, it is Topaz! Prince Topaz, of the land that no longer exists. I am sorry you ever had to learn the sad truth."

"Father?" Topaz swallowed hard as he uttered the strange word. "Father?" he repeated it just to hear himself say that word.

Falgar rose, placed his hands on Topaz's shoulders and solemnly said, "Tobar, son of Falgar of the House and lineage of Andar, King of Abundant in all its glory. That is what I wanted for you, and can never give you."

Topaz was overcome with emotion.

"Father, I have an amendment to that statement, if I may. Topaz of the Prince, of the High King who reigns in the City of Light, formerly known as Tobar, son of Falgar of the House of Andar, the Great and former king of Abundant, who does not have to be a king to be loved and remembered by his family."

Falgar closed his eyes and embraced his son.

"We must speak no more of this lest someone overhear and report to Malpha. I do not want to give him the satisfaction of knowing he has indeed captured the son of the king."

"One thing I must know. Why does Malpha keep you locked up year after year? What does he hope to gain by it?"

"I am a symbol of victory over the former kingdom so that he reigns supreme. He believes there is a hidden treasure."

"Treasure? Is it true?"

"That is my secret, and I will never tell."

*

"Your Ultimate Rulership, you were right. We put the young man in the room with Falgar and overheard them say that he is the son of Falgar. Not only that, the trinket known as the Komatal is here in Tenebrose."

"Where is it? I want it. I must have it," Malpha yelled.

"The son said it is held by a friend. We are trying to find out who his friend is. There is a suspect."

"Who is it?" screamed and angry ruler.

"It is the man you appointed Chief Samaran, your Ultimate Rulership."

"What? Bring him here immediately. How can this be?"

*

Diamond hurried down the hallways and corridors to Malpha's throne room. The messenger's alarming words pushed him with all possible haste.

"Your Rulership, what is it? Has something gone wrong?"

"What is it that I hear? You are a friend of this son of Falgar? Why did you not tell me? What are you hiding? I will find out, you know."

"I am not hiding my knowledge of this young man, your Rulership. I met him when I was the Prison Master. He was a prisoner, and a wood carver. I know nothing more about him other than he was seeking to find out who his father is. I had no knowledge that he might be the son of Falgar. Is it true that he really is that man's son?"

"Do not play with me. I am not a child. You must have known more than you are telling."

"I swear to you, I did not know any more about his family or connections."

"Has he entrusted you with any of his possessions? An amulet perhaps?"

"No, Your Rulership. He may have mentioned that he had such an item, but I have never actually seen it."

240

"Who are his friends? Where are they? I must know!"

"He did say he had a friend. He wanted to know how to contact him. I could not help him as I did not know where to look."

"You had better be telling the truth. I have placed you in a very high position and I can remove you to the very lowest place if I choose. Do not fail me. Do you understand? My spies will continue to investigate. If I find that you have had a part in this, you will suffer."

"I understand." said Diamond as meekly as he could. He bowed and backed away out of the room, turned and found his way back to his chambers.

"Watch him," Malpha ordered the Chancellor who stood nearby.

*

Back in his chamber, Diamond pondered the significance of the interrogation by Malpha. *Why is the Ultimate Ruler interested in Topaz's amulet? If Topaz is indeed the son of Falgar, what part does an amulet play?* Thinking back to Jewel's necklace: how it sparkled in the light, how its gold and emerald jewel held the very promises of the High King; a suspicion occurred to him. *Could it be that the amulet has some kind of power not unlike my diamond, or Gem's key, or Jewel's emerald?*

CHAPTER 32

DOURMALINE

The flat field in front of the palace was alive with activity. Like ants, laborers carried beams of wood along toward the edifice that rose before them at the far end. A high platform was taking shape that would be the stage for the great celebration the Ultimate Ruler was having for himself.

Gem proved himself worthy of his employment once he picked up the carpentry skills required to participate in the project. Unlike most of the slave or prison workers, he was a volunteer, having the freedom to come and go. Several times he had been able to slip away and walk the long distance to the home of Jasper. Having that connection to the others made the pointlessness of his work seem bearable.

Sitting in the shade of the east wing of the palace afforded a cool place for a break from the intense lifting, carrying, and pounding demanded by his work. Gem drank from his metal cup and thought of places he would rather be. From around the building he spied a familiar man approaching.

"Surprise. To whom do I owe the honor of a visit from the Chief Samaran himself? Are you allowed to talk to the common laborers?"

"I am being watched so do not get too familiar just now." Diamond struck a pose of haughty superiority for anyone who might be observing their conversation.

"What did you do wrong? Are you in trouble?" Gem asked trying to look like a humble servant speaking to his Chief.

"Take a message to Ameth," Diamond instructed in a barely audible voice. He waved his arms and gestured as if giving orders to a worker. "Topaz is in the dungeon with Falgar. Topaz has been identified as his son. A friend of Topaz is being sought in regard to a certain amulet. Tell all to be very careful."

Gem rose to his feet and bowed to his brother. "Yes, Chief Samaran. I hear and obey." He hoped that his response had looked like he was receiving details about the platform construction. Sensing a risky adventure, Gem tingled with the thought that finally he had been given something to do that would make a difference. How to do it without raising suspicion would be the challenge.

Diamond went to several other workers about the area: speaking to them in a similar manner, asking questions about the construction, and making suggestions. Gem watched and understood his strategy.

He did not leave right away but waited. Stealth was a specialty for Gem. He had made mistakes in the past and he wanted to make sure he had fully learned to not repeat them. At the end of the day, he left the grounds through the main gate. He walked in the opposite direction until the daylight faded. Darting into an alley, he pulled a dark tunic and a cap from his shoulder bag. Anyone watching for him would lose him quickly.

Late at night, he knocked softly on Japer's door.

"Gem, is that you? At this late hour? Come in"

"I hope that I am not being followed. I think Diamond is in trouble."

"What is it? Does it have to do with Topaz? We know that he was taken by the palace guards. Do you know more?" Others in the household were roused and drifted downstairs to see who had come.

"Tell Master Ameth that Topaz has been identified as Falgar's son. Diamond said that Topaz's friend who has the amulet should be very careful."

"I see. Malpha must know that someone has the Komatal. He will be looking for it. Was it possible someone might have followed you here?"

"I do not think so. I changed my clothes in the dark and came very indirectly. That is why I am so late."

"And so you must leave again the same way. Another change of clothes and a different route should do it. Can you find your way?"

Jewel spoke up. "Is Diamond in trouble? Do they know who he is?"

"He did not tell me anything else. He said he is being watched. If he has any other messages, he knows where to find me."

"We will send our boy to the gate to look for you. He will be able to take messages." said Jasper.

After the addition of a dark cloak, Gem was on his way again. By early morning, he had hidden the cloak and reported to the gate for admittance.

"Had a night on the town, eh?" asked the gate commander.

"I sure did. I will be sorry today," said Gem truthfully. He was exhausted and the day's work lay ahead.

*

Finishing touches on the gigantic platform found Gem standing high atop, inspecting the railings that surrounded each side. A covered stairway zigzagged its way up the back of the structure. Insuring the safety of each person who would go up the stairs and stand on the platform had been assigned to a young carpenter whose skills the bosses had come to trust. Gem had been a good student, despite the temptation to cut some corners. He imagined an unfortunate accident happening to Malpha. He thought again. That was not the way the Prince would deliver the kingdom into rightful hands.

The day had come for the Chief Samaran to inspect the project. Gem stood alert for any signals or messages that Diamond needed to send him. Soon guests would be arriving; crowds would be milling about.

In the distance, Diamond appeared, followed by a group of the Ruler's men; some he knew would be keeping an eye on the Chief Samaran's every move. Gem descended the stairs to report on the results of the last inspection.

"Have the railings been made to my specifications?" asked Diamond of the carpenters.

"They have, Chief," replied Gem.

"Take this measure, stretch it out above and make sure that it is exactly as I have ordered." Diamond handed Gem a length of rope. Gem trudged up the staircase feeling around it for any foreign, non-rope texture. His hand touched a slab of thin wood. Sliding it into his shirt, he continued up and completed the measure of the rails.

"All is correct," Gem shouted from the platform. The men who accompanied Diamond looked at one another and nodded their heads in approval. The Chief Samaran continued his inspection until all was seen and checked off his list.

"Good work, men. The Ultimate Ruler will be pleased." Diamond and Gem acknowledged with a mutual wink.

*

Gem waited until dark once more. He walked away from the main gate as if going for a casual stroll. Once out of sight, he passed the wooden slab to the waiting spy; it was carried away into the night and safely into the hands of Ameth.

*

Tensions mounted as the day of the celebration grew near. Bustling here and there were nervous servants, slaves, officials, and courtiers. Everyone was aware of the great import of the event. Everyone knew that failure would result in the previously-threatened consequences. No one wanted to find out exactly what those might be. The Ultimate Ruler had struck great fear into the hearts of all his subjects, which was exactly what he planned and desired.

Diamond still was not sure how disaster could be achieved. There was a plan, Ameth had been alerted, and all the players would soon be in place. Now, all he could do was to cry out to the "One" who could bring about success.

"Great Prince, wherever you are, do something miraculous. This is the moment of truth. You are the one who sent us to overthrow the evil ruler. Show yourself to the people of Tenebrose. Use the gifts you have given us to bring light to the darkness."

*

In the damp, stone dungeon, Topaz tried to encourage his father. "There will be triumph, I know. Many people who wish Malpha to be overthrown will be behind us. Diamond, Ameth, Jasper, and the others will be out there. We will not fear!"

"My son, how strong you are. You lift up my heart and strengthen my weary soul. I had given up hope."

"The Prince will not fail us." Topaz lifted up his voice and directed it to the dark, empty ceiling. Falgar followed his gaze and saw nothing.

"Mighty Prince, you are the one who helps those who cry

out to you. We cry out and ask that you do something miraculous to defeat Malpha and his evil cohort. May the High King rule once again in the whole kingdom."

*

Ameth gathered the little group together for a final word of encouragement. They all joined hands and looked to the Master as he raised his voice to the sky. "You are the "One" who helps in time of need. Let this be the day that Malpha is ruler no more. Diamond has devised a good plan. May you come and show yourself mighty before the citizens of Tenebrose and beyond. We look to the day when there will be no doubt who is the real King."

*

A stream of servants and overseers plied the Chief Samaran with last minute questions and problems. Below his chambers, people began to arrive for the celebration. Gerwin kept a lookout from an upper window for the arrival of particular ones.

"They have come, Chief. The ones you asked me to look for," said Gerwin to his master.

"Yes, I see. Go to the entrance hall and do as I instructed you," said Diamond. Taking off the symbols of his chiefly position, he donned the ordinary clothes of a peasant worker and slipped out of his chamber. Down a staircase at the far end of hallway that was normally used by servants, he found his way to a dingy room and waited.

Gerwin opened the door and ushered in a tall figure dressed in a long, dark gown and hooded cloak. Dismalia looked up and saw her son standing amidst stacks of garden vegetables.

"Damon! My son, whatever are you doing here? Where have you been?" She threw herself forward and wrapped her arms around her lost son without any hesitation. Shocked by her behavior, Diamond laughed and hugged her in return.

"Mother, I am glad to see you too. I am well. I see you are

247

also well." Now that the moment had arrived, he did not know what to say. How would he begin to tell her about his life? Would he tell her? She would find out soon enough, and his cover would be in danger.

Dismalia stepped back and smiled at him. "My son, I have missed you so. This is an answer. Thank you! Thank you!"

"Thank me for what?" asked Diamond.

"I am not thanking you. I am thanking the "One". You see, after you left my life was very miserable. I was locked into a lonely prison cell of my own making. There was nothing left. Even my own daughters did not come to visit or seem to care about me. After many weeks of weeping, I went up into the room, the one that Julen found. I tore down the hideous dragon image and ripped it to shreds. I saw the message on the wall and, in desperation, I did cry out to the "One". After that I had a dream in which a man told me that I would find the way. I would be delivered from my prison. Until now, I have remained in that state, only, I had hope."

"How was it that you were allowed to come to Tenebrose?"

"It was the invitation. I received my own personal invitation from the Ultimate Ruler. Even though I despise that man, the invitation was a chance to leave. They let me go since it was my own invitation. Oh, Damon. You are here and maybe now I will not have to return to Bellacosa. Will you help me?"

"I will do what I can. There are some things you need to know about me."

"It is alright. Whatever you have done, I forgive you."

"I married Jewel."

"That is wonderful. I am happy for you. I am sorry I rejected her. That was wrong. Everything is different now. I promise."

Diamond looked into his mother's face and saw that she told the truth. She was different. The change was good.

"I hope you are telling me the truth. Lies and deception seem to be the standard fare for our family."

Dismalia held up her hand in front of Diamond's eyes and showed him a ring on her finger. "Do you see this? It is called a dourmaline. I found it. Is it not beautiful?"

"It is. Where did you find it?" asked a curious son.

"I found it in the hidden room. When I put it on, it sparkled so brightly, I was almost blinded. It is just for me, Damon. It is who I am now. It is a sign."

"Dourmaline. I like it."

"Here is Dourmaline's son," Diamond said as he produced his sparkling jewel from a pocket. They held their gems together and marveled at the brilliance, even in the dim light of the room.

"Where is Julen, I mean Jewel?"

"That is what I must now explain. Sit down for I have much to tell you."

CHAPTER 33

THE PROMISE

"Tedious business, all this planning. It will be splendid, will it not? It will be thrilling or…."

"Yes, your Rulership, dire consequences," said Diamond finishing the sentence.

"I want perfection! I want superiority! The whole empire must know that I am the supreme ruler. No one dares to stand in my way." He stopped momentarily to take quick gulps from his flask.

"Do not worry, your Rulership. First will come the singers and dancers. Then you will enter along the path I have outlined." Diamond pointed to a diagram of the entire palace grounds. "You will climb the stairs with the Lord Chancellor and, once on top of the platform, you will greet everyone."

"Where will you be?" asked Malpha. "Will not the Chief Samaran also appear for this occasion? Yes, you must be there as well."

Diamond thought for a moment. This would mean a change in his plan, but it could still work.

"Whatever you wish, your Rulership. After a short speech of

introduction, you demonstrate your power by transforming into the ferocious dragon, breathing fire and all that," said Diamond as the two nodded heads simultaneously. "While everyone cowers in terror, the best part of the evening will commence. Falgar and his son will be led in and paraded past the audience. This will be the most spectacular part of the ceremony."

"Ho. Indeed! I can see it all now. It is a good thing I shall be upon the high platform, or the fire of my breath would roast everyone alive." Malpha laughed a dry, crusty laugh. "Make sure that Falgar and the boy are up high enough for every to see their humiliation. Right up front. In heavy chains. Yes, very heavy chains."

Diamond appeared to be writing down the instructions saying, "High. Up front. Heavy chains. Good. We will conclude with fireworks, then the parade of banners and singers will file out again. There will be feasting and dancing and ….."

"That is it? Fine. I must leave now. I have a very special guest arriving today," the ruler confessed through a lecherous grin.

"Yes. I have everything under control, your Rulership." Diamond stepped back and made what resembled a half-hearted bow. Curious to see who the special guest could be, he followed several paces behind as Malpha made his way out of the room and down the long hallway.

Witnessing the interaction, Lord Drain turned to a fellow dignitary next to him and said in a low voice, "I suspect Mondo of mischief. He has been seen speaking with strange people. Why would he do that unless he was up to something?"

"How would he dare do anything against the Ultimate Ruler. Surely he knows of the consequences."

"I have investigated Mondo's background. He was a criminal, a thief, caught in the act way in the north. Lord Crumblestone bought him very cheap. And here, he passes him off as being trained by royals. Did he think we would all be fooled?"

*

The throne room of the palace buzzed with talk of the newly arrived guests. Every room in the palace bustled with either visitors or servants. A fortunate few found accommodations there, but most had to find rooms in the city. One guest, in particular, had requested an audience with the Ultimate Ruler. Malpha hurried along the corridor followed closely by his usual entourage. Diamond continued to follow, noting the improvement in the Ruler's temperament as he anticipated the encounter. A dark-haired woman stood, waiting for him. She was dressed in a lavish, black gown, accessorized with fine strands of blood-red stones.

"Lency, my sweet. You have come at last!" cooed Malpha grabbing Violencia's hands.

"Malphy, you adorable man. You are looking wonderful! It is so good to be back in your palace. This is my favorite place to be in the whole of the empire." Violencia curtsied and flashed her long eyelashes.

"My dear, you know I love it when you call me that," said Malpha with a sickly smirk.

Hearing the name of the visitor, Diamond came to an immediate halt and took several steps backward, mingling with the others to stay hidden. Was Violencia on such friendly terms with the Ultimate Ruler? He had no idea she had spread her net of influence so wide.

"What have you done with that husband of yours?" asked Malpha. "Last I heard, you had him well under your spell."

"Oh, that ridiculous man. He is no problem. He wanders around in a daze, like a ghost. I am sure he will be dead soon. Oh, I had better keep my voice down; he is lurking here somewhere."

"You are a clever woman, my dear. How many men have you deceived and stolen their fortunes? How glad I am to have you on *my* side."

"Speaking of fortunes, have you recovered Falgar's gold yet?"

"Hush, my dear. Not so loud. No. I'm afraid another round of

252

torture is in order." They laughed.

"I do so look forward to the celebration. How have you accomplished so much in such a short time? I must meet the man who has organized this for you. What did you say his name is?"

Diamond turned and fled; his false identity held by a tenuous thread.

*

In the dungeon, Topaz and his father prepared for their entrance.

"What is this? asked Falgar, as Topaz brought over a pile of clothing.

"This is what Mondo sent to us. These are the clothes we are to wear tonight. Now, let me help you get dressed."

"How did he get these?"

"How does Mondo do anything? He is brilliant, I tell you. I do not know what his plan is, but I know he has one."

*

Diamond, dressed in his formal regalia, tried to make his outlandish headgear hide his face as much as possible. He would have to appear and participate as one of the important officials.

A light, knocking sound alerted Gerwin who stood guard in the event of unexpected interruptions. Opening the door just the width of his face, he beheld the lady in black.

"I wish to be introduced to the Chief Samaran. I am a friend of the Ultimate Ruler and have his permission to enter this chamber. Open the door and allow me to enter," she commanded with theatrical authority.

"I am sorry, Mistress. The Chief Samaran is preparing his dress and is not available."

"I insist!" she continued as she pushed against the paneled door. Gerwin was stronger and was able to push the door closed in her face.

"I am insulted. Do you hear? I shall report this to the Ultimate Ruler." She heard nothing from inside the chamber.

253

Sulking and angry, Violencia stalked away.

*

Below, the broad, palace grounds were filled to capacity with people from every corner of the kingdom. Torches placed at intervals around the field splashed just enough light upon the attendants for them to see their way into the standing masses.

In back of the palace waited the hundred participants: singers, dancers, and banner-wavers. In the halls, cooks and servants had prepared table after table that held platters of the best food in the land.

Last light faded; torches blazed. Daylight was gone; darkness was the signal for the festivities to begin.

*

Malpha took one last look at himself in his looking glass. The robes of dyed-green fur and velvet, the high-heeled boots, and the towering headdress added all-important bulk to his physique. Standing at a distance and squinting his eyes, he could almost imagine that he looked young again. But, there was no denying it—age had taken its toll. Satisfied with the overall impression, he grinned as he patted down the abdominal bulge. Fishing in a deep pocket in one side of his royal robe, he found the familiar flask.

"I must make sure this is full before I begin the ceremony. I must be at my best," he spoke aloud to himself. "One last drink of my very own juice of the koma tree." The flask was now only half full. "Montar! Fill this before I leave."

The Ultimate Ruler's personal slave stepped into the room and obeyed his master.

The Ruler opened a locked cabinet revealing the sacred pome that, along with the koma juice, had been his source of evil power all these years. As he removed the glowing ball, he rubbed its surface with one hand.

"Promise, indeed," he said with utter contempt. "Promise of what? Empty Promise for them; the dragon's promise for

254

me." Immediately, he stood straighter and taller, there was a bounce in his step, his complexion grew slightly more youthful, and slightly more green.

Carefully, he placed the pome in the other deep pocket until just the right moment on the platform when he would again amaze and terrify the entire population of Tenebrose.

The Lord Chancellor coughed, signaling his presence outside the door of the ruler's chamber. He knew that his powerful master became very annoyed with such conventions as knocking.

"It is you. Is everything ready?"

"Yes, your Ultimate Rulership. It is time."

"Is she here?"

"Yes, your Ultimate Rulership. Lady Chiselstone has come to accompany you in the procession."

"Good. Is the Chief Samaran here yet?"

"No, your Ultimate Rulership. He will join us as we enter the palace grounds."

*

Diamond stood in the entrance of the palace giving instructions to the torch lighters. There was to be enough light for the guests to see their way onto the ground, but not enough light to drown out the effect of the elements he had prepared.

A large, standing crowd had assembled. Once all the spaces around the edges were filled with people, he would give the signal for the singers and banner-wavers to enter.

"They are coming," said a servant who leaned into Diamond's ear to be heard by him only.

Diamond immediately darted out the door and positioned himself on a path that was invisible from the entry way where the ruler and his small group of officials waited for their turn to move forward.

"Where is Mondo? He should be here," barked Malpha.

"I want to meet him," cried Violencia. "He is quite elusive,

255

is he not? He would not even allow me to be introduced to him in his chamber."

Lady Chiselstone's final words were cut short. Diamond had given the signal for the singers to begin their entrance.

Dressed in colorful gowns and flowing robes, the group of one hundred slowly marched three abreast along the back and down the center of the field. Their song had been composed by one of Malpha's courtiers and was an attempt at sounding joyful. The song lacked the energy to impress the Ultimate Ruler and he grumbled under his breath, "Who are these numbskulls? Do they call that singing? Mondo, where are you?"

While hundreds of spectators watched, the singers filed in and lined up across the front of the gathering. Only a small gap remained where the Ultimate Ruler would proceed to climb the high platform for his speech.

Diamond quickly stepped into the cluster, bowed low, and held his arm out with his hand pointing to the platform. When he rose to an upright position, he looked straight at Violencia and smiled.

"Well, let's get going. What are we waiting for?" Malpha demanded.

"You may proceed now," said Diamond.

"Is this the young man you told me about?" Violencia asked suspiciously. "He looks very much like someone I knew once. Could it be?" she demanded.

"Go now and stand alongside your husband, Master Chiselstone. We will look into this later, my dear." Malpha turned and began the walk to the front, followed by the Lord Chancellor and Diamond. Violencia stood speechless. "It is not possible. It could not be Damon, could it?"

Banners waved, singers sang, and the audience stood in rapt silence. The Ultimate Ruler, in all his pompous regalia, began his march to the platform, hearing the feint voice of

Violencia in the distance yelling, "Wait. Something is wrong. That is Damon. You must hear me." Malpha reached the stairs and began to climb. The noise of the singers drowned out all other sound.

Once at the top, the Ultimate Ruler, the Lord Chancellor and Diamond stood and faced the crowd. From a short distance, Harraster Chiselstone and his cousin Lord Crumblestone stared at the dignitaries on the platform. "What do you think of that young man?" asked Crumblestone. "Does he look like someone we know?" Diamond's father tried to focus on the faces but found it too difficult. Violencia recoiled at the question.

"What are you saying? That is Damon? How? Why?" Suspecting a plot, she quickly darted away through the crowd to warn anyone she could find who would listen.

"Stay, my dear. Be patient," crooned her husband's cousin as she swept past him.

Someone else heard the conversation. Dismalia could not believe what she was seeing. Was that Damon, her son, standing with the Ultimate Ruler? Without making any disturbance, she slipped away into the darkness to follow Violencia.

*

The Chancellor stepped to the front to introduce Malpha and give him time to recover from the exertion.

With inveigling words, the Chancellor praised all the achievements of the ruler, going on for some time.

"Even the most outlying towns and kingdoms have come to recognize and bow down to the great Ultimate Ruler who..." he stopped in mid-sentence, feeling a sharp pain just below the rim of his prodigious headpiece. Turning slightly, he could see the ruler's scowl and realized the source of the pain was a finger poking the long-winded speaker's head. It was time to step back.

"Welcome, the Ultimate Ruler, Malpha the great..."

257

Malpha cleared his throat loudly. The Chancellor bowed and stepped aside. The great, green-robed ruler came forward and grasped the items in his hidden pockets—one hand on the flask, which he now raised surreptitiously to guzzle the remainder of his koma concoction, and the other hand brought forth the stolen Promise of the High King. Dropping the flask, his two hands were free to hold the treasured ball and rub it with all his might. The desired effect was not long in coming. A puff of green haze shot out in all directions and, from the midst, rose the specter of the great, green reptile. His dragon head was thrown back as if to laugh before it came forward in a mighty blast of fire and smoke.

Sounds of fright emanated from the audience as they ducked down and crouched low where they stood. Having achieved the desired response, he commanded that the defeated King of Abundant and his only son be marched into the arena for all to see.

"Look upon the former king! See his chains. Know his downfall, and know who is the ruler of all, now and forever!" shouted the Great Dragon amid the smoke and fire.

Falgar and Topaz stumbled into view, pushed from behind by soldiers with sharp, pointed spears. Layers of chains encircled both men weighing them down so they could hardly walk. Slowly, they dragged past the horrified onlookers. The expected applause did not erupt as Malpha had hoped. A hushed veil of whispers settled over everyone.

"Have faith, father. All will be well," Topaz whispered.

Their journey to their designated, lower platform in the front of the crowd seemed to take forever. When at last they reached the destination, they both stood, a forlorn site bowed down with the weight of chains.

A robed figure in the crowd stepped forward and stepped up onto view on one side of the chained royalty. From the other side, another figure appeared and stood beside them.

Malpha looked on, smugly appreciating the Chief Samaran's plan. However, a quizzical frown overtook the benign smile as he observed the kingly clothes each prisoner wore. Despite his disapproval of the chosen attire, he nodded his ugly green head and waited for what was to come next.

One robed figure held up a shining object for all to see. It was a key with a glowing blue stone at the top. In an instant, Gem and the key did their work; the chains lay on the ground around King Falgar's feet.

A buzz of alarmed voices stirred the back of the crowd. "Stop them! Treason!" they yelled.

Then the other robed figure held high an amulet and put it around the neck of Falgar. Ameth turned the King toward the audience to behold the rightful ruler of Abundant. He cried out in a loud voice, "Great High King, send your son to illuminate this gathering. Show everyone who is King in this land!"

At this, the dull stone in the center of the amulet lit up like a beacon spreading light into the night sky. Topaz's eyes were wide with wonder as he saw the familiar ornament transform before him. Ameth turned the King once again; this time, the beam of light was aimed at Malpha who stood transfixed by the unexpected sight. The light hit his red, dragon eyes. His short, clawed arms rose to block the glare, but it was too late. Fire and smoke disappeared into a wispy cloud of green mist as the dragon shriveled down into the lowly form of an old, old man.

A hard object hit the surface of the platform producing a thud that few noticed. All eyes were fixed on the spot-lighted ruler. Slowly the object rolled, picked up speed, and then dropped over the edge and disappeared from sight.

Shock and anger erupted from the platform as Malpha realized what was happening. "Treason! Guards, take them!" he tried to shout, but found only a whisper would come.

No one moved. The beam from Falgar's amulet grew and spread, turning the field from night to day.

Malpha screamed in horror, but his shrieks went unheard by the crowd. The sight of the great ruler shrinking, shrinking, shrinking down, swallowed up in a mass of green velvet, was enough to rivet the attention of all present.

The Ruler's ardent followers wondered if this was another of his amazing feats. Most backed away into the dark. Some stood unbelieving and in shock. Violencia screeched, "No! What have you done? You have ruined everything."

Mucosa Drain could be heard to say from somewhere in the dark, "I knew it. That Samaran was not one of us!"

At Diamond's invitation, Jasper, all his household guests, and every follower of the Prince that could be mustered had been scattered throughout the field. When they saw what was happening, each knew what to do.

Jewel brought out her green necklace and held high the sparkling stone. Light from the Komatal brought the jewel to life and filled the night with words of comfort and love. Ruby began to sing. Flashes a tiny lights swirled above her head and moved through the sky. It appeared that hundreds of those faithful to the High King were present. They all joined in, shining their jewels into the heavens. As the lights blended together in all their color and splendor, a shape formed above them—the unmistakable shape of a horse and rider.

CHAPTER 34

A NEW KINGDOM

The bearers of the lights moved forward to form a group, shouting praise in celebration. Ameth, Falgar, Topaz, and Gem stood in the center raising, their hands in victory. Diamond descended and wrapped his great robe around the former prisoner.

"Hail to the King!" shouted Diamond. "Falgar, of the House of Andar, King of the new kingdom of Abundant." Cries of victory and shouting lasted several minutes until the aged prophet raised both arms to silence them all.

"Where is the Promise?" yelled Ameth into the crowd. "Did someone find it?"

A silent figure worked through the tightly packed bodies of joyous people. "Here it is!" she proclaimed. "I have it."

261

Onlookers fell back and allowed her to come through. Dourmaline held out the treasure she had discovered as she stood below the platform, waiting to see if the Chief Samaran was indeed her son, Damon. Diamond met her, received the pome and embraced her in a powerful hug. Smiling, she put her arms around him in return as tears of joy flowed from her eyes.

"Dear lady, I believe you are the mother of this remarkable young man. He has led us tonight in a great victory for the High King and the whole of his vast kingdom. You should be very proud."

Jewel, Ruby, Rista, and Jasper squeezed past the last human obstacle and reached the knot of celebrants.

"Come!" shouted Diamond. "A feast awaits. Eat, dance, celebrate the installation of the real king." At this, the joyous mass moved away towards the palace and the tables full of delicious food.

King Falgar chose to find a quiet spot to sit. Everything had happened so quickly, it took his mind some time to catch up to the reality. Diamond and Topaz sat with him as he recovered his composure.

"It has been so long. I am quite dazed."

"Here Father. Someone has brought you a drink. Perhaps this will refresh you." Falgar took the cup and drank slowly, then smiled.

"I know this taste. It is the sweet juice of the koma tree. How I have missed it. Who brought this to me? Let me reward the one who has been so thoughtful."

"Whoever it was has gone as quickly as he came," observed Diamond.

The aged, former prisoner closed his eyes and relaxed against his high-backed chair; a flush of color came into his cheeks. The wrinkled, grayness of his flesh seemed to turn a healthy shade of brown.

"I believe I will join the celebration."

*

The crowds thinned. The tables that had overflowed with food were bare. Servants who remained and wished to serve the restored king busied themselves with the clearing and cleaning.

"Come!" Diamond beckoned. "Come into the palace and hear even more revelations."

Falgar, Topaz, Gem, Jasper, Ruby, Ameth and Jewel. followed, wondering to themselves what Diamond referred to. Once inside the great entrance hall, Falgar looked at each person present wondering what were the connections between the participants. Ameth saw the look of curiosity and stepped in to help.

"My friends, we must now find out how our brother Diamond—a man of many names—has brought us all to this moment in the history of our beloved kingdom." Ameth motioned to Diamond to begin the narrative.

"First, allow me to introduce you all to each other. When I was the Prison Master for a short time, I met Falgar, a prisoner for many years, who we now know is the rightful King of Abundant. I also met Topaz, otherwise known as Tofar to some of you. He traveled here with Amethyst, known more familiarly as Master Ameth. Topaz came in search of his family history, and if he prevailed, the knowledge of his father's fate. He has succeeded in this, and we realize now that he is the heir to the throne of Abundant, being the only son of the King.

"Long live King Falgar and his heir, Topaz the Fearless," shouted Ameth, who even at the late hour was demonstrating remarkable energy.

Diamond continued. "Master Ameth, would you introduce your friend, as I have not had the pleasure of meeting him?"

Ameth, speaking with great solemnity, "I cannot tell you what this moment means to me. I have believed for so many years that this day would come, but I had no idea how it would take place. The Prince has used each and every one of you to accomplish this feat. My dear friend, Jasper, has been in communication with me for quite some time, taking the pulse of the times and helping me sense when the Prince was indeed moving. He has sheltered me and these others as we waited for today to arrive."

Jasper sensed his turn had come. "Thank you, Master Ameth. We come now to my dear sisters, Ruby, Rista, and Jewel. These women have told me their stories, and it is the stuff of miracles. They too have been part of the greater plan to free the kingdom from the clutches of Malpha, the dragon ruler." The three stepped forward and bowed before Falgar. Ruby stepped back and stood near to Jasper, smiling up into his appreciative face. Jewel joined Diamond who put his arm around her and squeezed her tight. Rista skipped across the room to Gem and threw her arms around his neck, squealing with delight.

"We cannot forget Gem who has been our spy and chief communicator. I believe Gem is your brother, Diamond."

"Gem is my brother, and Ruby is his mother. Without Gem, we could never have coordinated our plan." The older brother smiled sheepishly, as Rista looked up at him with adoration and pride.

"Let me introduce my mother, formerly known as Dismalia, now to be known as Dourmaline." The embarrassed mother held up her hand to show the group her bright ring. They all admired it and thanked her for saving the Promise from anyone else who may have snatched it.

"I have one last great surprise for you all. I have something to show you. Wait here." said Diamond. They all looked on wide-eyed with anticipation. Diamond left the room and returned a few minutes later carrying a dusty volume and opened it to a marked page.

"This is the record of family history for the House of

Andar. Here on this page it records that a son, Tobar was born to Falgar."

"My real name was Tobar," said Topaz in response. "My mother changed it."

"Yes," said Diamond. "Now let me read to you from a another page." He flipped back the page and began to read aloud. "Born to Falgar of the House of Andar, a daughter. Her name is to be called..." he paused for dramatic effect, "Julen."

Jewel's hands went to her mouth; her eyes were wide with shock. Everyone in the room turned their gaze to her. "That was my name!" she cried. "Father!" She ran to Falgar, weeping, and embraced the dazed man.

"And do not forget, your brother, Topaz as well," said Diamond.

"I have a brother? I do not remember you, Topaz. I am sorry. Father, how is it that I have a brother?"

"And you have a mother," added Topaz who was still reeling from the revelation. "She did not tell me I had a sister. Why is this, father?"

Falgar now spoke. "Many years ago, the kingdom of Abundant was a joyful, contented place. It was prosperous, even rich in the pleasant fruit of trees known as koma. When Malpha arrived, he wanted the riches for himself. Through his dragonish deception, he overthrew the kingdom and destroyed the koma trees, saving only those he would grow for his own use.

"When it was obvious what was about to happen, the Queen and I decided to split the family and flee. She took my son and traveled to a far country using some of the wealth that we had accumulated. We hoped that, if I died, at least a son would survive to take my place. I took my daughter and hid in a tower that looked out to the sea. We were discovered; I was captured, imprisoned, and tortured to reveal the location of any other wealth I had hidden. Malpha always believed that there

265

was hidden treasure somewhere on the grounds of the palace.

"I never knew what became of my daughter, Julen. She was taken away, and I did not hear any news of her. I did not want to ask after her, lest Malpha use her to make me reveal my secrets. I assumed that she did not survive."

"Father, I did survive. In the strangest way, it was for the best. I was sold in the slave market as a small child, and this kind lady bought me to protect me," Jewel reached out to Doumaline and touched her arm. "I was further protected by Emerald, who it turns out, was very close to Ameth before I came to Bellacosa. Then I met Ruby, who became my friend in the service to Dismalia Chiselstone, now Dourmaline. It is a long story, but in time you will see how every circumstance has worked together for this moment that we are together again."

Both Ruby and Dourmaline bore a look of shame as Jewel recounted the story of her life, realizing that they had both treated her with contempt for being a low, ignorant slave. It began to dawn on them both that Jewel was the daughter of the King, a position higher than either could have ever imagined.

Jewel looked into Diamond's face, "How long have you known this, and you did not tell me?"

"There was much at stake. I could not say anything until now. Remember how, when I met you, I called you a lady and you said you were not a lady. Did we ever dream that you are instead a princess?"

Falgar stood with his arms around his newly-found children, rejoicing to be together again. "Never did I imagine this day would come. I had given up hope. Here you both are at last."

"There is an addition that none of you have anticipated. I sent for Topaz's mother some time ago and she should be arriving soon here in Tenebrose. So your family will be complete again."

Tears filled Falgar's eyes.

"And," added Ameth, "Jewel, you have the home and family forever that was promised to you."

"Let us all retire, for it is late. Tomorrow we will begin again in the new kingdom of Abundant.

*

The sun dawned and threw its light through a gathering of golden clouds on the horizon. Topaz stood on the balcony of his new apartment in the palace and was awestruck by the beauty of the new day.

A shout from inside brought him back to the present.

"Prince Topaz! The Mirabelle has docked and the carriage arrives soon. Come down for the welcoming ceremony." The servant quickly left and ran to the next rooms to make his happy announcement.

"Topaz, brother!" Jewel ran into the room and hugged the young man with such strength that he nearly fell over. Ruby had dressed her hair with colorful ribbons. There had been no time to purchase grand gowns, but the emerald necklace more than made up for her princess-like appearance.

"Jewel, sister. How strange it is to say that word. You waste no time in making me part of the family. I could have no better family in all the world."

"Oh, Topaz. I am so nervous. And happy and excited and sad all at once," Jewel exclaimed.

"Why are you sad? This is the day you will finally meet your mother. You will love her just as I do."

"I am sad that I have no memories of growing up with a mother and barely any memories of a father."

Diamond appeared in the doorway and summoned the pair. "Come. It is time to gather below." The three joined the others waiting in the grand entrance hall. Ameth, Jasper, Ruby, Gem and Rista stood by with a crowd of men and women who had remained faithful to the High King. Wafting through the room, the smells of a sumptuous feast reminded all that a celebration was about to take place. The royal family would soon be complete.

Diamond put his arm around his wife and they held onto each other in nervous excitement.

"The carriage approaches!" yelled a palace guard.

The matching white horses trotted down the drive and stopped. A servant opened the door. A tall, dignified woman dressed in bright colors of red and green stepped down and stood waiting for what was to come next. Around her neck a necklace of large, shining beads caught Jewel's attention. A memory of her dream flashed before her.

Jewel could no longer stand the formality of the welcoming. She darted out the door, stood at the top of the steps and looked into her mother's face. With feet barely touching the stones, she ran down into the outstretched arms and warm embrace of Jebel. Through the blur of tear-filled eyes Jewel noted her mother's appearance and knew that this was the moment that she had dreamt of.

"My beautiful daughter, and my handsome son! Take me to your father, the King. How I long to hold you all in my arms."

*

This is an official proclamation from the
Royal Palace of Abundant
There shall be a re-coronation of King Falgar
and a recognition of the Royal Family
at mid-day, five days hence
in the Royal Courtyard.
All are invited to witness the rebirth of
the Kingdom of Abundant
and hear the decree of King Falgar on the future of the kingdom.

268

A New Kingdom

*

Without fanfare, the small kingdom by the sea known as Abundant was again flourishing. Those who had followed Malpha made themselves scarce, some leaving by ship to find some other people to oppress. Those who had secretly remained true to the High King came out in force to support the former ruler and acknowledge his rightful place on the throne of Abundant.

The royal symbol of kingship, the Komatal, remained around the neck of King Falgar. He blessed and thanked all who had returned to bring back Abundant as a peaceful and prosperous city state. Wanting to avoid undue ceremony, he chose a simple program in which he designated and appointed future leaders for the kingdom. But not before he presented his reunited family to the audience.

"I have waited for a very long time to have the privilege of presenting to you the royal family. Queen Jebel, Prince Topaz, and Princess Jewel rose from their seats on the stage.

"Prince Topaz will now become your future King-in-training. Your queen and princess will oversee the welfare of the citizens of Abundant, making sure that all are treated fairly and no one suffers as a slave in this kingdom.

"All of you have a place in the future of Abundant, as it will be called once again. I call forth my servant, and son-in-law, Diamond. Bow before me and swear allegiance to me and to the High King who reigns in Illumah, the City of Light."

Diamond bowed before the king. "I appoint you Lord High Chancellor of the Kingdom. You will oversee all the business ventures of Abundant and make sure all is done with wisdom, honesty, and care for even the lowliest persons."

Falgar called Gem to join his brother on the platform. "Gem, I wish you to serve me as the Head of Security and Defense. You will oversee the safety of the kingdom and alert me if anyone again threatens the peace of our land."

269

The two brothers looked at each other acknowledging the new positions they would hold.

"Jasper, I would be honored if you would serve as an ambassador from Abundant and go into all the kingdom to tell them the good news that Malpha and the dragon are no more. See that they return to the rule of the High King. And I suspect you may want to take someone with you that you have grown very fond of by the name of Ruby." Jasper blushed and reached out to hold the hand of his soon-to-be bride.

At this time, Ameth spoke without being called on by the King. "And I, Amethyst, must take the Promise and return it to Illumah, the City of Light, and the High King. The Promise shall again be the symbol of the never-ending reign of the High King."

"Yes, Master Ameth, I do not forget that you have a solemn duty to perform in regard to that which was stolen from the High King," added Falgar. "To mark this day as the one in which the Promise is once again the sign of the Rule of the High King, I proclaim this a national holiday from this day forth."

Cheers went up from the crowded courtyard.

"There I will dwell and there I hope to be reunited with my one true love," Ameth added quietly.

*

Dancing, feasting, and merriment commenced and did not conclude until late in the night. In the meantime, the new royals gathered in what had been the room for interrogating errant Tennebrosians, but had been turned into a comfortable sitting room for the family.

"I thought we were all going to the City of Light. Is not that what we have had as our goal all these months?" asked Jewel.

"You will reach that fair city in time. Right now there is need for you to reside here and help to build the next generation of Abudnantites," replied Falgar. "Your friend Ameth and

270

others will be there waiting for you and all of us when that time comes."

"Father," continued Topaz. "Was there any truth in the rumor of your great wealth supposedly hidden from Malpha?"

"I think the time has come to reveal the secret of Komatal at last," said Falgar. At this everyone sat up to attention.

"When your mother and I parted ways those many years ago, we divided our wealth so that she and Topaz would have enough to live on for years to come. We did not know what would happen to the kingdom. I took the remaining gold and made a hiding place for it."

"Do you mean there really is a treasure?" asked Diamond.

"There is indeed a hidden treasure. In fact, it is here in the palace." Surprise and shock showed on the faces of all present.

"Diamond was very close to finding the first clue. Bring the book of records here and I will show you."

Diamond quickly left the room and returned with the dusty volume. Falgar held the book and turned to the final page. Written on it were strange scribblings that made no sense. "Look closely. There are four sets of lines." Falgar bent over the book and placed the Komatal upside down on the page. On the back side of the amulet were lines that completed the pattern and formed what looked like the layout of a room.

"Is it a room of the palace?" asked Diamond.

"It is. Come and we shall see for ourselves." Falgar walked slowly up the grand staircase and headed for the chamber that had become the Ultimate Ruler's. Once inside, Diamond laid the book on a table and again put the amulet in place on the final page.

"I see. This is the room." Gem oriented himself to the space and the lines on the page and asked, "Where is the treasure?"

"It is right where the stone is centered on the other side." said Falgar.

271

Gem quickly found the spot in the middle of the room and looked to Falgar for the next clue. The king pointed to the floor and instructed Topaz to remove a tile. Between the two men, they pried up the polished stone. Underneath, a small sunken handle could be seen. After removing more floor tiles, an entire trap door was revealed. They opened the trap door and held a lamp over the top of the cavern below.

"It is late and dark. You may take my word for it that in this vault you will find the treasure stored that was so long sought by Malpha. All this time it was right under his feet."

*

After a time, the group dispersed and went their various ways. Gem and Rista found a home in the palace, as did Diamond and Jewel. Dourmaline found her role as a grandmother of lovely, olive-skinned babies.

Jasper and Ruby married and traveled through the land as ambassadors of the Kingdom. Topaz gradually took over the duties of King as his father aged. He married and had three offspring to insure a future ruler for the kingdom.

As for those who had followed Malpha, most slipped away hoping not to be discovered and penalized for their faithlessness. What happened to the rest? Well, that is the stuff of further adventures.

Ameth found his way to the City of Light with the Promise. Walking down the aisle towards the great throne through a throng of celebrating courtiers, he came before the High King and his son, the Prince. Bowing down, he held out the Promise and placed in the Prince's hands.

"My servant, Amethyst," said the King. "You have done well. My treasure is returned. All my treasures are safe. Your reward will be great. Welcome to my city that has no end. You are forever blessed."

The High King waved his arm from right to left. Spread out at his feet, an array of bright jewels appeared and shone bright and clear. Ameth gazed into the jewels and recognized each one as the members of his new family. He smiled and felt a thrill of new energy and youth.

From the corner of his vision, someone approached. He turned to see standing before him a beautiful woman, dressed in gold with a sparkling green jewel at her neck.

"My dear, Emerald."

"I have been waiting for you. It has been a long time, but I knew you would come. Welcome," said Emerald as they embraced. "We are together forever in the City of Light."

Ameth, with Emerald, received a hero's welcome. That night there was joyful dancing in the streets of the city. Displayed for all to see was the Promise that had been restored and would stand forever and ever.

Great lights flashed from the throne and sent rainbow-colored rays of words of blessing into the sky. Love, joy, peace, truth, goodness.

ABOUT THE AUTHOR

Carol Lee Anderson lives in Spokane, Washington. After 34 years serving as a missionary in Papua New Guinea, she taught at Moody Bible Institute Spokane for nine years. She now works with English language learners. She and her husband, Neil, have four grown children and ten grandchildren.

The Treasures of the Promise is a sequel to Carol's first fiction book titled *The Treasures of Darkness.*

86588639R00154

Made in the USA
Columbia, SC
16 January 2018